Mowzl's story takes the reader on advent
a child or a grown up, this tale, like all th
ages. From the very start, you will find yo
are transported into the magical world o
The story is deftly woven between our da
Mowzl, some long time in the future, to v
his human friends and brings children and adults alike close to ...

confronting them with the painful realities of our planet's sickness. Realising how
much they have lost touch with nature they find the courage to be transported within,
to a deep understanding of healthy, abundant nature.
This is a story of hope and encouragement. I most earnestly recommend it to you.
Rick Vick Artistic Director, Stroud Festival

Reader responses to Volume 2: First Purlings

Mowzl is ace and I wish I could meet him really truly and I want to learn purling, so
I can talk to animals. I like stories of our world and Mowzl's all mixed up. It's lots of
levels and fun and challenging. Thanks, Mowzl!
Will Beckwood Age12

Amazing! I slipped right into it and simply DEVOURED, I was so hungry for more
all the way through! The story is deep, full of feeling and it made me think and
sympathise more as the book went on. The story felt so real to me that I was shocked
to be pulled out of it to find that I was not purling with the others, chatting with
animals in the Glade.
Leela (A.K.) Age 10

This book inspired me – and hopefully others too – to do as much as I can to repair
the wild web. It's great that it's addressing what we've done to the Earth, as so many
people need to start helping the environment. I think the world would be a much
better place if everyone read this book!
Charlotte Blue Age 12

Visit www.mowzl.co.uk to find out more and write reviews.

The Adventures of Horatio Mowzl

Volume Three
The Great Rising

The Adventures of Horatio Mowzl
(Volume Three: The Great Rising)

By Paul Thornycroft

Published by MowzlPrint Publishing 2019
ISBN: 9781916198142

All internal illustrations by the author
Cover illustration by L H Trevitt

***

www.mowzl.co.uk

For all children everywhere, for the wild web they share
and for those countless living things whose habitats are
disappearing . . .

Volume Three
The Great Rising

Contents

Nothing in the cry
of cicadas suggests they
are about to die

~

Haiku attributed to Basho
1644–1694
Japan

Chapter One

Creatures

Pop! Pop! Pop!

"Wha-at? What's happening?" cries Pip, swerving the car as purlers appear in front of his eyes.

"Purlaz iz appnin, Pippee!" says Emmy, laughing.

Pop! Pop! Pop! Pip's car fills with excited purlers, all laughing and whizzing about.

"Hallo!" cries Larky.

"Where are we going?" says Penny.

"Wait a minute," says Pip. "What are you all doing here? Wait, let me find somewhere to stop – hey, don't purl in front of my eyes, I can't see where I'm going!"

Pip drives on, looking for somewhere to pull off the road.

"Phew," he says, sighing, at last able to stop driving. "Alright, you lot, what's going on?"

"Pip, I'm sorry," says LuLu. "I let slip that you and Emmy might be going to the seaside. We were purling over Tillings Wood and suddenly, here we are!"

"Are you really going to the sea?" Penny asks, hopefully.

"Yip, weez vizitin oshn."

"Emmy! Please may we come?" Larky pleads. "Pleease!"

"May we come, Mr Pip?" says Stomper. "Please?"

"Is anyone else coming?" asks Pip. "Let's see now, who have we got here: Stomper, Billy, LuLu, Larky, Penny, Nosey, David, and who's this?"

"It's my Grandpa, Mr Pip," Billy explains. "'Is name's Frank."

"Hallo, Frank, welcome to purling."

"It's the best thing ever, Mr Pip."

"Is that everyone? Anyone else?"

"Don't know, Mr Pip," says David.

Pop! "Allo, Donna!" Emmy cries. "Yooz cummin too!"

"Hallo, everyone! No way I'm missing out on this trip, Emmy."

"Hallo, Mummy!" Larky is feeling very pleased because she has been able to 'call' her mum with her heart.

Pip greets Donna. "Hallo, Donna, I'm glad you're here. Now listen, everyone, I know you're all happy and excited at the moment but if we drive to the sea, you'll get further and further away from your bodies and your wool pouches..."

"We'll be alright," says Stomper, confidently. "We've been practising a lot and now we can purl a long way, don't worry."

"Well, I don't think I could do it. Emmy, what do you think?"

"Theysll be orite, Pippee, n weezl b meetin creachaz wotll b teachin uman cubz, so letz b goin."

"But what if something happens to your bodies back at home?"

"Pippee, you's nevva to be wurryin, weezl be pulld wen weez pulld. Letz be goin to oshn."

"Alright, if you're sure."

The purlers cheer as Pip drives back onto the road, heading west towards the hills. He opens the window a little. Stomper hovers on the edge of the slipstream that sucks at the opening.

"Ha-ha! This is fun," she cries. "Oh-oh, whoops!"

Suddenly, the wind sucks her out of the car; she tumbles in the air while her pouch rights itself, speeding along to catch up. Pip slows down so the other purlers can jump into the slipstream too, joining Stomper outside; he opens the other windows and the purlers practise going in and out of the car, and soon they are purling round and around, through the car and up over the roof, chasing each other and laughing.

"Let's purl up to the top of that hill," cries Stomper, "We'll meet Pip and Emmy on the other side!"

"Alright, Stomper Jack!" calls Pip. "I'll find a track that goes up. See you up there!"

"Yeah! Come on!" Billy yells, and off they go.

Pip glances at Emmy. "Don't you want to go too, Em?"

"Iyz keepin cumpanee wiv yoo, Pippee."

"Thanks, Emmy, I'll be fine. You go, if you want to."

"Yooz appy?"

"I's appy, Em."

"Fankz."

"You're welcome."

"Bi."

"Bye."

Emmy disappears with a pop.

~

The hills below the purlers look soft and rounded except for the ridges where rocks stick out above the vegetation. Plantations of

conifer trees look like geometric patches sewn on to the landscape, like a patchwork quilt. Most of the ground is grass-covered, with moorland plants such as heather, bilberry and rushes here and there. Dotted about over the hills are white blobs, which seem to be moving.

"What's all those white blobs?" calls David.

"They look like maggots!" cries Larky.

"They're sheep, I think," Penny observes, peering down.

"Sheep! Let's go and say hallo to the sheep!" Larky suggests.

"Let's go to that funny patch of trees," yells Stomper. "Come on!" She's already moving fast, and the others follow, leaving Larky feeling a bit miffed.

"Don't worry, Larky," Penny calls back reassuringly. "We'll say hallo to the sheep later."

"Look out!" warns David. "There's a bird chasing us."

They turn to look, without slowing down.

"'E's a red kite," Billy shouts. "'Allo, red kite, don't try eatin' us, we'd be tastin' 'orrible."

The kite catches up, flying alongside; he's stripy chestnut and black, and his long wings have black feathers like fingers at the tips. He examines the purlers, his eyes yellow and fierce.

"Hallo, strange birds, or whatever you are. Don't worry, I'm not hunting. I'm not very good at hunting in the air, it's much easier for me to carry off carrion – ha-ha! Get it?"

The purlers exchange smiles. They've slowed down now, and the red kite circles round them, his wings spread wide, and his forked tail tilts and flicks as he turns.

"My name's Billy," says Billy. "What's yours?"

"I'm called Tricky," replies Tricky.

"N mi naym iz Emmy n Iyz a mowse," Emmy cries, appearing suddenly in the middle of the cloud of purlers.

"Emmy!" says Larky. "Where did you spring from?"

While the purlers turn to look at Emmy, Tricky swoops under them, flipping over as he goes, plucking Emmy out of the air with his talons. He flies off at top speed towards the forestry plantation.

"Yiiikes!" cries Emmy.

"Oi, Tricky, you trickster!" yells Billy. "We's comin' for ya!" The purlers give chase, easily catching up with Tricky who, it turns out, hasn't hurt Emmy at all; even though his talons are sharp, they are not digging into the mouse.

Tricky flies over the plantation and down to the treetops, where two oak trees grow in a patch of land that was not planted with conifers. The foresters must have liked the oak trees and left them unharmed with a bit of room to grow. The conifer trees have grown more quickly than the oaks and are already taller, but the oaks still get enough light to survive.

Tricky flies to a nest near the top of one of the oaks where another red kite is busy building a nest. The purlers gather round, cautiously keeping at a safe distance.

"Where is he?" demands David. "Where's Emmy?"

"Iyz ere n Iyz orite. Trikkee aznt urt Emmy."

"Let him go!" Penny commands. "Why did you do that?"

Tricky releases Emmy from the cage of his talons.

"Just can't help it, you see, collecting things, you know."

Billy glares at Tricky. "Emmy ain't a thing!"

"Sorry," says Tricky. "This is my beloved Pinch."

"Hallo, Pinch," says Donna.

"Krrk," says Pinch, ruffling her handsome rufous feathers. "Tricky brings me presents. Look at all these!"

She pecks at the things that Tricky has collected for her: bits of coloured string, plastic bags, an empty tuna mayo sandwich carton and an empty shotgun cartridge. She stands up to stretch, revealing her chick, a large fledgling red kite.

"This is Kirk."

"Allo, Krk," says Emmy.

"Krrk," says Kirk.

"That's why we call him Kirk," says Pinch.

"Did you collect all this stuff, Tricky?" asks Larky. "Did you catch Emmy just to decorate your nest?"

"Yes. I'm sorry, it's only a bit of fun," says Tricky.

"Trikkee, Iyz kno-in yooz eatin Emmy xcept Iyz toy mowse."

"But, Emmy, you're purling!" cries Penny. "Tricky can't eat any of us when we're purling, can he?"

"Yooz rite, Pennee, Iyz forgettin."

"Come on, you lot." Billy is impatient to get going. "We 'as to find Mr Pip."

"Ang on a mo, befor weez leevin letz be lookin about," says Emmy, purling towards the ground. The others follow, including Tricky, who's curious to see what they are up to.

"B lookin n tellin."

"Telling what, Emmy?" asks David.

"B tellin wot yooz seein n earin n feelin."

The purlers look around. The oak trees shade the ground, and soft green light filters through the leaves. The branches of the oak trees are festooned with mosses and lichens, and on the ground are larger ferns and woodrush and bilberry.

"It's a bit like the Glade, only smaller," observes Donna.

"It's dark as night under the pine trees!" says Grandpa, who's drifted off to the edge of the plantation.

"They's spruce trees, Grandpa," says Billy.

"Iyz wontin yoo to b opnin yor earts n feelin great wave," says Emmy. "Wotz yoo feelin?"

"I feel sadness," says Larky. "Why is that?"

"Sad? What's you meanin', Larks?" asks Billy.

"Don't know, Billy, just it feels different to the Glade."

"It's worse than sad over here," says David, who's followed Grandpa to the edge of the plantation. "There's nothing under these trees except needles, loads of them. It's dark as night in there, like Grandpa says."

Tricky flies down from his perch in the oak, curious to know what's going on. "What's all this about? What are you looking for?"

"We're learning to feel the unwords," says Penny, simply.

"Ah! Yes. Hmm. The wave is very slow here, slow and quiet. You must be patient."

"Why's that, Tricky? Is something wrong?" Penny asks.

"We can feel the great wave here, where these oaks are growing, that's why we built our nest here; the great wave is slow, waiting, waiting on the mountain too, and in the dark trees."

"But the moorland looks so beautiful!" cries Donna. "Why is the great wave waiting?"

"I bet it's the maggots!" says Larky.

"I get it!" cries Stomper, excited. "Wildness can't grow, that's what it is. I've felt this before, at home, the very first time I was purling over the town. I can remember feeling the wildness trapped in the ground, squashed down into the ground because of the roads and buildings and machines and everything."

"The moorland would be scattered with trees if the seedlings weren't eaten by the sheep," says Tricky. "It can never grow to be what it wants to be, and so the great wave waits."

"What about these dark trees?" David peers into the gloom.

"It's spooky in there. I don't want to go in," Donna says, shivering.

"I think the great wave is squashed in there too, look," says Stomper. "The trees are jammed in like sardines in a tin, there's nothing else!"

"Maggotz n sardeenz! Ha-ha!" says Emmy, singing. "Letz b findin Pippee. Bi, Trikkee, fankz."

"Goodbye, Emmy, come back and see us soon."

Emmy purls up to the nest. "Bi, Pinch, n goodbye, Krk, weez leevin."

"Krrrrrrrr."

"Krrk"

Emmy rounds up the purlers. "Weez findin Pippee!"

The purlers fade away, disappearing all at once with a loud pop. "Hmm," murmurs Tricky. "P'raps I should've tried eating one."

~

Pip bumps along in the car following a track that leads up the hill, but a locked gate stops him. He's been looking for a way to get up the mountain, but with no luck so far. As there's no room to turn, he reverses back down the track. Suddenly the car is full of purlers, whizzing in all directions, blocking his vision.

"I can't see a thing! Help! Stop!" he cries, just managing to stop before crashing off the track. "All right, you lot, you'd better tell me. I can see that you're excited."

"Hallo, Mr Pip! You'll never guess..." cries Larky, and so begins the telling of Emmy's capture by a red kite on the mountain and all the other things that happened. Pip is relieved that Emmy is not hurt, and he's amused by the maggots and sardines.

"I've got something to show you," he says, when they have finished their story. "Well, it's somewhere actually. I think you'll like it after what you've just seen. It's further down the track, I'll have to reverse down until we find room to turn."

Soon the track widens where the forestry people sometimes stack timber and load lorries; Pip turns the car and drives on down the hill, with the purlers lining up on the dashboard looking out of the windscreen, blocking his view and making it difficult to drive.

"I can't see – please keep low down, or at the top of the windscreen, not in the middle! Thanks."

"La la laa la laa! Maggotz n sardeenz la laa la!" Emmy sings. "Emmy!"

Where the moorland comes to an end, there's a cattle grid; the wheels of the car rumble over noisily.

"Drrrrrrm!" says Larky, laughing.

"Drrrrrmm!" Emmy sings along. "Laa la la! Maggotz n sardeenz!"

The track ends at the main road, and Pip finds somewhere out of the way to leave the car. "Come on, follow me!" he calls, as he sets off along a stream side path.

"Ha! Mr Pip! You'sll be followin' us!" cries Billy, as he and the rest of the purlers race ahead to explore the woodland.

After walking for half an hour or so, and with no sign of the purlers returning, Pip finds a place to settle himself down to rest and have a good look at things – and a good listen. He closes his eyes, listening to the stream as it chuckles and chockles its way between rocks. He hears birds in the woods, and nearby a dipper zinks and warbles, sounding like the water itself.

Opening his eyes, he sees the dipper bobbing his white bib, then flying upstream. He notices trees covered all over with lichens, mosses and ferns. The ground, too, is thick with plants and young trees. There are the big oak trees of course, and ash, birch, alder, lime, hazel and rowan. If you were to count the little things too, the list would go on and on. There are some dead trees still standing, stark and bony, and trees blown over in storms lying on the ground across the path and stream; these too are covered in growing plants. The older fallen trees are melting into the ground as they decay, feeding the fungi and creepy-crawlies. One of the fallen oaks has recently shed its bark, which lies like giant flakes of skin on the ground, either side of the trunk. Perhaps an animal peeled the bark off to get at the beetle larvae burrowing beneath. With the bark peeled away, the spiralling grain of the tree trunk is clear to see, the spiralling strength that once roped the tree into the sky.

Pip watches a family of tree creepers chasing each other around the oaks, in and out of tangled branches, hiding in clumps of moss and fern, chasing each other and catching insects as they go. Blue tits tease and chase each other up in the canopy. Pip might have gone to sleep if the purlers hadn't returned at that moment.

"Pip!" cries Larky. "Emmy and Donna have disappeared! What shall we do?"

"Don't worry, Larky," says Pip. "Emmy did warn me that purlers might be pulled back at any time. Emmy and Donna must have been pulled back; they'll be alright." Pip in fact feels a bit disappointed that Emmy has gone, and worried, too.

The purlers slowly calm down and take notice of where they are.

"What a lovely wood!" cries Penny.

Pip clears his throat to speak. "Hurrm. I was thinking about what you said earlier about the plantation up on the hill and the moorland. The little glade where the red kites are nesting is a remnant of a wood like this. 'Remnant' means a bit left over, a fragment that remains when the main part is gone."

"'Ere we go!" says Billy, laughing. "Mr Pip's talkin' 'abitat!"

"But this isn't sad, Mr Pip, not like up on the hill!" says Larky. "It's laughing!"

"You can feel it, then?" Pip asks.

"Oh yes, it's strong and clear," says LuLu.

"Right, good," says Pip. "But we have to remember that this lovely bit of wood we're in now is also a remnant, it's a remnant of the rainforest, or wildwoo–"

"Rainforest?" cries Larky, interrupting. "That's in Brazil, and hot places!"

"Yes, you're right, Larky, but that's tropical rainforest and this is temperate, or 'Atlantic' rainforest, but still rainforest. Once it covered all this land, all the hills and all the mountains, up to the treeline. Once there were big herbivores that browsed on the trees and plants, their munching and trampling creating diverse woodland pasture, and there were big predators that hunted and ate the herbivores, keeping their numbers down. We've lost all that, for the sake of a few sheep."

"Do you mean that if there weren't any sheep or humans, it would all go wild again?" says David.

"I don't mean no sheep or humans!" cries Pip. "What I mean is there could be big areas of land that humans don't meddle with and these wild bits could be all connected up, with no roads or fences."

"What about the magg– er, sheep, I mean?" says Larky.

"It's not their fault, is it?" says David. "It's humans that put the sheep there!"

"Right," says Pip. "We humans could choose not to put sheep on the hills, or at least not so many, so we could have woodland pasture and big animals again over huge areas of land!"

"Farmers wouldn't be 'avin' it, Mr Pip," Billy comments.

"No, you're right, Billy, they wouldn't. But the wilded land could be worth more to them than the few sheep these barren hills support. The hills would be less prone to wildfires and would absorb more rain, reducing flooding in the valleys. The farmers can make a better living in other ways than sheep farming. Oh dear, I'm getting wordy again. Come on, let's go to the sea!"

"Hooray!"

Pop! Pop! Pop! The purlers disappear, leaving Pip to walk back down to the road; when he arrives back at the car, he finds them there, but not quite all of them.

"Mr Pip!" cries Billy. "Grandpa's gon' missin'."

"And I haven't seen Nosey for a bit either," says Penny, worried. "Has anyone seen Nosey?"

"Nope," replies Billy.

"He's been very quiet," says Stomper. "Is he alright?"

"I hope he's alright," says Penny. "Did Tricky snatch him?"

"No, he was with us a minute ago," says LuLu. "I saw Nosey when we came to the woods."

"They've both been pulled away somewhere." Pip reminds them all. "Remember, you're purling because of the magic that Emmy brings, and it's to help you to learn from creatures. You never know where purling will take you next – it might be back to your body or it might be to somewhere far away. Don't worry about Frank or Nosey, they'll be all right. After all, the invisible ones are looking after them. Now, shall we go to the sea?"

"Yes!"

"Yes!"

"You bet!"

"Come on then, let's go."

They drive on, with the windows open enough for the purlers to practise their flying skills. An hour later they crest a hill and see the gleam of water.

"The sea!" cries Larky. "The sea!"

"We won't be long now," says Pip.

They go through a few towns and villages on the way, where people stop and look curiously as the car goes by, thinking there's something a bit odd about the birds flying along with the car, or are they huge bees? People stare, not knowing quite what it is that they have just seen.

Pip drives to a place he knows, near the sea, where there's a car park in a field especially for people who want to catch a small ferry to a nearby island. At this time of day, the field is empty and there's no one around. He parks the car, dons his backpack, and sets off on foot for the beach, with the purlers high above him. They race about, excited by the cliffs and seabirds, the wind and the sound of the waves breaking on the rocks below the cliffs. Pip walks across the shingle to a narrow strip of sand at the edge of the sea.

"Mr Pip, I want to go in the water!" says Larky, excited.

"Larky, you can go into the sea, of course, but you won't get wet. The invisible ones will bubble you," says Pip.

"Bubble me? Let's see!" says Larky, waiting for the next gap between the waves before she dips into the water. Her pouch goes under, then her arms, and then her head; in another moment, out she pops, dry as a bone. "Hey, this is great! Come on, Billy, come on, David!"

The purlers disappear into the sea like slipping shadows. Pip squats down on the sand, looking and listening, waiting for them to come back. Closing his eyes, he lets the sounds and smells fill his senses. The purlers are gone for such a long time, he decides to walk up to the clifftop above the bay to watch the sunset. He climbs to the top of the headland where the grass is closely cropped by rabbits; tufts of sea pinks grow near the edge of the cliff. He sits to watch the sun until it disappears over the horizon, the sea and sky blazing with light.

"I wonder where the purlers are?" he says out loud, just to hear the sound of a voice, but no one answers. "Let's go down and make a fire. Emmy, I miss you."

He walks back down to the beach to find a sheltered spot among the rocks, gathering twigs and driftwood from above the high tide line. None of it will burn easily, he knows that, because everything is salty from the sea and salty things are always a bit damp, but eventually he gets a fire going. Settling down beside the little fire, he opens a tin of beans and pushes it into the embers at the edge of the fire to warm.

"Hallo, Pip, we're back!" whispers LuLu, purling out of the twilight.

"Ah! There you are! I was beginning to think you'd all gone away to a magical place at the bottom of the sea!"

"Well, we did!" says Stomper.

"We've seen some wonderful things, Pip," says Penny, wistfully. "We've talked with fish and dolphins, gannets and other creatures, and they've talked to us about the wild web. They want to show us more and invited us to return. The dolphins told us that humans have been taking too many fish, and doing it for a very long time, and many species are extincting. They showed us the bottom of the sea where trawlers pull nets along the bottom with weights – everything is dead for miles and miles. They showed us the horrible rubbish that kills creatures because they get stuck in it, or it blocks their gills or their tummies; even a little plastic bag can kill a creature that eats it, thinking it's a jellyfish, and the noise is terrible with ships' engines and propellers all the time, and the water's poisoned with oil and chemicals... It's really horrible!"

"I hate us!" says Larky, sobbing. LuLu purls to her side.

"It's true," says David, quietly. "The sea creatures say it's really bad. There are huge 'dead zones' in the oceans, and the worst thing of all is that the sea is getting warmer – everything's changing too quickly for creatures and plants to adapt or move. Things are dying. It's so sad."

"That's climate change, David. I can tell that you've been learning a lot purling in the sea!" says Pip. "Climate change is the thing that humans don't want to talk about or admit to. It's too frightening to face up to. That's why what you are doing is so important. There isn't much time. Climate change is runaway."

LuLu comforts Larky; no one speaks for a while. Pip pokes at the fire, sending a stream of sparks into the air; they burst into more sparks, cascading down like fireworks in the dusk. The purlers move about avoiding the sparks and the smoke, but then realise that the smoke doesn't make their eyes water or make them choke.

Larky begins to get over her upset. She gives LuLu a hug, well, as close to a hug as is possible for a purler in a pouch.

"Mr Pip," she says. "I really want to get wet in the sea, but I can't. I can't even make myself cry properly in this smoke. I want to be in my body! I'm fed up with this, and it's all so sad anyway, and I felt so sorry for the dolphin with the propeller wounds on her back."

Larky does actually begin to cry now, not because of the wood smoke but because she is so upset. LuLu purls close to her again, putting an arm around her shoulders.

"We all feel it, Larky," says LuLu, gently. "It's horrible. But there's a reason why we are purling and that's so that we can find out for ourselves about the wild web. It's time to get back to our bodies and recover, so we'll be strong enough to go back to the dolphins."

"Thanks, LuLu, I want to go back to my proper body now."

"You're right, Larky!" says Stomper. "Let's all go back and get wet and dirty – and eat something!"

LuLu has known all along that purling would be difficult for the children. It is fun, and it's exciting – it's miraculous! You can understand the wild talk, even feel the unwords, but you can't get muddy and wet, you can't get sweaty and hungry, you can't cut yourself, bleed or fall over a cliff. The purlers are missing the creatureness of their own bodies, creatureness that they have never thought about before because it's just normal – you take it for granted.

"I want my body back!" declares Stomper. "I want to smell the sea properly and taste it and get wet in it."

"You'll have to travel here in your real body to do that, Stomper," says Pip. "Purling allows you to see what's behind things, the deep Nature, but you need your body to experience these things with your senses."

"Is it real then?" asks Penny.

"What's that, Penny?" says Billy.

"Purling."

"It's real, Penny," says Pip. "Imagine the invisible ones: they are formless and have no way to taste, or feel thrill, or to hurt. They are the unwords, the deep Nature."

"So why are we purling?"

"Wildness is the wild web *and* the great wave; it's not something imagined. You can know deep Nature when you are purling, which humans have separated themselves from and forgotten. Now that you know this, you can truly be wildness in your bodies. That's why you're all longing to be in your bodies."

"I know what you mean, Mr Pip!" cries Stomper. "My first purling was brilliant, and when I woke up my body was a hundred times wilder!"

"That's right," says Pip. "It's different levels of seeing and feeling; it's different levels of awareness. What do you say to going home to your bodies, recharging, and purling back tomorrow – if you want to?"

"Can we do that? It's so far," wonders Penny out loud.

"Yes, Penny, you can, it's not far for a purler. You've probably been further than that just now, under the sea."

"I'm for doing that, Mr Pip," says Billy. "See you tomorrow!"

"Goodnight, Mr Pip!"

"Goodnight!"

The purlers disappear, each one making a little pop as they vanish. Where the firelight had a moment ago shone on their tiny faces, the air is now empty and black.

Pip finds a spoon in the backpack and sits back to eat the beans. He gazes at the embers of the fire, listening to the waves whispering on the beach. The evening is still; the sea is calm. The shrill piping of an oyster catcher echoes from the cliffs, reminding Pip of the other trip to the sea with Emmy, when he found out that Emmy comes from the future – where there are no humans...

~

Pip wakes the next morning, cold and aching, in the back of the car. He needs to stretch his limbs and warm up, so he climbs to the top of the headland again and sits among the tufts of sea pinks near the cliff edge.

The air is loud with the jakka-chack of jackdaws and the kruk-kuk of choughs. Pop!

"Allo, Pippee, iz yoo merembrin?"

"Emmy! How wonderful to see you, I've been missing you. Yes, I'm remembering. It was on cliffs like this that you told me about the wild web, and that you are from the future where there are no humans..."

"Prapz."

"Perhaps?"

"Prapz no umanz."

"You wouldn't tell me even if you knew, would you, Em?"

"Iyz nevva kno-in, Pippee."

"Emmy, things have been getting a bit hectic with the purlers doing all sorts of crazy things. I need your help. I don't know where it's all going."

"Yooz avin Emmeez elp alwayz, Pippee. Purlaz iz avin to reelise for themselvz n yooz avin to b payshunt."

"Realise what, Em? Last night they were really missing being in their bodies. They were upset because they couldn't get wet in the sea."

"Iyz missin mi boddee n all, so Iyz kno-in wot theyz feelin."

"Of course, Emmy, sorry, I forgot."

"Sorite, Pippee."

They are quiet for a bit. Pip looks out to sea watching a few gannets skimming low over the waves. As he watches, one bird gains height and plunges, folding its wings like a dart just as it disappears into the sea.

"Wen theyz purlin, theyz kno-in wot wildniss iz, n wen theyz in their boddeez, theyz bein wildniss."

"You mean we can't be both at the same time?"

"Xaklee, umanz iz feelin themselvz az seprat."

"Separate from the wild web?"

"Yip, wot az to appn iz, umanz az to b lernin ow to b bof."

"What if humans can't do that, Em?"

"Umanz iz abl, n itz time, n purlaz iz showin ow."

"Oh, Emmy, what's happening? I don't know what's happening."

"Itza mystree, Pippee. Sumfinz appnin wotz nevva appnd before. Weez avin to b trustin great wave."

"Thanks, Emmy. Come on! Let's go to the island!"

"Undastandin appnz bakwudz."

"Em?"

"Yooz lookin, n itz cumin be-ind you."

"Ah! I'll just keep looking then!"

Pip jogs down the hill to the car, with Emmy purling along just above his head humming a little tune that blows away on the wind.

"Iyzll b seein yoo on ilnd, Pippee!"

"Alright, Emmy, see you later."

"Bi!" calls Emmy, and off he goes, purling high and out to sea.

Pip watches for a moment, thinking how small Emmy is. He seems so vulnerable, but that little speck of a mouse has turned his life upside down. He shoulders his backpack and walks down to the beach, finding a path along the foot of the cliff that leads to steps up to a gate; beyond the gate, metal stairs ramp down to a floating pontoon, where the ferryboat will come.

A few people are waiting by the gate and Pip joins the queue; more people arrive, and by the time the ferry comes, there's a long line of chattering people and excited children. The ferry nudges against the pontoon while the seaman hands each person aboard, lifting the smaller children into the boat.

The waters between the mainland and the island are turbulent because of the tide rushing through. Sometimes, this 'tidal race', as it is called, is quite fierce and the water swirls in whirlpools; the ferry master has to work hard to steer the boat in the right direction, while the boat lurches unpredictably. There are lots of seabirds to be seen, some of them floating on the water in groups, or 'rafts', and some flying to and fro in a chaotic sort of way. The children on the ferry are looking out for puffins, and anyone with binoculars shouts out and points to the birds they see.

"Puffins! Look, over there!" yells a boy with curly yellow hair.

"What's that flying with them?" says one of the grown-ups.

Pip uses his own binoculars to have a look in the direction the man is pointing. He sees razorbills and guillemots flying about, a raft of razorbills on the water, and there's a group of puffins flying towards the island; in the midst of the puffins is a small but familiar shape – it's Emmy!

"There's another – and another!" says the man. "What *are* they?"

Looking carefully with binoculars, Pip sees that some of the purlers have returned and are purling with Emmy and the puffins, but they are too distant to make out their tiny faces.

"Maybe they're young puffins," Pip says, mischievously.

"No," says another passenger. "The pufflings haven't quite fledged yet. This is the last of the adults."

"Do you mean the parent birds leave the chicks alone?" says Pip.

"Yes. The pufflings leave in the next few nights. They go in the dark."

"Extraordinary."

"Never seen the likes before," says the man, referring to the tiny things flying with the puffins.

"What about small birds, like warblers, flying with the puffins for fun, or protection?" suggests Pip.

"Nah! I haven't got a clue what they were."

"Oh well, never mind."

"It might be a rare 'un."

"Probably very rare," says Pip, putting his binoculars to his eyes, trying to hide his grin.

~

Once disembarked and safely on the island, the visitors listen to a talk, given by one of the wardens, about the wildlife on the island and what you must be careful not to do. The most important rule is, everybody has to keep to the paths because there are thousands of birds nesting in burrows underground; if you stand on the grassy bits, you might crush a nest, and that would be simply awful. If you do that, you have to be thrown over the cliff into the sea. Only joking. The warden laughs.

Wanting to be on his own, Pip waits while the other people walk on and disappear along the various trails. He walks slowly and finds a place on the clifftops where he can daydream properly, as Stomper would put it. He's been worrying because the purlers have been having quite a hard time and it's all a bit distressing. What he needs right now is to be alone in a wild place, where he can smell the sea and hear seabirds yelling – a chance to feel free for a minute or two.

Well, that was the plan, but what happens is that he goes to sleep. He goes to sleep hearing the seabirds clamouring and waves crashing into the rocks below, and he dreams of the same; he dreams of puffins and finds himself talking with a puffin on the clifftop. The puffin says that she's only three years old and not old enough to lay an egg yet.

"My name's Whirligig. Come and have a look in my burrow. I'm practising for when I'm ready to lay an egg. It might be next spring."

Pip follows the puffin down into the burrow, seeing that the tunnel forks several times, going to other nests.

"Not down that one!" cries Whirligig. "That's my shearwater neighbours. We don't want them to start screaming."

Pip follows Whirligig to the chamber where, one day, Whirligig's egg will be laid.

"This is where the nest will be!" she says, proudly.

"Where's Mr Whirligig?"

"I haven't met him yet. Soon I'll be going back out to sea. I won't see land again until we come back to this burrow next spring. All that time at sea! I'll find him at sea or he'll find me! It's funny being on land; all that time at sea makes the land move about under my feet."

Whirligig tells of seeing whales and dolphins, and huge squid, and sharks and strange creatures from the deep, and they have told her of the warming oceans and changing currents, and of creatures that can't find food where they used to find food, and there are not

so many fish because humans are catching so many. Pip is beginning to get a bit fed up with listening to Whirligig and is relieved when a voice interrupts their conversation.

"Hallo, Pip!" He hears Donna's voice, and there she is, purling, in the burrow beside him. "You're purling, Pip, did you know? You're so far away from your pouch! It's in your bowl of things at home, isn't it? That's amazing."

"Goodness gracious me! I'm purling!" cries Pip. "Whirligig, this is Donna – Donna, this is Whirligig."

"Hallo, Whirligig, I've been purling far away at sea, and seen puffins that might be your family. I expect you will soon be going back to sea, won't you?"

"Yes, Donna, any day now."

"How do you choose when to go?" asks Pip.

"The wind has to be right," says Whirligig, "but if I'm grumpy because the shearwaters have kept me awake all night, then I won't go till I've had some sleep."

"I've seen some amazing things at sea," says Donna. "But there have been some very sad things too. I love purling, and seeing so much of Nature and the world, but it breaks my heart to see the wild web so torn. I need to go home, Pip."

"I know the feeling!" says Whirligig. "Back to your burrow!"

"You can just go, Donna – just wake up at home!" says Pip.

"No, Pip, I need to go in the car with the others and travel the miles. I'm so tired. The others feel the same."

"Alright, but we need to get to the car on the mainland, and I have to wake up and go on the ferry."

"Yes. I'll purl to the car," says Donna, "and, Pip, there will be the others..."

Donna disappears with a pop, which amuses Whirligig very much. Pip thanks Whirligig and says goodbye, wishing her luck flying over the ocean, and then he, too, disappears.

~

Rousing himself from sleep, Pip looks out over the sea, savouring the ease that he feels. Remembering his mission, he jumps to his feet and sets off to catch the ferry back to the mainland. He must have slept for quite a while because he is only just in time for the last boat of the day. A queue of chattering people threads its way down the steep steps to the makeshift wharf. When Pip arrives at the boat, he has to stand in the last remaining space available.

He listens to the conversations around him, the children excited about what they have seen, pleased with how their binoculars have helped them see more things and identify species from far away. Even as the boat moves away from the island, there are happy shouts from children watching the puffins flying close by, and great excitement when a herring gull alights on the boat's radio mast – it seems huge, so close.

On the waves are rafts of puffins, razorbills and guillemots; on rocks by the headland, seals have hauled out to bask in the remaining sunlight. The water itself is churning, tugging at the boat, as the tide squeezes through between the island and mainland.

Having safely disembarked and walked to the car park, Pip finds the purlers already there: Donna, Billy, Penny, LuLu, David, Larky and Stomper. They are strangely silent.

"Are you alright? What's up, Donna?" Pip asks.

"Pip, please would you put your sleeping bag on the front seat, folded, so we can all snuggle in and be close to each other, and close to you too."

"Yes, of course." Pip does as Donna asks, and watches as the purlers snuggle into the folds. He rearranges the sleeping bag to make sure they are all tucked up and safe.

"We have seen things, Pip," whispers LuLu, "both wonderful and terrible. The terrible things are enough to break our hearts, and we are hurting now so very much that we cannot speak. Please forgive us. We need to travel the miles with you. We don't have the strength even to purl home."

"I understand," says Pip. "You are all safe now, and I'll take you home. I hope Emmy's alright. Have you seen him?"

"He'll be alright," says LuLu, lapsing into silence.

That's all she says. Pip drives.

The purlers remain snuggled up in the folds of the sleeping bag for the whole journey. It is a long way, and when Pip turns off the engine, he sits quietly, enjoying the silence after hours of road noise.

"We're home," he says softly.

The purlers emerge from the sleeping bag and, without a word, disappear into thin air. At last, they return to their bodies wishing more than anything to sleep, but their sleep is filled with troubled dreams.

~

The next morning, waking from their troubled sleep, the purlers immediately think of yesterday's purling under the sea. Memories of their adventures come flooding back, making them all very sad.

It is still early morning, and Larky is in the little arbour in the back garden, a place she loves to be. Her thoughts are miles away, but, suddenly, she is alert.

Pop! It's Billy, purling.

"'Allo, Larks, is you alright?"

"No, Billy."

"Me, too."

"I'm happy to see you, Billy, but why are you purling?"

"'Cos I needs your company."

"That's nice, it's good to be with you too, but you could've walked over."

"Larks, what about we all meet in the Glade, and be together – not purlin', I mean in our bodies."

"Good idea, Billy, let's do it. Today?"

"Yeah, I'll tell 'em all. That's why I's purlin'."

"Alright, Billy, what time?"

"You'll know! Bye!" Billy disappears.

He purls the rounds – pop, pop, pop – from one friend to the next; when he's seen everyone, he wakes from his purling to find himself lying on his bed. He lies still for a long time, just thinking, just feeling. He feels different. He used to get cross and angry when he saw humans doing things that hurt Nature; he'd sort of thought he was the only one that cared, and it wasn't something that mattered to anyone else.

Now he knows how much the creatures care, and how much his friends care; now he has seen for himself the huge scale of the hurt to Nature, and he has understood what the creatures have told him about the wild web being so badly torn. He knows that Nature is disappearing; creatures and plants and living things are disappearing. Extincting. Habitats are extincting. Whole ecosystems are extincting. It is happening now, and the damage gets more every day. It's all over the whole world – it's a nightmare.

Billy has thought a lot about *'What can we do?'* He knows that everything we do is important. Saving a hedgehog, or a sparrow, or a bumblebee – every action is helping to change the world; making a bug hotel or a pond in the back garden is helping, Nature reserves, everything! Everything helps. But now he knows that there's more that could be done, more that must be done, and he wants to find out what that might be. That's why he wants to go to the Glade, but not on his own. He needs to be with his new friends and to find the answers with them. The Glade has healing power: maybe there they will see what to do; maybe their hearts will sing once more.

He must have drifted off to sleep, because an hour later he wakes up knowing at once that it's time to go to the Glade. He runs downstairs to find Nan in the garden, weeding the herbs.

"Is it alright to go to the woods, Nan?"

"Yes, Billy, we'll be alright. Back for tea?"

"Yeah, thanks, Nan."

Billy runs through the house and out of the front door, shouting goodbye to Grandpa as he pulls the door shut behind him.

~

On the way to Tillings Wood, Billy meets up with Penny and Stomper, and together they catch up with David and Larky. They greet each other, but otherwise are silent. Now and then they stop walking to stand still and listen.

"I feel so different," whispers Larky.

"Purlin's changed us, Larks," says Billy. "Come on, let's get to the Glade."

"It seems such a long way to walk!" says Penny. "I've got used to purling already! We could purl there in a moment."

"We's needin' our proper bodies, Penn," says Billy.

Last night's rain has made the ground soft and muddy. The

children love the squidgy mud and the smell of damp earth and leaves. They are soon muddy up to their knees. Larky slips as she walks round a puddle and falls in; kneeling there in the mud, she looks at her muddy hands and smiles, spreading the mud over her bare forearms and making marks on her face, like war paint.

"This feels great!" she cries. "Purling is fun, but I've missed getting dirty!"

Billy scoops up some mud and copies Larky. "Yeah! That feels good!"

David, Penny and Stomper all have a go too, and soon they are all covered in mud, and laughing, released from the deep sadness that had gripped them.

"Come on! Let's go to the Glade!" cries Stomper.

They walk on to the Glade, making their way to the talk-stone where they wait patiently. The vegetation has grown a lot since they were last here; the plants have toughened up their leaves and stems in preparation for autumn. The ferns are no longer soft, fresh green furls; now they are big and tough looking with spores spilling out in billions from the undersides of the fronds.

"Hallo, Rindill," David calls out. "May we be here for a bit?"

Rindill appears from the undergrowth and flies to the talk-stone, trilling his trill. "Hallo, human cubs, welcome to the Glade. It is still a strange feeling for me to be talking with humans. Would you like me to call the creatures?"

"No, thank you, Rindill," says Penny. "We just need to be here."

"May I ask why?"

"We've been doing a lot of purling, which is when we are very small..."

"Yes, I know what purling means," says Rindill.

"Well," continues Penny, "we have learned such a lot from creatures, about the wild web and the wild talk. What we have seen, Rindill, is making us feel very unhappy; we thought that purling would teach us what to do but it's made things seem worse."

Rindill looks at the children carefully before replying. "You need not worry about what to do, Penny Unwords, you are all being made new. It's very good that you've come to the Glade, because here you can simply be. The mud is a very good idea."

"Thank you, Rindill. Is it alright if we stay?" asks Penny.

"Yes, it is."

"Can we get logs to sit on, Rindill?" asks Billy.

"Yes, Billy, mind out for the creatures," says Rindill, slipping like a shadow from the talk-stone down into the undergrowth.

"We will, Rindill!" cries Larky.

After searching around for a while, they find some logs not too rotten and not too big to move. Lifting them carefully, so as not to harm the creatures underneath – beetles, centipedes, woodlice and many other species – they carry the logs to the middle of the Glade where they make a rough circle.

"What are we doing now?" asks David, sitting down.

"Bein'," says Billy, matter-of-factly.

They sit in silence; they are all feeling very strange. The ocean purling has changed everything. Each child soaks up the sounds, smells and sights of the Glade, feeling wonder and happiness grow in their hearts. This is what they need.

"Are we all feeling this?" Penny whispers, after a long quiet.

There is no word spoken, but Penny feels the unwords from all her friends – yes!

At last she speaks. "Just now, Rindill said that we are being remade... That reminds me of Emmy talking about being re-knitted, you know, when Pip was ill. We are being remade, and that's why we feel so strange. Being here is just what we needed, thanks, Billy."

"Bein' 'ere sort of joins us together," says Billy, happily.

"And joins us to the wild web!" says Larky.

"What's hard for me," says David, "is that when we're purling, we feel the wild web and we love that, but we can see how much it's damaged, and that hurts. We've seen what Emmy's meaning about the wild web being all torn. Now we know. But at home people don't know it's happening, or if they do, they pretend it's not."

No one says anything for a while. David has just broken the spell of wonder and happiness they were all feeling.

"David?" says Penny, gently.

"Yes?"

"You've changed so much."

"We all have."

"Yes, but you... You... It's like you've climbed out of your old self, climbed out of the skin of a horrible bully and become somebody else. What happened to you?"

The others are surprised that Penny is able to ask David, just like that. They've all been wondering, but not wanting to upset David by saying the wrong thing, or even asking about it.

"I'll tell you a story," David says. "It's about a boy whose dad wasn't his real dad, but a stepdad. His real dad used to hit his mum and hurt her, and he hit the boy too, and hurt him, and the boy got more and more angry and hit things and smashed things and bullied everybody, and it was all because he couldn't protect his mum.

"One day, the boy's dad walked out and never came back, and mum found another man – but the boy couldn't get used to him, and got more angry and nasty, and he forgot how to be anything else.

"Then one day the boy met a mouse and started to split open because his heart had been all closed and locked up. And now the boy feels like he has split open so much his whole skin has peeled away. Underneath is a little boy learning all over again how to be alive, and the new skin is thin and sensitive, like it's just hatched, and that's why the boy doesn't say much."

There's a long silence after David finishes telling his story. His friends stand up, pull him to his feet and circle him, putting hands on his shoulders. The healing power of the Glade unites them.

"Thank you, David," says Penny, quietly. "Now I know why Rindill said that your name had changed. Now you are David."

"What can we do now we have seen what we've seen?" whispers David. "Like I said, at home everyone pretends it isn't happening, they think what we say isn't true."

"People's all busy livin' their lives," says Billy.

"They're in a bubble!" moans Stomper.

"Bubblenormal," says Penny.

"What's that, Penny?!" cries Stomper.

"Unwords just happened – bubblenormal."

"Meanin' what, Penn?" asks Billy.

"Purling takes us outside what we see every day. Every day is like a bubble – it's normal because it's every day."

"So, er, where's we goin' with that?" asks Billy.

"What if everyone at school got taken out of bubblenormal?" cries Stomper.

"Ha! You'd never get 'em back!" says Billy.

"What if everyone at school was purling?" says David. "They'd feel like we do!"

"I don't want to talk about school," Larky murmurs.

"What then, Larky?" asks Penny.

"The sea," says Larky, softly.

"Ah!"

They are all quiet, remembering.

"Did we stay together?" says Penny. "It was all so fast, and we went so far. It's hard to believe it really happened."

"I can remember us being together some of the time," says Stomper. "But not all the time – I think I was on my own when I was with the jellyfish."

"I remember seeing the jellyfish too, Stomper!" says Billy. "There was millions of 'em."

"I remember seeing a lovely coral reef," says Penny. "I've always wanted to go scuba diving to see a coral reef, but there we all were, purling underwater, and it was so beautiful. And then in a flash we were somewhere else, and we were seeing dead coral. It was awful. It was all pale and dead, bleached by acidic water."

"I remember the dolphins," says Larky. "Telling us that humans take too much from the sea; they showed us the huge ships and the damage they do. It made me feel ill."

"We's all feelin' like that, Larks, you's not alone," says Billy softly, to reassure her.

Pop! "Allo!" says Emmy, appearing out of nowhere.

"Emmy! Hooray!" cries Larky. "We haven't seen you for ages!"

"Hallo, Emmy!" they all chorus.

"Iyz feelin yor unwurdz n mi eart urtz for yooz all."

"We're really sad, Emmy," says Penny. "Purling has changed us. We don't know what to do."

"Weez all bein reknittd, Pennee," says Emmy. "N our eartz iz urtin coz weez feelin wild web badlee torn."

"We weren't 'xpectin' it to be so bad, Em, or that we'd 'urt so much," says Billy.

"Iyz been wiv LuLu coz sheez poorly sorted sintz oshn purlin."

"We didn't know, I'm sorry, Emmy," says Penny. "Can we do anything for her?"

"Sheez needin loneniss."

"So, we are not the only ones feeling bad," says David.

Rindill flies to the talk-stone, trilling to get attention.

"May I speak?" he says.

"Allo, Rindill. Weez needin yor wize wurdz," says Emmy.

"You are here in the Glade where the great wave is strong. When you are strong enough in your hearts, as you now are, you will know that you *are* the wild web – what else could you be? You no longer need to believe that you are separate, or that the wild web is something to be frightened of.

"Yes, our hearts are hurting because the wild web is torn, but

let the great wave lift you so that you can return to your world and tell of what you know. Tell all the human cubs, tell all the humans! Don't let a little hurting stop you!"

The children look at Rindill in wonderment. This tiny bird has just chased away their despair and sadness. No wonder he is the keeper of the Glade.

"Thank you, Rindill," says Penny, with tears in her eyes.

"Thank you, Rindill," chorus the others.

"Rindill sez wize wurdz orite," says Emmy. "Weezl bring orl uman cubz – orl ov uman cubz – to the Glade."

"How will we do that, Emmy?" asks David.

"Wen yooz avin Wot Appnd storeez at skool, Iyzll cum purlin."

"Hey, that's a great idea!" cries Larky.

"Iyz goin to LuLu, bi!"

"Bye, Emmy, give our love to LuLu, please!" says Penny.

Pop, and he's gone.

The children remain in the Glade talking things over. Rindill comes and goes, joining in from time to time. When they are ready, they say goodbye to Rindill and make their way through the woods towards home.

~

LuLu has not been well since the ocean purling and has needed Emmy's company. She is feeling sad and vulnerable, as though her skin is so thin she feels everything too much. She is shivery with cold and her energy is leaking out.

She remembers very little about the ocean purling; she remembers fragments, bits of a dream that surface and disappear again, leaving her unsettled. In darkness, with the doors and windows closed tight against the world, she tries to keep warm, and tries not to float away. *'I wish I could be purling all the time,'* she thinks, remembering the wonderful feeling of weightlessness and freedom. It's a feeling she remembers from when she was young, a feeling of something beyond the human world being within her, informing her, not with a voice, but as something felt.

This is why the unwords are not strange to her – she can feel the shared awareness, the sense of 'isness now', and feels that she belongs; here, she is not frightened.

LuLu is startled from her daydreaming by a voice, the voice of a memory.

'You are spirit, the source of all. Until it is time, we are stardust growing isness.'

LuLu remembers Willow the deer's voice, and she replies: 'Growing isness?'

'The great wave is made of all the isnessess that have ever been and ever will be.'

'Do you fear dying, Willow?'

'I do not fear dying, LuLu, for it is returning, but I do fear, because I am a creature. I fear danger and being hunted; I fear pain and loss, and I fear the fear itself, but that is not my isness.'

Willow's voice ceases; LuLu floats in memories of purling in places that made her feel good, like the Glade, like under the sea where she saw coral reefs, and kelp forests, and plankton-rich seas teeming with sea creatures; and she remembers dolphins – oh, dolphins! Suddenly, she snaps back to find herself in a dark room, cold and frightened.

"Emmy! I need you!" she cries out in anguish, feeling that she can't bear this any more, but in that moment, she understands something of Willow's words: 'I fear the fear, but it is not my isness.'

"Ahh!" she exclaims.

"LuLu? Iz yoo orite."

"Emmy! Thank you for coming, I've been so frightened, I need your help and company."

"Iyz ere, LuLu, wotz in yor eart?"

LuLu explains to Emmy how she has been feeling since returning from the ocean adventures; she saw wonderful things but can't remember anything.

"Why can't I remember anything, Emmy?"

"Yooz been un knittd n as to b re knut furst."

"Is that because I wasn't re-knitted when I first started purling?"

"Xaklee rite, LuLu, n yooz seen orribl fingz unda oshn."

"Yes, I'm wounded and frightened. Emmy, I'd like to go to the Glade. I need to go in my full-sized body, but I feel too weak to get there."

"Iyzll b wiv yoo, LuLu, yoozll b orite coz Emmeez pouch iz powafl."

"Thanks, Em, let's try, shall we?"

Emmy purls just a little in front of LuLu as she sets off on foot for Tillings Wood. She feels protected by him, and by the power of the pouch he is purling in. She feels wrapped and held, as though she is purling herself, and she feels invisible. The few people that she passes on the streets don't seem to notice her at all.

"Yoozll b orite," Emmy reassures her.

They make the familiar journey through the cemetery and into the countryside, walking through small copses and along the edges of fields, until they reach Tillings Wood. LuLu is very tired by the time they reach the Glade, and she sits down in the familiar place close to the talk-stone. Emmy moves away a little so that she can feel the energy of the Glade and be strengthened. She thinks of Rindill, and calls him with her heart, and then she waits quietly.

At length, Rindill appears from the low undergrowth and flies to a high twig, trilling loudly, then he flies to the talk-stone beside LuLu. No words are spoken at first, as they give themselves to simply being there.

"Rindill, I am hurting so much," whispers LuLu, at last.

"Let your heart speak," says Rindill. "Speak everything to the Glade, give everything to the great wave. You are ready now."

"I have seen terrible things happening in the world, acts of violence and destruction that I feel inside myself as though these things are done to me. I am wounded, and so shocked that I cannot see my way, I cannot stand without falling, so ashamed am I to be human."

Rindill flies to her shoulder, Emmy purls closer. The moment expands. With the unwords, Rindill asks LuLu to speak of what she has seen.

After a long quiet, LuLu begins to tell her story. "We returned home, after the first day purling by the sea, because we all needed to be back in our bodies to recover. The next day we went again, purling directly there, and made the sea crossing with the puffins, and with Emmy.

"The children were excited again, and very happy. Donna and I were feeling apprehensive. At a certain moment, we all knew it was time, and we slipped into the sea. From that moment everything became as a dream, as if it were a film made of random scenes stitched together. The ocean is another world, so unfamiliar is it to our senses. We were greeted by dolphins, who became our guides and guardians. We purlers could never tell who we'd be purling with next, it kept changing. Sometimes the dolphins were not visible, as though we had purled into a place that they could not enter, but they were always with us with the unwords, reassuring us and explaining what it was that we were seeing.

"We travelled all over the world, not travelling the miles but like Emmy moves, disappearing in one place and reappearing suddenly somewhere else. It was a surprise, a shock really.

"Of all the wild creatures I've met and got to know, dolphins are the dearest to me; dolphins are as I wish to be.

"Sometimes I was alone, sometimes with Donna, or with one or two of the children. Oh, the children! How are they now? They must be feeling this too..."

"I am sorry to interrupt your words, LuLu," says Rindill. "You should know that the children are alright. They came here to the Glade, in their normal bodies, as you have done, to be healed by the great wave, which is strong here. We had a good talk, and they covered themselves with mud and that helped them to recover."

"And Donna?" asks LuLu.

"Weez not kno-in," says Emmy. "Iyzll b seein er innabit, n yooz not to b wurryin."

"Please, continue," says Rindill.

"The dolphins showed us things, swimming with us as we purled under the sea, moving around the island. They explained what we were seeing, answering our questions about the creatures and plants that lived in those waters. With the unwords, they showed us the wild web of the sea in each particular place.

"The scene would change abruptly. One time, it was just Donna and me, and we found ourselves in a kelp forest with a dolphin we hadn't met before. We saw many different kinds of fishes and crustaceans, and other sea creatures, some of which grazed on the kelp and others sheltered in the kelp and filtered plankton from the water. Sea otters swam by, twisting and turning in the water as they hunted fishes. From time to time, the otters would take sea urchins and eat them; I couldn't see how they got through the spines. The abundance of life was astonishing. Then, like watching a time-lapse film, we saw the sea otters being hunted by humans – for food and for their fur. The dolphins told me that the humans wanting to catch fish to eat believed that if they killed the otters, there would be more fish for humans to catch. The time-lapse effect goes on until the otters are all dead and the sea urchins are no longer hunted by them, and as a result there were more and more urchins and they ate the sea kelp until nothing remained, and the kelp forest disappeared – all the creatures that lived there no longer existed.

"Without a moment's pause, the scene changed again. I was with Stomper, back with the dolphin we first met, and we were swimming with a huge shoal of herrings. We saw the herrings being hunted by dolphins and tuna fish, and we saw small boats floating above, fishing with lines, and gannets and guillemots diving in making the silver trails of bubbles as they plunged down deep to catch fish. Then we saw bigger boats arriving and the fisherfolk throwing nets and scooping out lots of fish at once; then there were bigger boats with bigger nets and then there were yet bigger boats with steam engines and much bigger nets, and then huge boats with powerful diesel engines and enormous nets that catch vast numbers of fish in one go... This went on until there were no fish left. In place of the herring we could see swarms of jellyfish rising and falling gently in the water.

"Without hesitation the scene changed again, making me swoon with vertigo, and we found ourselves on the bottom of a warm shallow sea with our dolphin guide, and we saw plants, and corals, and crustaceans, and a multitude of fishes. A huge ship passed overhead, the pounding of the propellers and the rumbling of the engine hurting our ears as we watched it pulling a great rolling beam across the sea floor. The beam had spikes that caught on rocks, lifting them; even big heavy rocks the size of a car were heaved up and rolled over. As this heavy beam was dragged across the sea floor, a net attached behind caught every living thing that tried to flee for its life from the carnage. The dolphin showed us the dead and broken remains of the ruined sea floor.

"The scene changed once again, and we were in another

shallow sea that was also warm and bright, and the water crystal clear. The sea floor was covered with turtle grass and this greenness extended in all directions for great distances. The turtle grass was home to a multitude of creatures, many liking to graze on the turtle grass itself, or to shelter within it. Green turtles were one of those species that graze on the turtle grass, and there were hundreds of green turtles doing just that, occasionally swimming lazily to the surface to breathe, and then down again to the sea floor.

"Again, we were given a time-lapse view of history. We saw humans come in small boats with spears and small nets and they caught sea creatures for food, especially liking to catch green turtles. We saw larger boats with bigger nets and better equipment catching more turtles and more fish; then bigger and better boats with more efficient methods of finding the sea creatures and better methods of catching them...

"Eventually there were not enough turtles left alive to graze the turtle grass, which grew tall and rank, collapsing onto the sea floor and rotting into a poisonous sludge that used up all the oxygen in the water. The ecosystem died, and nothing living remained.

"I was taken all over the world and shown how the ecosystems of the oceans are being destroyed by the ever-increasing predation by humans. I was shown seas almost lifeless, but for squid and jellyfish, sometimes nothing but blooms of red algae; even the krill hosts were shrinking. I was shown Nature being murdered.

"I was overwhelmed and frightened and wanted this relentless horror to stop. The dolphins swam in a pod around me, even though I was so small, and I found myself back at the island where we began. The dolphins cared for me until it was time for me to purl to the car and be taken home by Pip. It was very hard for me to leave them. They wanted to show me more, but I could not, having no strength left. Even with the pouch and the invisible ones, and the dolphins themselves who helped me so much, I could do no more.

"When it was time for me to go, the dolphins swam in circles around me, blowing streams of bubbles which floated me up and out of the sea. I thanked them and, without knowing how, I disappeared from there to reappear in Pip's car. I needed to go home but was too weak to purl any more."

LuLu stops speaking, sighing wearily, her eyes cast down looking sightlessly at the ground. Rindill flies to perch on her shoulder and Emmy purls close to her face.

"You have done well to remember so clearly. Thank you for

your words," says Rindill. "Your heart is strong and with the help of the great wave, you shall be remade."

LuLu looks up to find Emmy peering into her eyes.

"Yooz bein re-knittd, LuLu, itz nevva eezee."

"Thank you, Rindill, thank you, Emmy. I think I'll be alright now that you have helped me to remember, and to speak it. I'd like to stay awhile, Rindill, if that's alright."

"Yes, for as long as you need."

"Yooz onli avin to b callin," says Emmy.

"Thank you," she whispers.

Emmy fades slowly, disappearing into thin air, and Rindill drops down like a shadow, vanishing into the undergrowth. LuLu is a little frightened to feel so suddenly alone, but she calms herself with steady breathing and feeling for the great wave. She can feel the singing – at the very edge of hearing – and is lulled into sleep.

She dreams she is purling in the Glade; she is looking at her own sleeping body sitting by the talk-stone. She purls close to her own face and, as she watches, her full-sized body begins to fade; after a few minutes, it is hardly visible. Purling LuLu feels a great surge of happiness as she realises that her body is going to disappear. She feels no fear, or worry, that it will not reappear, for she knows, without knowing how, that her body will reappear where and when it is needed.

LuLu's full-sized body disappears completely; purling LuLu is ready to be with the creatures of the Glade. She becomes aware of the soft quiet of evening, and listening carefully, she hears the susurration of countless insects whirring their wings; she can hear a multitude of small creatures moving about, scratching, digging and chewing; she can hear birds singing as the day fades to darkness, and, carried by the soft quiet, the familiar voice of the dolphin comes to remind her of the ocean and the singing of stars.

A waning crescent moon rises, and the night sounds begin. A fox barks not far away, and Trundlweed can be heard setting off across the glade; a deer coughs under the dark canopy of trees and, far away, an owl is hooting.

Chapter Two

School

On the second day of the autumn term, Mr Weatherstone does something the children don't expect: he takes his class out on a Nature walk. He wants to get the children outside into the fresh autumn air, hoping that they can gather some leaves and berries to bring back to class.

The crocodile of excited, chattering children makes its way along the road towards the Old Cemetery. Walking alongside are the grown-ups in their hi-vis jackets – one of them being Mr Weatherstone himself, and two other assistants. This is Billy's class.

They turn into the cemetery at the main gates, only to find the road cordoned off and blocked by vehicles. A team of arborists are at work, cutting branches from a yew tree and feeding them into a chipping machine. The smashed bits of tree fly out of the chipper's spout, to be caught in a cage on the back of a small truck.

One of the arborists is up in the tree, wearing a harness roped to the tree so he won't fall, and so he can use both hands to cut the branches and swing them round to drop in the right place on the ground. Another arborist, on the ground, pulls the cut branches away from the tree and feeds them, thick end first, into the chipping machine; rotating cogs in the machine grip the branch and pull it in, while spinning blades shred everything to fragments.

The noise is so great that everyone in the school crocodile has to cover their ears with their hands. Mr Weatherstone wants to get the children away because it could be dangerous, but the children are rooted to the spot and take no notice of him as he tries to get their attention. Billy and Penny watch in dismay as a tree they know well is murdered in front of their eyes. They see the tree being cut and smashed to bits by machines, as though it is just an inconvenient thing in the way. They see the arborists dressed like aliens in their protective equipment, looking like machines themselves.

There are quieter moments, between mouthfuls, when the chipping machine is just whirring and waiting for more to eat; Mr Weatherstone uses the relative quiet to shout out an order. "This way, children, now please! It is not safe to be so close."

"Sir!" Billy shouts out. "They's murderin' my tree – they's breakin' my 'eart!" He runs to the tree and climbs, determined to save it.

"Billy, come back at once!" calls Mr Weatherstone, alarmed.

A few other children take courage from Billy and run to join him, following him up the tree. Soon there are half a dozen children swarming up the pegs of the sawn-off branches as though the tree were a ladder.

The arborist in the tree stops his chainsaw. The man on the ground turns off the engine powering the chipper; the whirring blades gradually slow down until there is silence.

With a sudden shriek, all the other children, except for Bottl and Luke, run to the tree and crowd round the bottom. The arborist abseils to the ground, taking care not to knock any of the children out of the tree, or cut them with the chainsaw. He unclips the carabiner from the rope and walks over to Mr Weatherstone. He's very cross.

"If you can't control these children, I'll have to call the police."

Mr Weatherstone smiles. "We don't need a sledgehammer to crack this nut, let's talk to them."

"We haven't got time for this nonsense. Get the kids out of the way right now, or there'll be trouble."

"Why, exactly, are you cutting this tree? It looks perfectly healthy to me."

"Council contract, we do what they want done."

The children have swarmed up the tree and are organising their shouting into a chant of 'save our tree, save our tree...' The arborist gets his phone from the cab of the truck and makes a call.

"Who are you calling?" asks Mr Weatherstone.

"Parks Superintendent. Oh, hallo – arborist here. We've got a bunch of school kids up a tree we're cutting. You can hear 'em." He holds the phone towards the tree to pick up the noise of the children yelling, and puts it to his ear again, listening. "Alright," he says, and ends the call, putting the phone in his pocket. "She's on her way."

When the Parks Superintendent arrives, she takes in the situation at a glance. She's used to this sort of thing, and she walks calmly over to the tree.

"Can we talk?" she says, looking up at the children. A few children stop chanting, and she calls out again: "Please, will you let me explain?"

The children gradually fall silent.

Billy glares down at her. "What's to explain?" he yells, his anger fierce in him like fire. "You's murderin' my tree!"

"Is it your tree?"

"It's the cemy, ain't it? Belongs to us all, don't it? Anyway, I loves it."

"What's your name? My name's Sandra."

"Billy." He sounds sullen.

"Billy, I understand what you feel. In my job I feel like that a lot, because decisions are made that mean cutting trees down, or cutting them back."

"Why? Who says? Who's the murderer? Why ain't we asked?"

"The council committee decides. It all takes a long time and surveys are done and people write in with complaints and requests. Decisions are made, and a contract for the maintenance work is drawn up. Some of the work is done by the parks department, but major tree work is put out to tender for professional arborists to bid for."

"What's that mean?"

"Professional arborists look at the work and tell the council how much it will cost. The council then chooses which contractor will get the job."

"Why's it bein' cut down? There ain't nothin' wrong with it!"

"It's not being cut down, Billy, it's being pollarded."

"That's like 'avin' me arms cut off, ain't it. Why?"

"The owners of the property next door asked for the tree to—"

"What right 'ave they got, they's only lived 'ere five minutes 'n the tree's been 'ere years 'n years, 'n what about the tree's rights?"

"I understand that you're upset, Billy, and I'm sorry," says Sandra. "I think you are very brave to protest the way you have, all of you. I'm sorry that you didn't know this was going to happen, it must have been a shock." Sandra pauses for a moment. "It's time to come down now, please, Billy."

Some of the children begin to climb down, feeling that the drama is over. Billy doesn't move; he clings to the top, tears streaming down his face. Penny climbs back up to him; she holds on to the tree with one hand and puts her free arm round his shoulders. They've spent the summer purling and feeling the unwords, and Penny feels for the tree too, and she cries too. She knows that Billy is feeling powerless to do anything, and it's the powerlessness that makes the anger keep welling up and exploding out of him in great sobs.

Penny gives Billy all her attention, and together they feel the unwords of the tree. The tree is hurting, but not dying; it is not angry, but forgiving. The aliveness of the tree is so great that Billy is calmed; his anger pours out of him, flowing through the tree into the ground. He thanks the tree, with the unwords and with his voice.

"Thanks, Penn, you're a real friend. I's got it now, let's go."

When they've scrambled down, everyone claps as they cheer and laugh. Sandra has meanwhile had a chat with Mr Weatherstone, and soon the crocodile re-forms, and the children walk off, heading back to school.

As soon as the children have left the cemetery, the arborist climbs the tree again to carry on the job. The branches are cut off leaving long pegs, but the small leafy shoots that will help the tree to recover are not cut off. It is a sad sight, but at least the tree will survive, and yew trees can live for over a thousand years.

~

The children are unusually quiet as they walk back to school. They've been shocked by what happened. Mr Weatherstone walks with them, sharing their feelings. He's not at all cross with them.

As their field trip was cut short, they get back to school before break time. Mr Weatherstone says to go to the toilet, if they need, drink some water, and come back to the classroom.

"We need to debrief," he says when they are back in the classroom again.

"What does that mean, sir?"

"Well, Siobhan, we've had a dramatic field trip and I would like us to talk about what happened. Who would like to start?"

"Billy was brilliant, shinning up the tree like that!" says Derek.

"Why did you do that, Billy?" Mr Weatherstone asks.

"I was awful angry, sir."

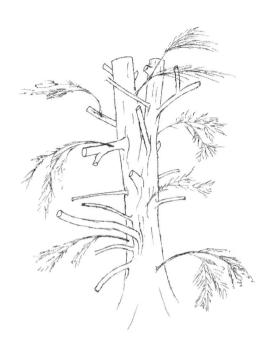

"We know that, Billy, I think. Tell us what happened."

"Up the tree, sir? What 'appened was, the tree soaks up all me anger. I's hurtin', 'n the tree was hurtin', but it were never mean 'n angry. It's alive 'n forgivin'.''

"I understand," says Mr Weatherstone.

"Why were you so angry, Billy?" says Olly. "It's just a tree."

"Not just a tree – it's a livin' bein' 'n part o' the wild web. We's all part o' the wild web too, so the tree's part o' me."

"That's good, Billy," remarks Mr Weatherstone. "Can you say any more about that?"

"Well, sir, I see 'ow the humans are like robots, sir, like the tree was just a thing to get rid of and smash to smithereens with that machine. They's feedin' that machine, like the machine's alive 'n the tree ain't. I feel like it ain't alright, sir."

"We all felt that! That's why we climbed the tree," Siobhan exclaims. "Billy's right, the tree gave us all something."

"You're all off your rockers," says Bottl, sneering. "I ain't 'eard so much twaddle in all me life."

"So, what do you think happened, Brian?" asks Mr Weatherstone, using Bottl's proper name.

"A tree gets cut 'n Billy 'as a tantrum, like 'e always does. Billy's soft in the 'ead, sir, that's all there is to it."

"Not true, Bottl," says Penny, gently.

"Penny's soft as well," says Bottl.

"Alright, alright," says Mr Weatherstone. "Billy, tell us more about what happened to you."

"Simple, really, sir. The tree's showin' 'ow me anger's like them machines, 'n I's not wantin' that. I's 'avin to find anuvva way."

"Another way to what?" asks Olly.

"Humans are tearin' the wild web apart 'n it ain't alright. I have to be doin' somethin' 'bout it."

"What's the wild web, Billy?" asks Paresh.

"All wild things, everything that's alive, is like a web: every bit's joined up 'n if you break the web, you kill what's wild. I want what's wild more than anythin' but we're 'avin' wildness robbed from us by grown-ups 'n machines."

The classroom is silent for a moment before Mr Weatherstone speaks. "Hmm. You are very passionate about this, Billy. Thank you for talking about it. We need a subject for this term's class project. Do you think we could do a project about this sort of thing?"

"Yes!" yell most of the class.

"Boring!" shouts Bottl.

"Sir, we were going to ask you," says Penny. "Billy and me–"

"Billy and I," Mr Weatherstone corrects her.

"Erm, Billy and I have got a project planned, and we want to ask if we could do it."

"What is it, Penny? Is it something the whole class could do?"

"Yes, Mr Weatherstone, that's what we're hoping. We've spent a lot of the summer holidays learning from wild creatures about wildness and the wild web, and how Nature works. What we've learned is different to what grown-ups tell us. We've been making a list of things we want grown-ups to do to help Nature, and another list of things we want grown-ups to stop doing because they hurt Nature. We would like to ask the whole class to help us do this – and Larky, David and Stomper's class too because they've been doing this with us all summer."

"'David' is it now? You're sweet on 'im," says Bottl, referring to David's change of name from Dungl after he met Mowzl Emmy.

"Hmm," says Mr Weatherstone, ignoring Bottl's interruption. "Penny, what will you do with these lists when they're finished?"

"We'll write letters to the PM, and to HRH, and to the

Secretary-General of the United Nations, and ask them to hear the voice of all of us children and to do what we ask for."

"Well said, Penny, very bold and passionate. I won't try to guess what they will say in reply, but I will say that I think it's a really good project. Who agrees that we make this a whole class project? Let's see a show of hands."

"Yes, me!" call out most children, putting hands in the air. Mr Weatherstone does a quick count.

"Not me, it's boring," says Bottl, groaning.

"Me too, sir!" Luke chimes in.

"Brian, Luke, the great majority of the class have voted in favour, so that's what we will be doing. We'll start tomorrow! Now, off you go."

The children begin their usual stampede out of the classroom for break.

"Sir?"

"What is it, Billy?"

"Thanks."

Mr Weatherstone smiles.

~

Later at lunch break, Billy and Penny talk over what's been happening. They can't quite believe that Mr Weatherstone has agreed to the class project idea.

"We need to look at those bits of paper that Tom gave us. You know, the lists we did?" says Penny.

"Yeah, I lost mine," says Billy. "Hey, Stomper! Larks!" he calls. "Come on over 'ere!" They come across with David, and Billy tells them what's happened in class.

"We should meet up at Pip's and talk about what to do in class tomorrow," says Penny.

"Or Tom's place, but how can we do that?" says Larky.

"I've got a phone now," says Penny, proudly.

"Let's see it, Penny! What is it?" says Stomper.

"It's pay as you go, and it works alright when there's a signal. I'll phone Mr Pip and ask him. I haven't got Tom's number."

Pip doesn't answer, so Penny texts him.

"He'll text back, I hope," says Penny.

Pip texts back before the end of break to say it's fine to meet at Tom's.

"I's got an idea," says Billy. "Why don't we ask Mr Weatherstone to come too?"

"What?" cries Larky.

"I's got a feelin'," says Billy.

"Good idea, Billy, let's ask him," says Penny. "I'll do it. See you all later at Tom's!"

~

Tom is delighted to have everyone come around to his place. The first to arrive are Pip and Mr Weatherstone. Mr Weatherstone says to call him John, so they do.

"Which children are coming, John?" asks Tom.

"I've no idea. Penny mentioned it and invited me to come."

"Ah yes, Penny, she's a mysterious one," says Tom.

"She is," says Pip. "She quietly holds everything together."

"Holds what together?" John asks.

"There's been a lot happening for the children this summer. They've had some challenges and upsets. Penny is the one who holds the compass steady, as it were, for all of them. You'll find out more in a minute – here they come!"

"May we come in, Mr Tom?" calls Larky.

"Yes, yes, come in, and welcome to you all!" cries Tom.

Larky is followed closely by David, then Billy, Penny, Stomper, and, to everyone's surprise, Siobhan, Olly and Derek, from Billy and Penny's class. They had asked Billy some questions at school and he just said the best way to get answers would be to come along to Tom's, so they did! Last to arrive is Donna, Larky's mum.

When all the introductions have been made, Penny stands up and nods at Billy to come and stand with her. Penny says that they need to get ready to start the school project, but first Billy wants to say something. Billy relates the story of the yew tree, and he tries to explain about the feelings he had at the top of the tree and how his anger had drained away. He then talks about their summer of purling.

"We's been purlin' all summer 'n seen stuff that breaks our 'earts, 'n we know we 'as to do somethin' – but we's not sure what. I's always been angry, you all knows me. But what I sees in me 'eart, when I's up that tree, was that bein' angry is bein' like machines. We can't fight machines, we'd be just like 'em. It's stupid, it's not from my 'eart. So, I's wantin' to start now by askin' 'what can we do?'"

"Billy and I have been talking about this," says Penny, "and what we have come up with is that we can share it. We can tell as many children as possible – and grown-ups if they will hear us – about what we've been seeing when we're purling. So, the school project is a way to get other children to join in."

"The problem is," says Billy, "they's not goin' to get it unless they learn purlin' too."

"We have to start somewhere, Billy," says Pip.

"Like you said, Billy," says Penny, "even for our friends to get what we mean, we know they'll have to feel it in their hearts first. We can't *show* anyone the great wave. They have to *feel* it."

"You've discovered a lot over the summer," says Tom. "You won't be able to tell it all at once at school. You'll need to draw people in, get them interested and ask about what *they* feel."

"Good idea, Tom," says Donna. "You'll soon get your school friends wanting to purl, and when they do they'll 'get it'."

"We'll never get the politician's purlin'," says Billy.

"Ha! Why not, Billy? You got me purling!" says Tom, smiling.

"'Cos they's locked in."

"Locked in?"

"Well, I dunno, they's only seein' one way, they's wantin' to control Nature 'n when there's problems they's wantin' more controllin' than before. It's gettin' worse every minute."

"But, Billy," says Pip. "It's the system that's like that, people are locked into a system; we never know what's in their hearts."

"That's right, Billy," says David. "Look what happened to me!"

"Come on, Billy," says Tom. "It's good to debate, but we must do some work here. Let's work on the list of words, so you've got something to take to all the children at school."

"Let's brainstorm now!" cries Stomper. "What about: 'what do we really care about?'"

The children shout out what they care about, and Penny tries to write things on the whiteboard. Tom helps, and in no time at all they've filled the board with words.

"It's enough to give me a headache!" cries Siobhan.

"How about starting with the list we did before?" says Penny. "I've still got mine even though it's a bit crumpled. Mr Tom, can you put it up on the screen again, like you did last time?"

"Of course, Penny, just a tick," says Tom, as he turns the various machines on. "Here it is."

What we want:

    We want everyone to care more about Nature
    We want green energy
    Make homes for wildlife
    Give back to Nature
    Make more wild places with wolves and monsters
    Make more woods. Plant squillions of trees
    Make more animal hospitals
    Nature's Rights: make laws to stop people hurting Nature
    Put them in prison when people hurt pets and animals
    Bring Wild Nature into towns where people need it

What we don't want:

    Stop climate change. No more smelly oil and coal
    Stop too many humans happening
    We don't want life without Wild Nature
    We don't want wild creatures being hurt or killed
    Stop slavery of humans and animals
    Stop poaching and hunting animals
    Stop cutting down trees and forests
    Stop covering Nature with concrete and roads and houses
    Stop making guns and bombs and wars
    Stop pollution
    Stop factory farming
    Stop machines smashing everything

The room is very quiet as they read the lists.

"Well?" says Pip, eventually.

"We did pretty well last time, didn't we!" says Penny.

"Erm, alright, but we ain't wantin' more bleedin' lists!" says Billy irritably. "We need a way for all of 'em at school to get what we're on about!"

"Billy," says David, "we're learning from creatures, and all the kids can do that. We have to trust... Imagine when they're all purling!"

"Well said, David and Billy!" cries Penny. "We can just be simple and in our hearts. We can ask everyone what they feel about Nature, like Emmy does, when he asks 'wotz in yor eart?'"

"You's got it, Penn!" says Billy, excited now. "And we can show what purlin' is – would you let us do that, Mr Weatherstone?"

John doesn't answer straight away; he is puzzled and

thoughtful. "I've been listening with great interest," he says at last. "But I don't really understand what you're talking about. I don't know what 'purling' is, Billy, and from what I've heard it sounds like 'purling' is the only way anyone is going to understand you. What is 'purling'?"

"This is purling!" cries Larky.

Everyone looks around for Larky but can't see her anywhere.

"I'm up here!" says Larky, giggling, up near the ceiling.

Gasps and shrieks come from Siobhan, Olly and Derek, who haven't seen anything like this before.

"Good grief!" exclaims John. "Extraordinary! Charlotte? Is that you? Are you alright?"

"Well done, Larks!" cries Billy. "Where's you sleepin'?"

"Behind the sofa," says Larky, purling down from the ceiling, where she had been watching and waiting for the right moment to announce herself. Stomper looks over the back of the sofa, to see Larky's sleeping body on a cushion on the floor.

"Yes, she's here alright!"

"Please tell me what's happening. Is Charlotte alright?" says John, visibly alarmed.

"Larky is purling, Mr Weatherstone," says Penny calmly. "She is asleep and dreaming into her pouch. She is alright, yes. In fact, she's very happy."

"Extraordinary. Why is she so small?"

"You can talk to me, Mr Weatherstone," says Larky, as she purls closer to John's face and gazes into his eyes. "I am small because the pouch is Emmy-sized. Emmy is the mouse from the future."

John groans. "Oh my god. This is getting too much for me."

"John, I understand exactly how you are feeling," says Tom, smiling broadly. "I had the same experience when I came back from my travels at the beginning of the summer. I couldn't believe what I was seeing. Slowly I understood, and I've even learned to purl a bit myself, but I'm only a beginner. The children are much better at it. You will be able to purl too, John."

"Why would I want to? So small, it's too strange! I don't understand what any of you are talking about."

"I have an idea!" exclaims Pip.

"Oh-oh, look out!" cries Billy.

Pip smiles at Billy's tease. "You may not know it, but Tom has been typing 'Wot Appnd' from the notes in the orange ring binder.

Tom, could you make a copy for John to read?"

"Easily," says Tom. "It still needs some editing as my typing isn't good, but it's readable. How about it, John?"

"What, exactly, is 'Wot Appnd'?"

"Oh, yes – sorry, John," says Pip. "It's the story of the mouse, Horatio Mowzl, and how the magic of the pouches happened."

"The mouse? What mouse?"

Pop! "Allo, evrywun, iz yoo callin Emmy?"

"Emmy! Perfect timing," says Pip. "May I introduce you to John Weatherstone, and this is Siobhan, Derek and Olly, from Billy's class at school. John is their class teacher."

"Allo, evrywun, mi name iz Oratio Mowzl, n Iyz a mowse. Iyz toy mowse in uman world but Iyz real mowse bak ome wiv an eart n real feelinz."

Emmy purls in front of Mr Weatherstone, close to Larky who's moved over a bit to give Emmy room. He looks into John's eyes with that look that goes all the way to the middle.

The room is quiet; Emmy moves from John to Siobhan, then to Derek, then Olly, then back to John.

"Mista John, weez needin uman cubz to b purlin, n weez needin yoo to b tellin storee ov Wot Appnd in skool."

John is speechless. Siobhan finds her voice first.

"Why do you need the children to be purling?"

"Allo, Shavorn. Weez needin umanz to b reelisin."

"Realising what, Emmy?" asks Olly.

"Allo, Ollee. Reelisin wild web iz dyin n yooz avin to b wakeful."

"What's the wild web, Emmy?" asks Derek.

"Allo, Derrik. Wild web iz orl ov Nature." Emmy turns to Larky. "Fankz for callin Emmy, Larkee. Bi, evrywun!"

Pop! Emmy is gone. Pop! Larky is gone.

"Larks?" cries Billy. "Are you alright? Are you awake?"

"Oh, yes, Billy, here I am," says Larky, yawning as she climbs over the sofa and comes to Mr Weatherstone. "Please will you read 'Wot Appnd' to us all at school, Mr Weatherstone?"

"Yes, Charlotte I will, to your class as well as Billy's. Why not the whole school! I look forward to finding out what it's all about. Yes, Tom, please give me a copy. You could email it to me if that's easier. Here's a card with my address."

"Right, John, I'll do that now."

John leans forward in his chair, puts his head in his hands, and groans.

"Are you alright, John?" says Pip.

"Shocked. I feel like I've been torn open and everything spilled out. Ideas, I mean, beliefs, you know."

"We understand," says Donna. "It's been the same for us all, and it takes time for it to sink in."

"We'll soon 'ave you purlin' too, sir!" says Billy.

"Me?" cries John.

"That's what Tom said, too!" says Larky.

"Tom's made his pouch," says Donna, "and you've been purling, haven't you, Tom?"

"I have indeed, Donna, thanks to you all, but as I said before, I'm only a beginner. Some of you have been purling all summer and have had big adventures."

"We have, Mr Tom," says Penny. "But it's not been fun exactly. We love purling. We love being close to creatures and being able to understand the wild talk. But what we've seen and what we've learned from creatures has made us feel sad. What humans are doing to Nature, all over the world, is hurting the wild web, and we've seen how creatures and plants are suffering and dying, and we have seen how humans are suffering and dying, and all this hurts us and breaks our hearts. That's why we've got to find a way to do something to help the wild web."

"Penny's right," says Billy. "And what I's gettin' from purlin' is I see what's missin', I see what's bein' robbed from us all, 'n I need it back – we've got to 'ave it back! We're urtin' in our 'earts 'cos we're missin' Wild Nature, 'n our 'earts are closed 'n we're all shut in 'n not seein' the 'arm what's 'appnin'."

Billy's voice grows stronger and more confident as he speaks, and when he stops talking the room is quiet.

"Billy, that's a strong message," says Tom. "Something for us all to think deeply about. I think we need to give John a chance to recover from all the surprises he's had this evening. Maybe it's time we finished up here. Penny, would you like more lists printed out?"

"No, thanks, Mr Tom, they've done their job. We'll make new ones now."

Pip laughs, quietly, as he watches the children filing out saying goodbye to the grown-ups, and 'thank you' to Tom for having them there.

"Amazing, there'll be no stopping them now!" Pip says.

"Are you happy about taking this on at school, John?" asks Tom.

"Yes, I look forward to it. Might need to bend the rules a bit."

"I think we are all being asked to bend the rules a bit, if not chuck them out totally!" says Pip.

"Tom, Pip, I could send 'Wot Appnd' to a good friend of mine who teaches at another school, I'm sure he would work with it. What do you think?"

"John, wait until you've worked with Billy and the gang, and then suggest it. This is their flame, it's up to them!" says Pip.

"I agree," says Tom. "But I'll not be surprised if a bush fire happens very soon."

John Weatherstone sets off home, feeling light-headed and excited. Later, he opens his laptop to check emails. There it is. From Tom Wylder. It's a PDF attachment. He saves a copy to the hard disk, then opens the file and starts to read, reading until late into the night.

~

The next day, Billy's class have arithmetic with Mrs Porter until break time. When the children return to their classroom after break, they find Mr Weatherstone there waiting for them. He is perched on the desk at the front of the class, squatting on his heels. He is tall and rather gaunt, and in this position strangely angular with his knees sticking out; his curly hair is tousled and wild because he was up most of the night reading a story. He looks like a predatory creature waiting to pounce on some unsuspecting prey.

In fact, the children know John Weatherstone better than to be frightened of him. They like him. They can tell that something different is going to happen, and there is a buzz of excitement as they go to their desks.

"Door, please, Jerome," says John Weatherstone.

Jerome, whose desk is closest, closes the door.

"Thank you."

Mr Weatherstone is quiet, looking around at the children for a few moments before opening the laptop computer on the desk in front of his feet.

"'The Adventures of Horatio Mowzl'," he says. "Chapter one – 'Typhoon'."

He reads Emmy's story until it's time for lunch break; he reads 'Typhoon', 'Allo', 'Time Capsules', 'Home Oak', 'Pouches and Things' and 'Snow'. Then he snaps the laptop shut.

"When you come back from break, we'll make a start on your class project."

~

"Billy!" Penny calls, outside in the playground. "It's so weird hearing Mr Weatherstone read 'Wot Appnd'!"

"Yeah, Penn, ain't it just. What's puzzlin' me is why he ain't sayin' it's about us."

"There's none of us in it until the chapter called 'Bowl of Things', when Emmy finds you in the woods. Do you remember?"

"Oh, yeah, course. What'll 'appen when they realise it's us?"

"That's when we call Emmy!"

"Purlin'! You's got it, Penn, perfect moment!"

"Billy, I think Mr Weatherstone wants to help us."

"Me, too, I 'ad a feelin'."

"It's such a lovely day!" cries Penny, skipping about. "I wish we had a classroom outside."

"Wild school! Good idea. Come on, we'd better get this project goin'."

Back in the classroom, Mr Weatherstone has cleaned the whiteboard and written up a new heading: 'Class Project'.

"Time to settle down," he calls. "Please, sit down and open your project notebooks. As we agreed yesterday–"

"We never agreed nothin', sir!" shouts Bottl.

"Brian, we had a vote, and a lot more than half the class voted for the class project."

"That's not fair, sir."

"Perhaps democracy is not fair, Brian, but it's the best system we've got at the moment. Where was I? Ah yes, we voted, and we have chosen to do a project proposed by Penny and Billy. Would you introduce it, please?"

"Well, sir," begins Penny. "What we–"

"Sorry to interrupt you, Penny," says Mr Weatherstone, "but please would you and Billy come to the front and talk to everyone about your idea; you can use the whiteboard to write things down."

Penny glances at Billy, knowing that this will be really hard for him. It won't be easy for her either, but she doesn't hate it like Billy does. Billy hates standing at the front and having to read something. It's even worse now, because he hasn't even got anything to read. Penny sees fear and anger flash in Billy's eyes and his face flushes; then he looks directly at her, and for a moment they feel the unwords uniting them. He stands up and escorts Penny to the front of the class. He looks at her again as if to say, 'you kick off, please, Penn, while I's findin' me wits'.

"Erm," says Penny, hesitantly. "Billy, me and some friends spent a lot of time this summer outside in Nature, and we met some really nice people who know a lot about Nature and wildlife. Anyway, we found out that Nature's in big trouble because of the harm that humans are doing, and we want to help. We must help. So, we thought of this project to find out what we all know, and what we feel about it and – and, well, and everything."

"So," says Billy. "We want to get talkin' 'bout all this with you all 'n to kick off we've got a question – Penn, can you write this down?"

"Can't you write yet, Billy?" yells Bottl.

Billy is shaking like a leaf because he's so nervous, that's why he asked Penny to do the writing. He tries to ignore Bottl's taunt.

"What's makin' us humans 'urt Nature 'n wild things?"

"What *do* people do?" calls a voice from the back.

"Alright, let's start with that," says Billy. "What do 'umans do that 'urts Wild Nature?"

"We don't hurt Nature that much. I get big spiders and woodlice in my bedroom!" says Gemma.

"I hate it when poachers kill elephants," says Holly, "just to cut off their tusks. It's horrible."

"And rhinos!" says Tracey.

"People who are cruel to pets should go to prison," says Gill.

"Killing badgers is cruel as well!" says Paresh.

"People stamp on things, that's cruel too," says Tracey.

"Cutting trees down is horrible, I hate that the most," says Siobhan.

"Alright! Slow down!" cries Penny, remembering the chaos at Tom Wylder's when they did the first brainstorm. "What about another question: 'What do you like doing outdoors?'"

"Skateboarding!"

"Going to the seaside!"

"What if I ask, 'What's your favourite wild place?'," says Billy.

"Arsenic factory!"

"Jungle."

"Forest!"

"Zoo!"

"The shopping centre."

"Beach."

"Wotsit Park."

"Help, Penny!" says Billy, worried because the class is getting noisier, and Mr Weatherstone will probably say something soon to shut them all up.

"Hurrm." Penny clears her throat. All eyes look to her. "We need your help to do a survey of our whole school, and maybe other schools too. We need to make a questionnaire for everyone in the whole school, asking what they think about these things, and we'll ask parents too, if they'll listen."

"Why?" says Luke.

"We want people to think about Nature more."

"Why, what's the point?" says Luke.

"None of us is seein'," says Billy. "None of us is noticin', 'n the wild web is bein' torn to shreds..."

"Ha-ha, Billy," says Bottl, jeering. "You sound like that story we had this morning – 'wild web'! Ha! It's a just a fairy story, Billy, get a life!"

Billy looks to Penny for help. *'Oops,'* he thinks.

Penny smiles. "We want to help Nature," she says, "and we need your help. Let's try to think up a good list of questions. What would you like to be asked?"

"Er, what's my favourite animal," Holly chips in.

"That's good, Holly, I like that," says Penny. "Any more?"

"What's your favourite spider?" cries Alfie.

"Why do people kill animals for fun?" says Tracey.

"Should we protect wildlife?" says Erin.

"Do you like being outdoors?" suggests Gemma.

"Why do people hurt wildlife?" says Derek.

"How could we treat animals better?" says Sophie.

"Good stuff!" says Billy. "We're gettin' into it now! Write stuff down if you think of anythin' else, 'n let me 'n Penny know."

"Well done, everyone!" says Mr Weatherstone. "We'll do some more on it tomorrow. Perhaps we'll be ready to draft up a questionnaire. I'll ask in the school office if they'll type it and print it for you. Off you go now, class dismissed!"

~

The next day, Billy's class has geography with Mrs Proctor up until break time. After break, Mr Weatherstone reads some more of 'Wot Appnd', but he doesn't get much further with the story because there's a bit of a disturbance. As you may remember, the chapter called 'Bowl of Things' is about Emmy purling in the woods, where he meets a little human called Billy.

When Mr Weatherstone reads the bit about Billy and the bivouac, someone in class starts choking and coughing. It's Bottl. Mr Weatherstone pats him on the back, worried that the poor child might choke to death.

"Are you alright, Brian?" Mr Weatherstone asks.

Bottl gasps. "I'll be alright," he says, and then wheezes and coughs some more. "I'll be–. It's 'im, sir, it's 'im!"

"What, Brian? Who's what?"

"Billy and–" Brian coughs again. "Billy 'n the bivvy, it's this Billy, I seen it! I's seen 'im!"

"Billy?" Mr Weatherstone turns to look at Billy.

"It's true, sir. Bottl 'n Dungl was spyin' on us."

"Billy, is it you in the story?" cries Siobhan.

"Yeah, it's real."

"Who's Mowzl?" says Tracey.

"Who's Pip and LuLu?" says Erin.

More and more questions get fired at Billy, until Mr Weatherstone calls for quiet and asks Brian to explain.

"I sees 'em in the woods, talkin' wiv fairies."

"Who?"

"Billy 'n Larky, sir."

They are interrupted by a tapping at the window; the children turn to see a bird clinging to the window frame, tapping the glass furiously with its heavy bill.

"It's Rattltap, sir! Can I let 'im in?"

"I suppose you'd better, Billy," says John, sighing helplessly, but smiling too.

Billy opens the window, and Rattltap flies in with cries of 'Tchak, Tchak'. He flies round the room looking for somewhere to perch, settling on a cork pin board attached to the wall; he has a good look at everyone.

"'Allo, Rattltap!" cries Billy. "We was callin' Emmy – me 'n Penny, I's meanin'."

"Tchikkltchakkatuk."

"He says Emmy asked him to come," explains Penny, being the only one able to understand Rattltap. Billy still can't understand the wild talk unless he's purling, or if Emmy's close by.

"You can't really understand that bird, can you, Penny?" says Derek, astonished.

"Yes, and when Emmy arrives, you'll be able to as well. Listen! I can hear Emmy now!"

"Who's Emmy when he's at home?" says Luke, with a sneer.

"Emmy is Mowzl in the story you've been listening to. Remember, in the cave with his cousin, Star? Star wanted to call him 'Emmy'."

"Laa la laaa la laaaa laaaa!" Pop! Emmy appears, purling, in the middle of the classroom.

"At last you're here, Mowzl Emmy," says Rattltap. "You know, these human cubs don't understand a word I'm saying – except for Penny Unwords, of course."

The children stare at Emmy, and then at Rattltap, and then back to Emmy, their eyes wide, their mouths open in astonishment.

"Allo, uman cubz, mi naym iz Emmy n Iyz a mowse. Iyz toy mowse in uman world, but trulee Iyz real mowse wiv an eart n real feelinz, n Iyz avin real boddee bak ome."

Emmy purls close to the children, looking into their eyes with that look that goes all the way to the middle.

"Iyz needin yor elp."

"Tchak!" says Rattltap in agreement.

"Iyz needin yoo to b listnin to Wot Appnd, coz itz real n troof, n wild web iz dyin coz ov wot umanz iz doin. Rattltap n meez cum ere so yooz kno-in Wot Appnd iz real n troof."

"Human cubs," says Rattltap, "it is the magic the mouse brings that enables you to understand the wild talk, but you can learn this for yourselves, just as Penny Unwords has already done. All the wild creatures are calling for your help, and there isn't much time. Listen carefully to the story that is being read to you, as it will tell you what to do. We wild creatures invite you all to come to the gathering in the Glade on the shortest day, what humans call the solstice. Now I must return to my beloved Tattlrap. Goodbye, for now! Tchakkak!"

Rattltap flies off through the open window, and away towards Tillings Wood.

Emmy purls close to the children, but not too close, especially around Bottl and Luke; he can see that Bottl and Luke do not like what's happening.

He purls to the centre of the room, drawing the children's attention so that he can say goodbye.

"Fankz, evrywun, Iyz opin yoozll all b elpin. See yooz innabit!"

Emmy fades away, disappearing with a pop.

"Aaawa! Where's he gone?" cries Holly.

"Sir, can we have more story, please?"

"Yes, Siobhan." Mr Weatherstone has a big smile on his face. "But not today, as we have other lessons to do too. Class! It's break time – off you go!"

~

The children talk excitedly about the visit by Rattltap and Emmy; soon everyone in the school is talking about it, and they want to know more. Mr Weatherstone gives copies of 'Wot Appnd' to other teachers and, with Billy's and Penny's agreement, he emails the story to teachers in other schools. Emmy and Rattltap find themselves being called to classrooms in these other schools, to surprise and encourage children who are new to the story. It's easy for Emmy, because he can purl to these places, but poor Rattltap has to fly everywhere!

Even though Bottl and Luke are outnumbered, they remain stubbornly determined not to join in. Billy tries talking with them, but it only leads to a noisy argument. Penny tries to make the peace, and they just pretend that she isn't there. Penny asks Emmy about what to do, and he says just leave them alone.

When they get more project time in class, Billy and Penny and their classmates soon work out what to put in the questionnaire, and when it's finished it looks like this:

Questionnaire about:
'What do you feel about Nature?'

Please would you write down your:
Name..Age.................
Your school....................................

1   What's your favourite animal?
2   Do you like being outdoors?
3   Where do you like to go outdoors?
4   What's your favourite wild place?

5   Do you think that humans do things that hurt Nature?
6   Why do you think humans do things that hurt Nature?
7   What should we tell the PM to do to help Nature?
8   What other questions would you put here?
Thanks for taking part!
Please hand in your questionnaire to your teacher.

There are spaces after each question, of course, for people to write down their ideas.

Mr Weatherstone takes the rough draft of the questionnaire to the school office for typing. The next day, Penny checks the typed version to make sure it's OK, then lots of copies are printed for the children to hand out to everyone in school at the end of the day. They ask everyone to take a copy for their parents, or brother or sister, or friend, or neighbour. Mr Weatherstone sends copies of the questionnaire by email to the teachers he knows in other schools, and before two days have passed, completed questionnaires are coming back, first in ones and twos, then in dozens – and then in a flood!

Penny has to think of a way to sort out the replies, and she comes up with a plan. Using a fresh piece of paper for each question, she writes the question at the top and goes through all the replies to that question, listing what people say. When two people or more say the same thing, she tallies it – like Scraggy did on board the *Wreckless* to keep track of the passing days. Like this:

4 What's your favourite wild place?

the zoo ~~IIII~~ ~~IIII~~ II	ocean II
canal II	skate park ~~IIII~~ III
moon I	arsenic factory I
I forgot I	my garden II
woods ~~IIII~~ ~~IIII~~ ~~IIII~~ ~~IIII~~ ~~IIII~~ III	
seaside ~~IIII~~ ~~IIII~~ ~~IIII~~ ~~IIII~~ ~~IIII~~ ~~IIII~~ I	
mountains III	jungle ~~IIII~~ I
yes I	cave I
allotments I	grass (for football) II
everywhere III	don't like outdoors II
chocolate factory ~~IIII~~	open spaces I
Nature reserve III	desert III

Penny sees at a glance: in her school, twenty-eight children (so far) have said they like going to the woods best of all, and thirty-one have said the seaside! Close thing.

Not all the questionnaires are back yet, so Penny asks in the office for some wallet files to keep the bits of paper under the name of the school that they have come from.

What Penny really needs is help with writing the letter to the PM. What will the other children say? Penny thinks that she mustn't be impatient, because the first thing is to get other children, and other schools, interested.

All the same, she is keen to get to question number seven, the one about the PM, and when she's tallied up the questionnaires that have come back so far, Question 7 looks like this:

7 What should we tell the PM to do to help Nature?

make Nature safe HHH HHH III
don't know III
make homes for wildlife HHH HHH HHH II
give sick animals medicine III
be nicer to pets II
start caring more I
grow more flowers II
make more space for Nature III
plant trees HHH HHH HHH HHH I
be good I
more animal hospitals III
recycle everything HHH-III
put poachers in prison III
make woods safe so trees aren't cut down HHH HHH II
give us a say IIII
put people in prison when they hurt Nature III
pay more respect to animals II

Penny works with Siobhan, Holly and Jerome, each of them doing a different question and tallying the results onto a piece of paper that they put up on the wall. They have a good laugh at some of the ideas that get suggested, like 'put people in prison when they hurt Nature', and 'chocolate factory' and the 'moon' for favourite wild places!

All this takes up their spare time for most of the autumn term.

Mr Weatherstone has read all of 'Wot Appnd' – all that's so far been written – to the class, and the children have begun collecting things for their 'bowl ov fingz'. They've been making pouches using anything they can find, and Donna has helped by sharing out the leftover wool from the wool gathering, but that's soon used up. Siobhan found some baby's booties that her mum had kept since she was a child – perfect! One night, when Siobhan is dreaming, she sees Emmy and he calls her over; she floats towards him, and when she gets close, he speaks.

"B lookin at yor footsiz, Shavorn."

Siobhan looks down to see the baby's bootie, not her feet, and at once realises that she is purling. It's getting easier for children to begin purling. Emmy helps children with their first purlings, and by the end of term there are lots of new purlers. The more purlers there are, the easier it is to get started. Parents are beginning to worry, because they find the sleeping bodies of their children lying around in strange places, and at odd times of the day – and they won't wake up! Sometimes parents are so worried, they call the doctor, or rush their child to A&E at the nearest hospital. The doctors do tests and frown and scratch their heads. The sleeping children are perfectly well, it's just that they won't wake up, and there's nothing to be done; they will not wake until they finish purling.

Parents are worried and need some answers. They talk to the children – when they're awake – and for many grown-ups, the stories the children tell are not easy to accept. "Purling? What are you talking about? Pull yourself together. We'll be having no more of this nonsense..." But, little by little, more and more parents are curious enough to want to find out more, and when they ask Mr Weatherstone, he says: "Ah yes! It's very interesting, isn't it? You should talk to..." And he suggests Donna, or Linda, or some other adult who knows all about it and is purling already. Soon, even the parents are beginning to dream into Emmy-sized old socks, mobile phone sleeves, and even a soft spectacles case with the closing bit cut off – and when they do, they discover a world of wonder forgotten since they themselves were children.

~

Excitement grows as the solstice date draws closer – the date for the gathering in the Glade. Penny prepares her shoulder bag, putting in the bits of paper with lists and questions written on, careful not to forget anything.

Emmy says that the creatures will hold their ceremony in the night-time, because the moment of the solstice will be before it gets light in the morning. The date will be 22nd December, but creatures don't use dates; all they need to do is feel the unwords.

Pip wonders how it is that the creatures can possibly know. Emmy explains. "Yooz bein too uman, Pippee, yoozll nevva b gettin it if yooz only usin uman bit ov yor brayn."

"I don't understand what you mean, Em."

"Uman brayn iznt joynd to wild web, coz umanz iz beleevin theyz seprat."

"You mean that humans are separated from Nature, even in their brains?"

"B keepin up, Pippee, thatz xaklee wotz rong. Umanz iz beleevin theyz seprat, so theyz iz."

Emmy also explains what the plans are for the gathering. The full-sized humans, and the purling humans, should arrive after daybreak; Pip will go as the only full-sized human adult, and Billy, David and Penny will go as the only full-sized human cubs. All the other children will be purling, and adults too if they go.

~

When the day comes, the four full-sized humans trudge along to Tillings Wood. The weather has been cold and wet, and the ground is muddy. They are wearing warm clothes and waterproofs. Pip wears his backpack underneath his waterproof jacket, the lump making him look like a monster; Penny, too, keeps her shoulder bag dry under her coat.

They arrive at the Glade, causing the usual ripple of unease and fear among the creatures already gathered there. Moving quietly and slowly to their usual place, they sit on rocks or logs. The purlers begin to arrive, appearing in the air with little pops, or floating and gliding in from the surrounding trees. There are lots of them! There must be a hundred or more! Birds, bats and flying insects take to the air and race about with the purlers, laughing, singing, making insect sounds, bat clicks – they are having a great time, a joyous time! The creatures that can't fly do their best to join in, by jumping up and down, or wiggling, humming or buzzing.

It may be play, it may be fun, but these purling children and the few adults that have come too are learning the wild talk, and they begin to feel the unwords. The Glade is filled with the happiness of reunion.

Rindill appears from the undergrowth; he trills his trill from a favourite twig, before flying to the talk-stone. At once, the creatures quieten and the purlers stop whizzing about; a deep silence opens the air.

Rindill welcomes the humans to the Glade, acknowledging the four full-sized humans as well as the purlers. He says that it is known that the human cubs have been busy all summer, purling to faraway places where they were shown, by the many wild creatures they met, what is happening to the wild web and the great wave.

"Because the human cubs have been able to do this," Rindill continues, "creatures from far away do not need to be here. For many of them, coming here would be very dangerous, and of course, the sea creatures could not be here anyway. Because the human cubs have been able to learn so much already, there is no need for further talk. The human cubs know in their hearts what is truly happening. I ask you all, creatures, plants, air, water, soil, rock, and humans all, please give your hearts to the unwords. The great wave is strong here in the Glade, even the new purling human cubs can feel it. We cannot mistake the meaning of the unwords. Be still!"

There follows a silence so deep, so big, that the countless beings present feel the great wave as though they are one being. No one could say how much time passes – perhaps a long time – a timeless long time.

Pip is suddenly aware of himself; he needs to speak but doesn't know what words will come. He is shy to break the magical silence.

"May I speak?" he whispers, at last.

"You may approach the talk-stone," says Rindill, moving aside.

"Thank you, Rindill," says Pip, moving his body slowly and carefully. "I feel the need to speak... I don't know what words to say, except that it's my heart's seeing of the unwords.

"The unwords tell our hearts that the wild web is dying, even as we feel such joyous reunion here in the glade, even as we have fun playing together in this magical place.

"Humans have become distant from Nature and no longer feel, or honour, the great wave. The unwords tell our hearts that the time has come for humans to open the eye of their hearts, and to honour once more the spirit in all beings.

"Time itself is shrinking, and it will soon be that the great wave will sweep humans, and all their works, into darkness. The time has come for humans to decide."

Feeling unsteady, Pip moves to step down from the talk-stone, but stumbles. Billy jumps to help him, taking his arm to give him balance.

"Thank you, Billy. I feel very strange; I feel faint and weak. I don't know where such words could come from, they seem – I don't know."

Trundlweed steps up to the talk-stone.

"The unwords come from all beings," he says, "from the great wave of being, from the stars themselves and from the smallest beings of all – but from humans? No longer."

"What about us?" cries Billy.

"You are but few, and there are billions of humans," says Trundlweed, sadly.

"But we can change it! We have a plan!" cries Penny, holding up her shoulder bag with its lists and drafts of letters. Suddenly, she sees how small and pathetic their efforts are against the whole world of humans. She sobs, her body shrinking down, so sad is she.

"Wait, please," says Pip. "I'm sorry, I must sit down... That's better. I must ask all of you, purlers too: do the unwords sing true in your hearts?"

There is a moment of hush before a strange sound begins to arise. It is a sad sound, sadder for the fact that all agree, and in one voice, as sad as ever has been heard, the word 'yesssss' fills the air.

"Then we must listen to Penny," says Pip. "Penny Unwords, please give us hope."

Penny moves towards the talk-stone as Trundlweed makes way

for her. She is silent for some time, her eyes closed, her cheeks wet with tears. The wave of despair slowly recedes, leaving her empty and vulnerable. The energy of reunion in the Glade slowly fills her, inspiring her, and lifting her spirits enough to speak.

"Thank you, everyone: all the plants, and insects, and creatures of every kind, thank you; and thank you, rock, soil, water, air, sun and moon.

"With the magic of purling you have taken us to places all over the world; we have seen wonderful things, and we have seen terrible things.

"We have seen forests, and we have seen forests burning; we have seen oceans teeming with life, and we have seen oceans plundered and dying; we have seen lands teeming with life, and we have seen land broken and dead, rivers dammed, waters poisoned; we have seen mountains covered with trees and teeming with wild creatures, and we have seen mountains barren and lifeless, broken and thrown down for the coal and minerals inside; we have seen vast forests destroyed for the oil beneath; we have seen vast numbers of machines burning what belongs in the ground and filling the air with poison. And we have seen terrible human suffering because of war, and we have seen fear and conflict because humans are scrambling for land and buried minerals that are in ever shorter supply.

"But all these terrible things are hidden from the everyday lives of many humans, and these people just do what they have always done, wanting to feel safe and have a job and somewhere to live, and to have a future.

"Now we have seen, and there will be more to see, there will always be more to see, of the deep wounding that is happening. And we feel this wound inside ourselves – we are not separate – we are the wounded too.

"What humans do to Nature, they've done blindly, unknowing. Now we see that humans can no longer pretend to be blind, because now we *do* know the harm we do to Nature. There are no excuses any more. Not a single one.

"Because of all we have seen, we know the truth of the unwords and we will do everything that we can to heal this wounding. With the help of the wild web, we will find new ways to change the way humans think of themselves. With Emmy's help, we have learned to understand the wild talk and to feel the magic of the Glade. We will take this magic into the human world, and the wild web will heal itself as humans find their hearts once more."

Penny pauses for a moment, a slight catch in her voice as she finishes. "We know in our hearts that we must do this – shall we do this? Will you help? Are we together?"

This time there is no sad pause, but a spontaneous 'yeeessssss!' from all the humans and all the creatures, each in their own way. The sound is like the gathering of a wave on the seashore as it builds, before plunging down; a sound that comes from the air itself, as though the air is the sea, bringing the voices of the sea creatures into the Glade.

Rindill flies to the talk-stone, settling on Penny's shoulder.

"Penny Unwords speaks truly," he says. "We wild beings have shown you what it is that humans have forgotten; it is up to you now to do what you have to do. Make your plans, make your lists, but not here. The Glade will always nourish and guide you, and you are always welcome here, but your work now is in the world of humans. May your hearts be strong!"

Rindill flies to his favourite twig, and Penny steps down from the talk-stone. Trundlweed steps up to close the gathering, thanking everybody for being here in the Glade and reminding them to remember the code. Rindill flies down to join him and after a few minutes' silence, Trundlweed rambles off, and Rindill slips away into the undergrowth.

With the formalities over, the purlers, birds and insects get back to playing, chasing each other and laughing, letting off steam and relaxing after the seriousness of the gathering. Pip, Penny, Billy and David sit quietly, enjoying the antics going on around them.

"Well done, Penny," says Pip. "You have been an inspiration."

71

"Is that what it's called? I have no idea how any of that happened," murmurs Penny, her voice tired and sad.

"The way you held off the feeling of sadness was amazing, Penny. Everybody was feeling it, and you transformed it."

"I don't know how, Mr Pip, I feel it just the same."

They are quiet, listening to the hubbub of voices around them.

"Where's Emmy, I wonder?" says Pip.

"'E said we 'ave to do this on our own now," says Billy.

"Let's find him, please," says Penny, wearily.

"Bet 'e's at LuLu's," Billy says.

"You're very quiet, David," Pip remarks.

"I'm feeling things, trying to understand," says David, simply.

"Come on, let's go," says Pip, standing and slowly moving to the edge of the Glade. The children follow, soon finding the path that leads through the woods towards home. They are all deep in their feelings, and they don't talk. After ten minutes or so trudging along, Penny stops to look at something in the bushes beside the path.

"I don't remember ever seeing that before."

"What, Penn?" says Billy.

"That wooden stake."

Penny points towards a wooden stake, or post, which is stuck into the ground a few metres away from the path. It's about a metre high and made of rough-sawn wood like you'd buy in a builders' merchant. The top fifteen centimetres of the post is painted bright yellow and written in black on the yellow paint is the number thirty-seven. The post is about ten centimetres square in section; the number thirty-seven is painted onto all four sides.

"Hmm," Pip says. "I wonder what that's for. Not sure I like the look of that."

"It makes me shiver," Penny whispers.

"Come on, I'm hungry!" says Billy, leading the way.

A few minutes later, they see another yellow-topped post. This one is number thirty-eight.

Pip sighs. "We must find out what these things mean," he says. "But I must get home, I am so tired. Have any of you got energy to go on looking?"

"Yeah, I's up for it," says Billy, forgetting about his hunger.

"Me too," says David.

"I need to find out," says Penny. "It's making me feel ill, I have to know."

"Which way?" asks David.

"Let's find post number one," says Billy.

"Good plan. And good luck to you all," says Pip. "Let me know when you get home, please."

"I'll text you," Penny confirms.

"Stay together – and look after each other!"

"We always do, Mr Pip!" cries Billy.

"Bye!"

"Bye!"

~

The three children walk back the way they had come until they get to post number thirty-seven, the first one that Penny found. They carry on walking, but the path to the Glade veers off slightly uphill, so they follow an animal trail that might be more in line with the two posts. It's hard to tell which way to go. They walk in single file.

"You was brilliant back in the Glade, Penn," says Billy, out of the blue.

"Thanks, Billy. I'm still feeling wobbly."

"There's so many purlers now!" David says. "What's going on?"

"The more of us there are purling, the stronger it is – the pull, I mean," Penny says, thoughtfully. "Do you remember when we first learned purling? It wasn't easy for most of us, but now it seems to be getting easier for the new ones."

"Right, Penn, them new purlers was gettin' the unwords straight away," says Billy.

"There's another post!" cries David.

"We should count paces next time," says Billy.

They find post number thirty-six to the side of the trail, in the undergrowth, easily visible because of the bright yellow paint.

"I'll pace this one out," says David, walking on with deliberately big strides, hoping they would be a metre; in fact, they are less than that. Sometimes there are fallen trees that he has to climb over, and that makes him lose his pace, so it's all a bit of guesswork.

"We've seen three now," says Penny. "Are they in a straight line, do you think?"

"'Ard to tell. Could be," says Billy.

"They could be marking the line of a fence or something."

"Fence? In our woods, Penn? No!" cries Billy.

"Billy, they're not our woods; they belong to someone."

"'Ow can woods 'belong' to someone? It ain't right."

"Twenty-eight, twenty-nine, thirty..." David counts.

Billy groans. "Oh, Penn! I's got a bad feelin'."

"Me, too."

"Thirty-two, thirty-three, thirty-four... There's one!"

They scramble through to the post, yes, it's number thirty-five.

"They're thirty metres apart – ish."

"David, well done," Penny says, smiling. "I think your paces may not be quite a metre. Let's say twenty-five, or less, even. How far is it to post number one?"

"Aww, Penny, I dunno." Billy is not good at this sort of thing.

"Let's have a think." Penny calculates. "This is stake number thirty-five, so there's thirty-five gaps of twenty-five metres before we get to number one. Thirty-five times twenty-five is...?"

"Eight hundred 'n seventy-five." answers David.

"David!" cries Penny.

"It just popped into my head," says David, mystified.

"Nearly a kilometre," says Penny. "That'll take us to the edge of the wood, I think."

"Yeah! We're 'eadin' for the top gate by the road!" says Billy, certain of his bearings.

They push on harder now, sometimes having to scramble through thick undergrowth where there is no trail to follow. Passing post after post, they realise that the line they make is curving round slightly, keeping almost level on the sloping ground, following the contour of the hill.

"Yep, I reckon we'll come out on the road a bit down from the gate," says Billy.

They eventually arrive at post number 2 tired, muddy and scratched, but still very determined. There is a little more light in the wood now, as though they are approaching the edge of the woodland. They expect to arrive at the road at any moment, but they are taken by surprise when they emerge from the thick undergrowth. Stopped in their tracks, horrified, they stare at the sight before them. They see a large clearing, where trees have been uprooted and bulldozed into huge, tangled heaps of tree trunks and stumps; a security fence has been erected along the roadside, with a big, metal security gate. There are signs of a fence being constructed between the clearing and the woods, but it hasn't been completed yet.

The clearing is crowded with machines parked in rows, and materials on pallets and in huge heaps. The ground has been levelled and covered with rubble and coarse gravel, rolled flat and solid; the surface has lots of strange square holes in it. A large, rectangular metal container, probably a secure tool-store, sits next to an even bigger portacabin that looks like a site office. Nearby are three portable toilets in a row.

The machines are excavators, bulldozers, dumper trucks and earth-moving machines, and there's a massive machine that looks like a roller except the big metal rollers bristle with square spikes. This is the machine that made the holes in the gravel.

"See that machine there?" says Billy, pointing, his voice trembling with emotion.

"Which one? There's lots," says David.

"Metal roller, with lumps stickin' out..."

"Yeah, what?"

"That's for makin' roads!" shouts Billy, very upset now. "They's makin' a bleedin' road through our wood! That's what them posts is markin' out! A ROAD!"

Chapter Three

Tooby Too

It's been a moon and a bit since One-Eye disappeared on his quest to rescue Scraggy and Whip-Tail Jack. At Burrow Cave, the first flowers of spring have faded, and now bluebells and wild garlic are budding once again – and that means Marigold and Ruby are looking forward to their birthday. Nettl and Bess prepare nice things to eat and make Burrow Cave colourful with wild flowers.

Flimsy and Pearl have been making presents for the birthday twins, and to hide from their curious eyes they have sneaked off to One-Eye's den. The Orb of light still floats in the air above the table, the empty lantern hanging above. Pearl has been crocheting scarves, using some of Ping Ling's finest wool, and Flimsy has been using coloured threads to make crests to tie on their heads.

Flimsy thinks often of One-Eye; every day she sits quietly, looking into the Orb, trying to give her heart to 'seeing'. But so far it has not happened; she has not been able to do 'seeing' since One-Eye disappeared. Dreamer too has been unable to do 'dreaming'.

The day of the party comes, and everybody gathers in Burrow Cave for food and stories and dancing. Ruby and Marigold love their scarves and crests, putting them on and dancing about. Sapphyr has made daisy chains for them both, and Acorn gives them some beautiful smooth pebbles he found in the woods. All the cousins, friends, aunts and uncles and, of course, Bess and Burrow Bill, their mum and dad, give them hugs and kisses, and little gifts of Nature's wonders.

It is such a lovely day, so the party spills outside under the oak tree. Friends come to join in the fun: Rippl and Chattabox, the squirrels, come looping along, and Dapper the jay comes too, screeching as always and looking extra smart; and Twitwit the nuthatch, Cheeky the robin and many others come too. When it seems like everyone has arrived, a sudden 'squaaaark–ak–kak!' makes all eyes look upwards, and there, coming down from the treetops, are two big birds.

"It's Gabbee and Waggl!" cries BillBill.

"Waggl's 'avin' fevvers now!" announces Waggl proudly, "Waggl fly now!"

"Hallo, Gabbee, hallo, Waggl," says Flimsy. "It's good to see you safe and sound. We've been worried that you were lost, and the winter's been very cold."

"Krrarrk! Lost we been and now we found," says Gabbee.

"Welcome to the party!" cries Pearl. "It's Marigold and Ruby's birthday!"

"Twin-twin meeces! Fly parrot?" says Gabbee. "Twin one fly Gabbee, twin two fly Waggl?"

"Ride on your backs? Can we really? Hooray!" cries Marigold. "May we really, Bess?"

"Yes, of course. But, Gabbee, don't go too far! Promise!"

"Gabbee not go far, meeces happy fly."

"Come on then, let's get you loaded up," says Burrow Bill, lifting Ruby on to Waggl's back while Scribbla lifts Marigold onto Gabbee's back.

"Hold firmly to the feathers!" cries Pearl, as the two parrots leap into the air.

"Squaaarrrk!"

The parrots fly around in circles, Ruby and Marigold shrieking in delight. "Let's go to Eagle Rock!" cries Ruby, and Waggl at once turns to fly in that direction, with Gabbee close behind.

"Don't go too far away!" cries Bess, but the parrots are already out of sight, flying over Eagle Rock and looking down at the river in the valley below.

"Waggl visit nest tree!" says Waggl.

"Krrarrk," agrees Gabbee, and they turn to fly towards the hollow cherry, where Mowzl and Scraggy first met Waggl. They fly above the trees of the wildwood, allowing Marigold and Ruby to see places they have never seen before. The parrots glide down to the hollow cherry, and perch on twigs near the entrance hole. Waggl jumps through the hole into the nest chamber.

"Baby Waggl was here, baby Waggl no fevvers."

"You've grown up now, Waggl. You fly so well and can even carry me!" says Marigold, laughing.

"We go back, we go back, Gabbee promise," says Gabbee and she leaps into the air, with Waggl and Ruby following close behind. Just as they leap from the cherry tree, two flashes of light occur, one when Gabbee leaps and one when Waggl leaps, and with these flashes, the two parrots and the two mice disappear from sight.

Back at Home Oak, it doesn't take long for everyone to realise that the parrots have flown further away than they should have done. Bess is worried.

"I wish they hadn't gone, but it seemed such a fun idea at the time," she says.

"I'll see if I can find them," announces Dapper the jay, taking to the air, showing off his magnificent feathers of white, black, pink and blue. He flies high enough to see far across the wildwood, but he can't see the parrots anywhere.

"I wish I had better eyesight, like Sparkeye the sparrow hawk, but I don't know where he is today." Dapper is always talking to himself. "I wonder if they went to the hollow cherry tree, for old times' sake?"

He flies towards the hollow cherry, but before he gets there he sees two bright flashes coming from that direction, one flash followed almost at once by the second. There is no sound, no thunder.

"Oh dear, here we go again. I seem to remember that Emmy and Scraggy disappeared in a flash of light just like this."

Dapper flies to the cherry tree and explores the nest chamber, finding no sign of the parrots or the mice. He is about to fly off when he spies a feather caught on a twig just by the entrance hole; he picks it up in his beak and flies back to Burrow Cave. He tells the story, and shows everyone the feather, and the mice are shocked and worried.

"The portal is open again," Flimsy murmurs. "Dreamer? You and I must go to One-Eye's den and try to do seeing and dreaming. Please come with us, Pearl."

"Bess," says Pearl. "Maybe they've gone to the same place that One-Eye went to rescue Scraggy. Perhaps they need to be there, we just don't know. Please don't worry. We'll find them."

Pearl, Flimsy and Dreamer go to One-Eye's den, while the

others say goodbye to the visitors and say special thanks to Dapper the jay, before returning to Burrow Cave. No one feels in a party mood any more.

~

Since One-Eye's disappearance, just over a moon ago, Flimsy, Pearl and Dreamer have spent a lot of their time in the den, talking and waiting, and looking into the Orb of light. Flimsy has tried to do seeing, and Dreamer has tried to do dreaming, but they haven't been able to make it work at all.

They have talked about Scraggy and Emmy and how much they miss them, and now there's Ruby and Marigold to think of, and One-Eye, and the parrots... Flimsy feels sure that what's happened today is a sign that things are changing, and she wants to do seeing. The three of them sit at the table in the den with the Orb floating under the empty lantern, and they remember their loved ones who are missing in other dimensions.

Looking into the Orb now, what can they see with their hearts' eye? Pearl is not gifted with the sight, and instead, she goes deep into her feelings and waits to be given insight. Dreamer goes into a trance but doesn't dream. Flimsy gazes into the Orb, wishing with all her might.

She is flying; she sees the world from on high. She is seeing the world from so far above she can see the curve of its roundness. She sees how colourful it is, with blue oceans and swirls of white cloud, and she sees land that is green and land that is brown, and she sees mountains and plains and deserts. As she watches, the world seems to go out of focus and the blurring jumbles the colours; appearing behind the blurry world is another world, a different jumble of colours, and behind that world another world, different again in colours, and there are more and more! Uncountable worlds!

Flimsy wakes from her trance with the singing still echoing in her ears. She understands the meaning of what she has seen, but somewhere so deep in her heart she cannot find any words at all to describe it; she sits in silence, remembering. She has heard before of the many worlds happening, but she has never understood what it might mean. She had imagined that the many worlds were different from each other and in different places, separated by space – by distance – so you would have to travel to go from one to another, if it were possible at all. And she can remember hearing the expression

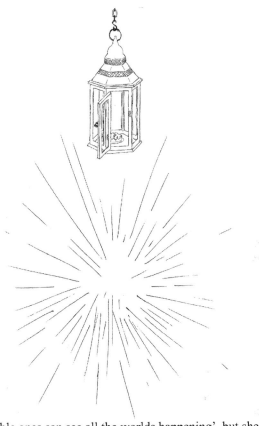

'the invisible ones can see all the worlds happening', but she doesn't know how or where she heard that, or who the invisible ones might be.

"Flimsy? Are you alright?" whispers Pearl.

"Uh, yes, I s'pose."

"You've had a vision, haven't you?"

"It is too deep, I can't pull it here..."

"Don't try to say anything, Flimsy. We are here with you, just rest."

Flimsy drifts away again, seeing flashes of the many worlds – on top of each other, only separate – and she sees how the colours are like a rainbow, but not an Earthly rainbow. She hears the colours. The singing, that's what it is! The singing is a rainbow of sound; the worlds are different sounds that meet, and excite, and withdraw, like dance.

She is in darkness now, the vision gone. Slowly returning, her awareness pours back into her body as she becomes aware of herself sitting at the table in One-Eye's den. She sits silently for a long time.

"I will try to word what I have seen," she says, weakly, speaking slowly and carefully, describing her visions to her companions. After she has spoken, there is profound quiet in the den.

Eventually, Flimsy continues to speak in the same slow, deliberate voice as before. "The portal is when two worlds are just touching the same sound, the same vibration. It is energy. Today, when the portal opened again, the parrots, Marigold and Ruby went through. It could be that the parrots must go back to the world they came from, but why our little ones had to go, I don't see.

"We will be able to do 'seeing' and 'dreaming' again, and we should send another parcel to Emmy. It is nearly time."

"Nearly time?" says Dreamer. "Nearly time for what, Flimsy?"

"I don't know. It is to do with the singing and colours, and the rainbow of sound. When One-Eye disappeared the first time, the portal was created. Emmy and Scraggy disappeared, and Emmy has gone even further, to a world we don't know at all. To get him back home, that world will have to be singing with this world *and* the world that One-Eye and Scraggy are in. What did he call it? Where's that drawing – the one he said was not a map, more a way of thinking?"

"I know where it is!" Pearl goes to the shelves, returning with a map tube. She opens it and teases out the rolls of bark inside. "Here it is, I remember now. He said that the 'zig-zag lines are lightning, and the worlds are 'ome', 'oshn', 'oomnz' and... and the 'ilnd ov myst' is in the middle.'"

"One-Eye already knew about the other worlds!" cries Dreamer.

"He must have known more than he told us," agrees Pearl.

"Maybe it's a mystery to him, too, and he can't talk about it either," says Flimsy, quietly. "This drawing is saying that the Island of Mist is 'in the middle'. The Island of Mist is where the songs meet; it's where the worlds meet."

Flimsy suddenly can say no more; she lowers her head down to the table and rests on her forepaws.

"Come, Flimsy, time to sleep," Pearl comforts her. "Dreamer and I will start making a new parcel for Emmy. You can tell us later what we should put inside it."

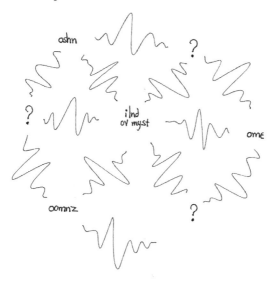

"I'll sleep here, don't worry." Flimsy lifts her head. "Dreamer, please start weaving a band to send... Get everyone to weave a bit into it. Pearl, could you write saying that he will be coming home soon, I know it in my heart."

Flimsy rests her head on her forepaws again, falling asleep in an instant.

~

When One-Eye disappears from his den – to rescue Scraggy and Jack – he finds himself high up on the main mast of the *Wreckless,* in the tangle of ropes beneath the crow's nest. Moments before his arrival, the ship had entered the fog and he can't see any further from his face than his paws. Loud shouts from nearby tell him that the human sailors are furling sails, following orders shouted from below. He can hear the feet of the sailor on watch, thumping and sliding on the crow's nest platform above him.

One-Eye is still holding the little head that he'd picked up in his den; reaching into the top of his backpack, he drops it in. He rummages in the backpack until he finds the short length of Ping Ling's strongest rope he knows is in there. Groping in the fog with his paw, he feels around for the ropes that go down to the deck, choosing the one he thinks will take him where he wants to go. Looping Ping Ling's short rope over the rigging rope, he throws himself into the fog, sliding down the rope at such a speed he is on the deck in seconds. Yes, he has remembered well. The rigging rope

runs down to a cleat on the gunwale near the stern of the ship. It's not far from here to the Hideout.

In the foggy gloom, it is easy for him to dodge the sailors, but dodging the sharp eyes of the rats is another matter. This time he is lucky as there are no rats about, and he is not challenged until he gets close to the first secret way towards the Hideout.

"Password, my friend, or show me your heels."

One-Eye doesn't recognise the voice and is puzzled. It is not the voice of a rat, so this must be a new pirate mouse!

"I'll just be sayin' 'Tooby' to thee."

"Hmm. That's familiar, you'd better come with me. Walk in front if you don't mind."

"I'll be no trouble."

One-Eye knows the way to the Hideout, making the correct turns even before the sentry tells him.

"You know the way, that's plain to see. How is that?"

"Many's the time I's been 'ere. I's come to rescue Jack 'n Scraggy."

"Ah, let me see your face... Yes, One-Eyed Tooby, I remember now, I have heard stories about you."

When they reach the Hideout, the sentry takes the lead, calling ahead to announce their arrival. Stump-Leg Stew is there, with Black-Boot Bess and Sieve-Brain Sally.

"Tooby!" they cry, all at once, crowding round him asking questions and touching him to make sure he's real.

"Who's this that brought me in?" Tooby asks, looking towards the sentry.

"Gaol-Break Jim," says Stumpy. "Jim, this be Tooby. Tooby, Jim. The 'uman sailors 'eld Jim prisoner in a cage, 'n Sad-Eyed Suzee too, but they 'scaped 'n found their ways 'ere."

"'N Kate?"

"Kate 'n Suzee's sentryin'. Fetch 'em in please, Jim."

"Aye, Cap'n."

"Captain?" Tooby looks at Stumpy in surprise.

"Ha! Only tempry like, till Jack does return," Stumpy explains.

"How long's 'e been gone?" asks Tooby.

"'E 'n Scraggy took off to the Island of Mist twelve moons back. Emmy was lost to typhoon three or four moons before that."

"Hmm. I see the little Orb's out 'n about."

"Aye, Tooby. Jack's insistin' we's practisin' every day lookin' to the light 'n stayin' awake, like you's always said, Tooby, but you never showed us the Orb."

"What's your plan, Stumpy?" Tooby asks, patiently.

"The fog's just 'appened 'n we's thinkin' we'll go lookin' for Jack – now you's 'ere."

Gaol-Break Jim returns with Kate and Suzee. "Tooby!" Kate cries, happily, hugging him. "It's so good to see you, you old pirate! This is Suzee, she was held prisoner by the rats, along with Gaol-Break Jim."

"'Tis good to see you, Kate," says Tooby, smiling. "'Allo, Suzee, I's very happy to meet you! Now then, Stumpy? What's we 'avin' for a celebration?"

"Ah-haa! We's 'avin' pickled raisins!"

"No point in wasting 'em, eh? Let's eat 'em up!" cries Tooby.

"Aye-aye, One-Eye!"

The pirate mice discovered pickled raisins by happy accident: some raisins borrowed from the human sailors were put in a bowl with some water to plump them up – but then forgotten about. The raisins fermented, and when Stumpy rediscovered them and tried one, he liked it so much he ate it all up. A few minutes later he was dancing about happily; his comrades were puzzled, but before long they all ate some and were dancing too!

Sally fetches the pickled raisins and passes the bowl around. It doesn't take much pickled raisin to make a mouse feel in high spirits and soon they are all singing and dancing as though they have no cares in the world. This is the first time that Suzee has felt such happiness for a very long time; she feels part of a family now.

Later, when they wake, the fog is still thick. Tooby and Kate go on patrol, listening intently and feeling their way with their whiskers. They can hear Gobbee squawking somewhere forward, and they hear human voices aloft, probably lookouts on the crow's nest platform. They hear the ship creaking as it makes its slow way through the fog. The humans are waiting for the Island of Mist to reveal itself.

Tooby and Kate creep through the darkness to the secret place that looks over the quarterdeck. It takes a long time to get there. A few lanterns hang, here and there, around the deck, so that the sailors don't trip and fall down the companionways, and by this light the mice are sometimes able to see the faces of the humans, faces that give away everything that the mice need to know; right now, the faces are looking excited and expectant.

"The lookouts aloft must have seen the island. The fog must be thinning," whispers Kate.

"Hmm. Kate, if 'tis the island, will thee be comin' along to find Jack 'n Scraggy?"

"Just try stopping me!"

"Good. Now, let's be callin' Gobbee."

They make their way under the poop to the fantail, where the steering ropes for the rudder go down under the sea. They climb out onto the huge oak timber that holds the top end of the rudder shaft and find the crevice in the wood where they are safe from falling into the waves. They make the highest squeaks that they can – as Stumpy taught them – wait a bit, and do it again. They repeat this every few minutes. This is the call that Gobbee will answer – if he hears it – but it means waiting for him to happen to fly past the fantail.

"Squaaaaaark."

"I hear him!" cries Kate.

Gobbee squawks, flapping about trying to find his way through the fog to where the mice are.

"Dark fly, Gobbee see nothing, where meeces?"

Gobbee hits the fantail awkwardly, scrabbling for a foothold.

"Aarrakakak! Why meeces call Gobbee in dark?"

"We's needin' a favour, Gobbee," says Tooby.

"Hallo, Toobee, hallo – favour always, promise, promise, but where's my Gabbee?"

"Gobbee, please," says Kate. "The humans are getting excited; the fog may be thinning, and the Island of Mist may be near. Would you fly up high to have a look, and come back to tell us, please?"

"Why-why-why?"

"We need to get to the island as quickly as we can. If we know it's near, we can hide in the longboat. We don't want to hide there if the island isn't near, it's too dangerous."

"Dangerous? Dangerous? Send Gobbee to danger in fog dark?"

"Oh, Gobbee, we's not meanin' no 'arm," Tooby pleads.

"Me joke, silly meeces. Gobbee fly meeces island."

"We thank thee, but please 'ave a look now for us."

"Gobbee go. Aarrakakak!" and off he flies.

"It would be much quicker to fly with Gobbee than to wait for the longboat to go," Kate points out.

"We needs a talk with Stumpy and the others. Gobbee could pick us up on deck if it's foggy still, t'would be safe enough."

"I can hear him already!"

"Aarrakakak!" Gobbee scrambles back. "Island near, island near, Gobbee see island, Gobbee fly meeces."

"Thanks, Gobbee. We 'as to talk with Stumpy first, we'll be callin' from the deck."

"Meeces bring dancing raisin."

"Ha! You've 'eard about them already! Yes, you'll get some."

Gobbee flies off into the gloom while Tooby and Kate make their way back to the Hideout. A plan is agreed with the others, and Tooby and Kate prepare their backpacks for the journey to the island. The only Orb remaining on board is the one in the fat light tube. Tooby decides to try taking a little bit from it. He opens an empty light tube and holds it close to the fat light tube. When the bung is pulled, the light moves like a thread of mist into the smaller tube. When it stops, Tooby puts the bungs back into both tubes, keeping the small tube in his backpack and putting the fat one back into the sea-chest. He instructs Stumpy and the others to let the Orb free every day, and to look into the light.

"You'll be know-in' in your 'earts what's to be done, 'n when," he says to them. "Keep lively, 'n be ready!"

"Do you know what's going to happen?" asks Bess.

"Nope. You just be ready."

Kate and Tooby make their farewells, Kate reassuring Suzee that whatever happens, she won't be left behind. Kate and Tooby creep out onto the deck, and, after a few minutes of squeaking their highest squeaks, Gobbee arrives. He eats the dancing raisin that they've brought for him while the mice climb on his back, and in another moment, they are in the air.

Gobbee flaps hard, climbing as fast as possible, straining with the extra weight of the mice on his back. As they draw level with the top of the mast, the fog thins, and they can see the glow of the sun showing through from above. In another moment they are in clear, sunlit air, speeding towards the tree-covered slopes of the Island of Mist. Tooby has the feeling of a hundred butterflies in his tummy.

Gobbee glides towards the beach, gaining speed as he goes, swooping up abruptly towards the clifftop to land. A sudden flash – closely followed by a second – makes Gobbee wobble and misjudge the landing; they fall, sprawling on the ground.

"Squarkark – oops!" cries Gobbee.

"Squaark-ak-ak-ak!"

"Who said that?" cries Kate.

"Look!" shouts Tooby, pointing.

"Two more parrots! Look, Gobbee!"

Gobbee flies off again from the clifftop to meet the two parrots, and when he gets close enough, he recognises Gabbee.

"Gabbee! Gabbee! My love, my life, my family!"

"Gobbee, we come, we home!" cries Gabbee. "Waggl, your Waggl this is."

Gobbee flies close to Waggl and Gabbee, and in their excitement they crash-land on the clifftop, Marigold spilling from Gabbee's back, and Ruby from Waggl's back.

Tooby stares in astonishment, recognising Marigold and Ruby straight away.

"Uncle One-Eye!" cries Ruby.

"Uncle One-Eye!" cries Marigold, and they run to him, tumbling into him, knocking him over in their happiness to see him. He's not really their uncle, but they are so fond of him that they've always called him Uncle One-Eye.

"Kate, this be Ruby 'n Marigold, from back home," splutters One-Eye. "How did you all get here?"

"Uncle One-Eye," says Ruby, her eyes bright with excitement. "It's our birthday today and we were having a party at Burrow Cave, and then Gabbee and Waggl suddenly turned up and took us for a birthday flying lesson and we went to the hollow cherry – and there were two flashes of light and here we are!"

"Ah-ha! The portal," says Tooby. "I's very 'appy to see thee 'n you's right welcome. I's reckonin' you'll not be gettin' 'ome today. Come on! Up the hill we go, find us some shelter 'n food."

"Gobbee, I'm so happy to see you reunited with your family!" says Kate. "It's been a long time. Welcome home, Gabbee and Waggl!"

"Shipwrecked long time," says Gabbee. "Waggl fly now, we come home."

The parrots fly away, screeching their heads off. The mice yell after them, 'see you again soon' and 'thanks for the ride', but the parrots are gone already.

"They's 'xtinct birds if the island truly be their 'ome," says Tooby.

"What on Earth do you mean?" asks Kate.

"'Tis a mystery, Kate. You's knowin' there's somethin' fishy 'appenin' 'ere. There be no land in this 'ere ocean, only the island in the fog. Everythin' 'ere be 'xtinct. Come, I'll show thee."

They scramble up the slope, finding animal trails to make the going a bit easier because it is steep, tangled with plants and strewn with rocks. After a while, they come to a place that Tooby recognises by the giant grasses that grow. It was here that he first saw bamboo.

"We'll find a cosy cave 'ereabouts," he says.

"I'm hungry," says Marigold.

"Me too," says Ruby.

"'Ere 'tis," says Tooby, poking about in the rocks at the bottom of a very steep bit, finding the entrance to the cave at last. "In 'ere, little 'uns! Thee too, Kate!"

Inside, Tooby finds the things that he left behind last time. He finds a few bamboo tubes that he hadn't quite finished, tubes he had used to collect nuts and seeds. They are still there, leaning against the wall of the cave.

"Here we are! Here's dinner. Help yourselves."

They eat and chat, Kate telling the little ones stories about the *Wreckless*.

"Are we going to rescue Whip-Tail Jack and Scraggy from the

Crystal Cave?" asks Marigold, hoping the answer will be 'yes'.

"We's 'opin 'tis so, Marigold! Tomorrow we'll be findin' out the answer."

"Can we come too?" asks Ruby, hardly believing their luck.

"Aye! We's needin' thee."

"Thank you, Uncle!"

The little ones sleep deeply, tired after an exciting day. Kate and Tooby talk about what to do tomorrow, but it's wait and see, and there's not much to plan. Soon they are sleeping too, their ears alert and twitching as always.

~

They wake before dawn and Tooby is keen to get going. The young ones are sleepy, yawning and unsteady on their feet, but they get into the swing of things soon enough. At first light, they reach a small plateau, or flat area, that is less tangled and there, browsing the bushes, is a giant tortoise.

"Lonely? Are you Lonely, the tortoise?"

"Ahh! What an unexpected pleasure! It is the mouse Tooby – and with companions! How splendid. What are your names?"

"I'm called Cutlass Kate..."

"Yes! A pirate mouse! How marvellous. And you two little ones?"

"I'm Marigold, and this is my sister–"

"Ruby!" interrupts Ruby, slipping on the rock they are sitting on, and scrambling back.

"Well, well. My name is Lonely, so-named by humans after they had killed all the others of my kind, and I was the last one left alive. As Tooby knows, they kept me in a cage for many years, until I died at the age of one hundred and eighty-nine and a half winters, but that was Earth time, not the Island of Mist, where time doesn't behave at all."

"Mr Lonely, how can you be telling us this if you are dead already?" asks Marigold.

"Well, my dear, everything on this island is extinct, every plant and every creepy crawly and every animal. Even the volcano on which we stand is extinct. I think it is all probably a joke, but not a very funny one. But you are not extinct, and so you must do what you have come here to do."

"What is that?" asks Kate.

"That is the wrong question, Cutlass Kate, please try another."

"Are we in time, Lonely?"

"Ah! That's a good question, as we don't seem to have moments that happen in a row, one then another, no, they are dancing about all over the place, so you can never be sure. But you are in time. I know this because if you were not, you would not be here."

"What sign will we see?"

"There is no word for the sign you will see, but you will know."

"Lonely, why have you got such a long neck?" asks Ruby.

"Oh, pure vanity, I like to look down my nose at the world. When you are as old as me, you will feel the same, I'm sure – but I joke with you, the answer to your question is 'giraffe'."

"More riddles, as ever!" says Tooby, laughing, but he's anxious to get away before the young mice are enchanted and can't move. "Lonely, I's glad to be seein' thee, but we's 'avin' to move on, so I bid thee farewell. Come on, you all, up the mountain we go!"

"Goodbye!" calls Lonely, watching the mice scramble up the hill. "May your journey be long and memorable!"

It takes them half the day to reach the entrance to the Crystal Cave, partly because they have to stop now and again for the little ones to rest, but also because there are so many interesting things to look at and creatures to talk to. But Tooby keeps the pressure up and eventually they get there.

"In we go! Kate, you be first, then Ruby, then Marigold, and 'tis

Tooby comin' behind. 'Tis squeezy, 'ere 'n there, but there's broader places too. Kate, you'll be 'avin to pull your pack along behind."

They reach the first wide bit, or cavern, and they rest for a minute, eating a few nuts that Kate had saved in her backpack. It's dark – darker than the darkest night Ruby and Marigold have ever seen. Kate goes ahead, exploring the tunnel further.

"Is it much further, Uncle?" asks Ruby.

"Aye, 'fraid so. Come on! Let's get to it."

After a few minutes, Kate shouts back along the tunnel. "Tooby! There's been a rock fall, I can't get through!"

"Come back 'ere then, Kate," Tooby calls, and when she has backed out of the tunnel and into the chamber, Tooby goes in by himself to have a look.

He wriggles his way along the tunnel until he finds the rocks that are blocking the way. He touches them, pushing and pulling to get some idea of how bad it is. Some of the rocks are small enough and loose enough to move, but he's got nowhere to put them as the tunnel is so small. He will have to wriggle all the way back to the cavern with each one. He tries to feel between the rocks; maybe if some of the smaller rocks could be taken away, there might be a gap to squeeze through. It would be too small for him; it would have to be Ruby or Marigold. He wriggles his way backwards to the cavern where the others are waiting, pulling along one rock.

"We's needin' to get some little rocks out, like this 'un, 'n open up a gap. It'll be too small for the likes o' me or Kate – one o' thee will 'ave to go."

There's a moment of silence.

"We'll both go!" says Ruby.

"Yes!" says Marigold.

"Ah! Good, I thank thee. Kate, please be fetchin' a rock from there while I's thinkin'."

"Aye-aye, One-Eye!"

The little ones like that and start to chant it while they wait, 'aye-aye, One-Eye', until Tooby growls at them and they are quiet again, twitching with excitement and nervousness. Tooby thinks about what the little ones could do when they get to the Crystal Cave – if they get there. First, Scraggy and Jack must be woken up from their enchantment. How could the little ones do that? Splashing water from the river onto their faces might do the trick, or tickling them, laughing in their ears, calling their names – anything! But what then? What if they do wake up? They won't be able to get out through the tunnel!

Tooby closes his eye and rubs it with his fist. He sees sparks flying, he rubs again, and again, seeing lights in his eye, but it's tight shut!

"Ah-ha!" he cries.

"What, Uncle?" says Marigold.

"I's forgettin' the light!"

Tooby searches for his backpack, which he'd put on the ground when they first entered the cavern. He opens the top flap and feels for the small light tube. He opens it; the light pours out, gathering into a small Orb. The two young mice gasp and stare; never have they seen anything quite so lovely. The Orb floats close to them, and Tooby waits, patient and quiet. He wants to ask the light if it can help them, but he doesn't want to interrupt the young ones' wonderment.

The Orb moves close to Tooby; he gazes into it, seeing, in his mind's eye, Scraggy and Jack in the Crystal Cave, close but unreachable. In that cave is the pool of light, from which Tooby had taken this very Orb. Tooby, Ruby and Marigold watch as the Orb extends itself, threading its way along the tunnel towards Kate, who is just wriggling back out with a small rock.

"You've released the Orb!" she cries.

"Aye! It'll 'elp us seein', if nothin' more. I'll go 'n pull out one more rock."

The Orb has stretched itself along the tunnel to the rock fall, going through the gap and on into the tunnel beyond. Now that there is light, Tooby can see that it will be possible to make a way through for Marigold and Ruby. *We need Burrow Bill here,'* he thinks to himself, grabbing another rock and crawling backwards out of the tunnel.

"One or two more, Kate, 'n we'll 'ave gap enough, I reckons."

"Is it safe, Tooby? Is it going to be safe enough for the twins?" says Kate.

"I can't budge the bigger rocks, they's well jammed."

Kate scrambles in and returns with another rock. "You're right, Tooby, the twins could get through now, and the light makes it much less scary."

"Ruby, Marigold, be listnin'!" Tooby calls for their attention. "You's knowin' you can be trustin' the light. Follow it. Follow till you gets to Crystal Cave. There'll be a river, 'n under you'll 'ave to go. Breathe deep before plungin' in. I's done that lots o' times 'n I knows you can do it.

"When you's arrivin', you'll 'ave to be wakin' 'em, 'n this'll not be easy. Try splashin' river water in their faces, shout 'n yell in their ear 'oles, yell their names, your names, anythin'! If they's not wakin', come back 'ere. Don't ever be fallin' asleep.

"If you's able to wake 'em, tell 'em Tooby says: 'speak with your 'earts to the pool o' light 'n ask for port'l to take y'all out of mountain'. Now, tell me what I's just said to thee."

First Ruby then Marigold repeat Tooby's words, getting them all right except they say 'porthole' instead of portal, but Tooby doesn't mind that at all because Jack will know what it means.

"Good, now off you go, me lovelies, 'n we'll guide you with our 'earts as best we can."

The two young mice hug Tooby and Kate and set off along the tunnel. The going is easier for them as they are smaller, and the light helps. At the rock fall they have to squeeze through the gap, trying not to imagine what would happen if the rocks tumble down even more. They follow the thread of light on into the tunnel beyond. There is more room now, and they can scamper along easily until they reach the river. The thread of light follows the edge of the water, before dipping under the surface when the river disappears into the ground.

"Come on, Ruby! Let's take the biggest breaths we've ever taken!" says Marigold. They plunge in, following the light through the underwater tunnel and then up, until at last they burst through the surface into the enchanting light of the Crystal Cave.

"Look!" Ruby gasps for breath, scrambling out of the water onto the sparkling floor of the cave. They gaze in wonderment. The light is soft, gentle and welcoming; it is... delicious.

"Marigold?" cries Ruby. "Marigold, don't go to sleep!"

"What? Oh, yes, of course. I remember. Where are they?"

"Look, over there, leaning against the edge of the pool of light."

They scamper across the glittering floor of the cave, calling Scraggy and Jack by name. The sleeping mice don't move; they remain sitting back-to-back, leaning against the rim of the pool. Ruby speaks her name into Scraggy's ear, then shouts his name and asks him to wake up, and she does the same to Jack. Not a murmur, not even a twitch of a whisker.

"Let's try water," suggests Marigold, running to the river and scooping up as much as her cupped paws can hold. "It's all spilling out, it won't be enough."

"I know!" cries Ruby, and she runs to the river and fills her mouth as full as she can, runs back and squirts it all into Scraggy's face!

"Ruby!" cries Marigold.

"Let's spray them both a few times," says Ruby, but even this doesn't wake them.

"Ruby, maybe it takes a long time to wake up from such a long sleep. Maybe they do hear us, and we have to be patient. Let's sit with them and sing to them. Do you remember that song that Emmy taught us before he disappeared? He called it the 'bat song'."

"I remember! It starts something like 'Bats is wakin'."

"That's it, Ruby, and that repeats, then it's 'up from the day'."

"Mmm. But it's a lullaby, Marigold, the last bit is about the bats going to sleep."

"Oh, alright. We could just sit with them and talk. We could tell them what's been happening, and about flying with Gabbee and Waggl, and about the porthole!"

"Yes!"

And that's just what they do. They talk about everything that's happened at Burrow Cave since Scraggy and Emmy disappeared, and about Uncle One-Eye's confession about stealing the light; everything they can remember. After a while they get tired of talking and fall silent. Marigold drifts off to sleep. Ruby thinks of Tooby and Kate in the cavern, waiting and wondering. She remembers someone at home telling her that wriggling your toes is helpful if you want to stay awake. She wriggles her toes.

~

"Ruby? Ruby? What's you doin' 'ere?"

"Uh? What? I was going to sleep, oh dear. Scraggy! You're awake!"

"'Allo, Ruby! Course I's awake, why shouldn't I be?"

"Scraggy, you and Jack have been asleep here for ages and Tooby has come to rescue you."

"Dad? Is 'e 'ere too?"

"Yes, he is, but the tunnel has fallen in and he can't get through. Me and Marigold could just squeeze through the gap. Tooby's in the wide bit, he calls it the cavern, and he's with Kate."

"Cutlass Kate! Hey, Jack! Did you 'ear that? Tooby's 'ere, 'n Kate!"

Jack groans and yawns. "Did you say Kate? Tooby?" He looks about him. "And who do we have here? Two young mice and one of them asleep?"

"My name is Ruby, and I come from Scraggy's world. This is Marigold and we came through the porthole, flying with Gabbee and Waggl."

"Ruby, it is good to meet you," Jack says, giving Marigold a gentle shake to try to wake her. "Now tell us, where is Tooby?"

Ruby tells the tale and Marigold wakes up in time to help recite the message that Tooby had asked them to say to Scraggy and Jack.

"Hmm," says Jack, "we knows the light makes the portal, but we isn't knowing how it be so. Tooby's always saying we has to ask the light, ask with our hearts!"

"You mean ask the light to take us out of here?" cries Ruby.

"Yes! But where? Back to the *Wreckless*, or to where Tooby is?" says Scraggy.

"Tooby and Kate are in the cavern... There's enough room there for us all," Ruby suggests.

"Alright, we'll ask to go there, to Tooby. Does this wisp o' light stretch all the way to the cavern?"

"Yes, Jack," says Marigold, sleepy and yawning.

"Marigold, hold one paw in the wisp o' light, and Ruby's paw with the other. Ruby, you hold Scraggy's paw, Scraggy you hold mine, and I'll put my other paw in the light pool. Good. Now, we've all been in the cavern before, imagine it – now!"

Four flashes pulse from the pool of light, through the mice, along the thread of light that stretches into the river and along the tunnel, through the rock fall, all the way to the cavern. The mice disappear from the Crystal Cave.

Tooby and Kate see the thread of light flash so bright they are dazzled for a moment, and when they recover their sight they see the four mice from the Crystal Cave sprawling in a heap on the floor.

"Ow!"

"Yikes!"

"Hey, you're squashing me!" This last complaint comes from Ruby, who has ended up with Scraggy sitting on her.

"Dad!" cries Scraggy, leaping up and hugging Tooby. "I's so 'appy seein' you."

"Jack!" cries Kate, giving him a hug too. "Hope you enjoyed your long sleep!"

"Long sleep? We only just–"

"Oh, no you didn't!" says Kate, laughing. "It's been twelve moons since you and Scraggy left the *Wreckless*."

"What? I don't believe it!" Jack exclaims.

The twins pick themselves up and stand shyly by Scraggy, waiting for him to notice them.

"Marigold! Ruby! Thanks for savin' us. Let's have a hug!" Scraggy laughs, very happy to see them.

The thread of light begins to change, pulling itself out of the tunnel and gathering into an Orb.

"Ah! The Orb's stayin' with us! That's a good sign, thank you, Orb," says Tooby, signing to the others to say it too.

"Thank you, Orb!" they chorus.

"Come on, let's get outside," says Tooby, turning to pick up his backpack.

"We left our backpacks somewhere here too," Jack remembers. "Let's have a look, Scraggy." They rummage in the furthest, darkest corner of the cavern.

"Yep! Found 'em!" calls Scraggy.

"Let's go!" calls Tooby, leading the way into the squeezy tunnel, followed by Ruby, Marigold, then Kate, Scraggy and Jack.

~

They emerge into sunshine. A gentle wind brings the smell of the sea. For some time, the mice stand still, soaking up the sunlight and feeling the fresh breeze in their fur; they stretch their limbs and breathe the fresh air deep into their lungs.

"This is good," says Kate.

"Let's just be here and rest a while," suggests Jack.

"Aye-aye, Captain!" cries Tooby. "Where's that Orb?"

"It's here." Kate cups her paws and makes a circular movement. "It's impossible to see in this bright sunlight."

"Ah!" says Tooby, reassured.

Just then a bird glides past, so close that the mice hear the wing-wind whistling.

"That wasn't Gobbee!" comments Jack.

They watch the bird swoop out to sea and curve back towards them, making a huge, slow circle. It prepares to approach again, eventually making a clumsy landing, almost falling over as it stumbles along trying to keep its balance.

"Oh dear, oh dear, I'll never get the hang of this!" says the bird, speaking slowly.

"'Allo!" Scraggy greets the bird. "My name's Scraggy 'n I's a mouse."

"Ah yes, I know you are a mouse," says the bird. "I met a mouse like you in the sky."

"Tell us! Tell us! What's 'is name? Is 'e alright?" cries Scraggy, beside himself with impatience to know if it was Emmy.

"First things first," interrupts Tooby. "My name is Tooby, 'n this be Jack 'n Kate, 'n these two be Ruby 'n Marigold."

"My name is Wandering Wings. I don't know what sort of bird I am; I have been flying for years and years looking for another bird like me, but there are none, and there was no land until the mouse in the sky helped me to find the fog and the Island of Mist."

"Was that after the typhoon?" asks Kate.

"Yes. After the turning-wind, the sky was full of fishes and seaweed and all sorts, and there was I, exhausted, unable to fly and about to fall out of the sky. It was very strange to see strands of seaweed coming towards me and wrapping themselves around my body, making a sort of nest – and I stopped falling! And then I saw a fish – in a nest as well – and then the mouse in a nest too!

"The fish was called Baloop, and he could breathe because of the seaweed and he didn't fall out of the sky either. The mouse was called Emmy–"

"'Ooray!" shouts Scraggy, jumping up and down with excitement. "Emmy! 'E's alive! 'E's alive!"

"Patience, my little friend, it is always good when journeys and stories are long. Emmy, the mouse, talked to his nest and called it a pouch, not a nest, and he named it Snugweed. I asked him to help me to find land and he said the only land is in the fog, and it's called the Island of Mist. We all three moved in our nests, or pouches as the mouse would have it, or bubble as Baloop would have it, and travelled very fast round the world many times – until we saw the fog, and then we slowed down and went into the fog, and Baloop and I found the Island of Mist, but Emmy called out that he was being pulled away, and his voice got further and further away until we couldn't hear him any more.

"We were sad to lose him, but we had found land and Baloop wanted to stay in his bubble for a bit longer, but then the seaweed unravelled, dropping him into the sea, and he swam away. My wings recovered their strength and my seaweed nest unravelled. I was flying again, and I've been flying round and round the island ever since. There are no birds like me, so I will never know what I am."

"Wandering Wings, you are an albatross," says Jack.

"Albatross? That is a splendid name, thank you."

Jack continues: "From the ship called the *Wreckless*, we have seen you many times, gliding on your great wings. I am sorry to have to tell you that you are the last of your kind and that is why you are here on the Island of Mist."

"Hmm. I might have known, just my luck."

"But where's Emmy?" says Scraggy.

"We's not knowin', lad," says Tooby. "But from what Wandering Wings is saying, 'e is livin' 'n breathin'."

Just then, a curious creature emerges from the bushes.

"Hallo," he says, in a slow, bored sort of voice. "My name is Pudge, and I am a Dodo."

"Pudge!" cries Scraggy. "We's met before, remember? I's Scraggy 'n this is Jack..."

"I remember, and now there are six of you, and a very large bird."

"Pudge, this is Wandering Wings. He is an albatross."

"Hallo, Pudge," says Wandering Wings.

"Hallo, Wandering Wings. I have been in the bushes listening to what you've been talking about, and I just had to meet you. You see, I am a bird that cannot fly, and you are a bird that cannot land, and so it seems to me that we shall be very good friends."

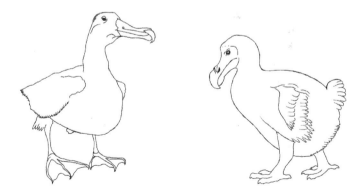

"Pudge, I do agree. Are there more like you?"

"No, I am the last of my kind."

"Then we are the same and will be good friends."

From the corner of her eye, Kate sees the Orb move a little. "Tooby! The Orb's on the move," she cries.

"Wandering Wings," – Tooby turns solemnly to the two birds – "we's grateful to you for givin' us 'ope that Emmy's livin'. Now we 'as to follow the light. Farewell to you! Farewell, Pudge!"

"Goodbye, farewell," reply the birds, each in their own slow way.

~

The mice set off down the mountainside, following the Orb which, as ever, waits for them to catch up when the path is difficult. They reach the cave where Tooby made the first light tubes, whereupon the Orb stops, hovering at the entrance. The mice gather round while the light threads itself through, re-forming into an Orb in a corner from where the light spreads across the whole cave.

"The Orb's sayin' we stays put," says Tooby. "We'll call it Bamboo Cave."

The mice settle in to their new home, collecting dry leaves and grass for bedding, seeds and fruit and whatever else they can find to eat, storing the food in bamboo tubes. Tooby shows Kate how to work the bamboo and asks her to teach Scraggy and the twins how to make things from it.

Tooby is restless, pacing about and finding it hard to sleep. When he does sleep, he dreams. He spends a lot of time gazing into the Orb and sometimes he 'sees' Flimsy. He's not certain what the message is, apart from 'it will be soon', until one day the message is clear – 'get them all from the *Wreckless*'. That it is urgent, he has no doubt. It is time to act.

"Jack, I's needin' to get to the *Wreckless*, will you be comin' along?" says Tooby.

"Yep. Now? Is it there?"

"The *Wreckless* is at anchor, and yes, we'll go this very day. We'll stow away on the longboat."

"May we come too, please, Uncle One-Eye?" pleads Ruby.

"I's needin' you all 'ere. We'll be back in two shakes of a shark's tail. It's urgent we get everyone here from the ship."

"How are they going to get here, Tooby?" Kate wonders out loud. "They won't all be able to hide in the longboat."

"You're right, Kate, especially with the rats too."

"Rats? You're joking, Tooby, aren't you?"

"My 'eart tells me I's 'avin' to give 'em a chance."

"Yes, you're right," Kate agrees.

"Away, Jack, let's go. We'll be back before you knows it. Watch the Orb, it'll tell you what you need to know."

~

Jack and Tooby scamper down the mountain as fast as they can go. From the clifftop they see that the humans are not yet back from their hunting, so they speed on down to the beach and along the mooring rope to the longboat. Sitting on the gunwale, they enjoy the sights and sounds of the sea until, when they hear the humans returning, they hide and listen as the longboat is floated and loaded. At last the humans climb aboard, ready to row to the *Wreckless*.

When the cargo has been unloaded, the sailors row back to the island and do another load, fetching things that have been stacked at the top of the beach, under the cliff. When the sailors are far enough away up the beach, Jack whispers to Tooby: "They're taking everything back to the ship! They're about to set sail! We's just in time, Tooby. How will we get back to the island?"

"The light, Jack, it'll be the light."

~

After another two trips the cargo has all been brought back and the longboat is hauled up to the deck of the *Wreckless*. By now, the two mice are tired and hungry and want very much to get to the Hideout, but they are not going to get any rest just yet. They run from the longboat as soon as the sailors are looking the other way, and the first thing that happens is that two rats challenge them. Jack and Tooby run for their lives – down a hatch and through a cargo bay – to the nearest rat-proof hole. It's a hole through an iron strap where one of the bolts is missing. It's an emergency escape route that they can rely on because the iron strap cannot be chewed by the rats to make the hole bigger.

Arriving at the Hideout, Tooby and Jack are greeted by the rest of the crew. Jack receives hugs from his crew; they are all so happy to see him they forget all about formalities.

"Right, my hearties," says Jack. "What news? Are we ready to go?"

"Cap'n," Stumpy replies. "We's 'ad a little skirmish with the rats like, 'n two of 'em wants to be comin' with us."

"Two?" says Jack. "I'll bet one of them's Black-Eyed Bart, but who's the other?"

"'E's called Coal-Face Carl 'n 'e's a big 'un."

"Where are they?" asks Jack.

"Emmy's Hold." Sally smiles. "They're hiding there."

"Let's all get along to Emmy's Hold now," says Tooby. "Is that where Emmy was taken by the typhoon?"

"Aye," says Stumpy. "We's remembrin' 'im by it."

"Let's see what we's needin' to take – lively now!" says Jack.

They lay out a row of things on the floor that they must take, including the fat light tube, other light tubes with maps and things in, food, two tiny daggers that Stumpy had borrowed from the sailors, a compass that might be too heavy to bother with, their cutlasses and belts, two backpacks, three little heads made of stone, and some bits and pieces of string and shells.

They wear their belts and weapons, carrying the other stuff out of the Hideout before packing the backpacks. In moments, they are ready to go. Suddenly they realise – this is it! They are leaving the *Wreckless*, their home for so long!

"Goodbye, Hideout!" Jack announces solemnly, facing the little entrance hole to the place that has been so good to them. "You've served us well, and we thank you."

"Goodbye, Hideout!" chorus all the others.

With the packs loaded, they set off for Emmy's Hold.

"Bart?" Jack calls as they get near.

"Who goes there?"

"Whip-Tail Jack."

"Ah, Jack, how good to know you're back safe and sound from the island. Now I was wanting to tell you..." Black-Eyed Bart shuffles out from the shadows, looking nervous. "I was wanting to tell you that I wants to come along with you like you offered, and there's another here who feels likewise."

"Come forward!" commands Jack.

"My name is Coal-Face Carl," says Carl, stepping out of the shadows. In the low light from the hold's only porthole, his face appears as black as soot; his eyes, ringed with white, look as though he's rubbed them with his paws and rubbed the soot off. The mice are a bit edgy being close to such a big rat, but they soon realise that he is a gentle giant.

"Carl, we welcome you," says Tooby. "We'll talk later, but now we must make haste. Pay attention, you all, every one of us must be lookin' at this light..." Taking the fat light tube from his backpack, Tooby opens the plug allowing the light to stream out and form into an Orb. The rats are especially surprised and gasp in astonishment, never having seen anything like this before.

Tooby waits patiently so that everyone has the time they need to say hallo to the light, and then he speaks out loud to the Orb.

"Orb, we's not knowin' how to ask this, but we's needin' your 'elp. Please be makin' a portal for us to get from the ship to the Island o' Mist, outside Bamboo Cave. We's not leavin' you 'ere unless you needs to stay, so I's keepin' the tube open for you if you needs it."

The Orb pulses, pulsing brighter and softer and brighter several times. Gradually, it spreads to form a circle, at first a flat, round sheet of light; then a point of blackness appears at the centre, growing larger until the light is reduced to a ring surrounding the blackness – a blackness that is blacker even than Coal-Face Carl's face.

Tooby peers into the blackness. He pokes his hand forward into it, but he can feel nothing the other side. He moves his head forward...

"Tooby! Don't!" cries Bess, afraid.

"Bess, 'tis now or never." Tooby leans forward, pushing his face through the blackness, feeling with his whiskers the slightly sticky texture of it. Opening his eyes, he sees the Island of Mist and Bamboo Cave, and he sees Ruby and Marigold playing tag with a lizard. He moves back into the dark hold of the ship.

"Come, my friends," he says, calmly. "Mice 'n rats together. I'll go last cos o' the light. I'll be 'oldin' the tube ready for the light if it needs. Jack, you lead the way, Kate 'n all other mice follow, then Bart, then Carl 'n me. Take heart!"

Jack steps forward, prepares himself for a moment and steps into the blackness. The mice and rats follow, one by one, and Tooby, coming last, walks through backwards holding up the open light tube. As he steps onto the ground of the Island of Mist, Tooby watches the circle of light spread over the blackness, disappearing it. He watches the light re-form into an Orb and thread itself gently into the light tube. When it is all inside, he replaces the plug.

~

There's a big party that night, as you might imagine. Stumpy had been wise enough to put the last few pickled raisins into the backpacks. The only problem is that the entrance to Bamboo Cave is too small for the rats to enter, so they search for another cave with a bigger way in for the rats. A quick share out of bedding and food and everybody is ready to party! As the new dawn brightens the eastern sky, they are all sitting on the clifftop looking out over the bay. As the sun rises, the *Wreckless* sets sail, turning slowly to catch the wind, and moving out of the bay towards the open ocean.

The eleven mice and two rats watch as the ship turns towards the south-west. Not one word is spoken. They don't know what's going to happen, or where they might go... They feel a shiver of apprehension as the ship sails away. It has been their home, their security, and now they face the unknown.

"Come, let's be 'avin' a look at the Orb," says Tooby. "I'll fetch it 'n meet thee all at Bart 'n Carl's cave."

In the darkness of the cave, the light flows from the light tube and forms the Orb. Gazing into the light calms and reassures them. It doesn't drive away all their fears, but they are strengthened, ready to face whatever might come.

Later, Scraggy dreams of Flimsy. She tells him that it won't be long now before the many worlds sing together and the sky glows bright. Scraggy doesn't understand, but he tells Tooby anyway. Tooby nods his head thoughtfully.

"We's in the nick o' time," he says, sighing.

To pass the time, waiting for whatever will happen next, Jack and Tooby keep everyone busy collecting food and bedding, and tidying the caves. When these jobs are done, Tooby sits making things with bamboo while the others explore the Island of Mist, meeting old friends, introducing Gabbee, Gobbee and Waggl to Lonely, Pudge and Wandering Wings.

Tooby, ever watchful, keeps his one good eye on the sky, his ears alert, and his wits sharp.

Chapter Four

Trouble

January has been cold and wet; the children haven't walked to Tillings Wood very often. But they have purled there quite a lot, enjoying spending time with the new purlers. Most of the local children are purling now, and some of their parents are learning too.

At school, Penny and her friends are looking at the questionnaire forms that have come back so far. There's a lot of them, and it takes them several 'project' classes to tally them up. Penny can't help feeling that something isn't quite right – the forms are missing the point somehow. She's been feeling this ever since coming back from the sea purling last summer. Her helpers have been learning to purl and have purled to the Glade to learn the wild talk and spend time with wild creatures. They, too, are beginning to feel that something is not quite right.

"Penny," says Siobhan, with a sigh. "Doing these questionnaires was good to get us all thinking, but now we've been purling it's different. Well, I feel different anyway. We wouldn't do it the same now, would we?"

"Yeah! You're right." Jerome shakes a fistful of questionnaires in the air. "These are too lame."

"That's what I'm thinking as well," says Penny. "But I didn't want to say anything..."

Mrs Weeble brings in another cardboard box. She sees Penny, and comes over, smiling her big, friendly smile. "Penny, these are from the office, for you, I think."

"Thanks, Mrs Weeble."

"You're welcome."

Penny opens the flaps, which are not taped up, to find a stack of recent survey returns from other schools. These are different. These are shouting!

"This is more like it!" cries Jerome.

"Fabulous!" says Siobhan. The children set about tallying up the results using a blank questionnaire form. It's Question 7 that's shouting the loudest, and it looks like this:

7 What should we tell the PM to do to help Nature?

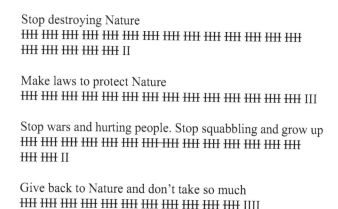

Stop destroying Nature
卌 卌 卌 卌 卌 卌 卌 卌 卌 卌 卌 卌 卌 卌
卌 卌 卌 卌 卌 II

Make laws to protect Nature
卌 卌 卌 卌 卌 卌 卌 卌 卌 卌 卌 卌 卌 卌 III

Stop wars and hurting people. Stop squabbling and grow up
卌 卌 卌 卌 卌 卌 卌 卌 卌 卌 卌 卌 卌 卌
卌 卌 II

Give back to Nature and don't take so much
卌 卌 卌 卌 卌 卌 卌 卌 卌 卌 卌 IIII

Stop climate change. Do green energy. Leave fossil
energy underground
卌 卌 卌 卌 卌 卌 卌 卌 卌 卌 卌 卌 卌 卌
卌 卌 II

"Wow! That's totally different!" cries Holly.

"There must be lots more people purling now than two weeks ago," says Penny. "Look how it's changed what they're seeing!"

She is right. Children in more and more schools are having 'Wot Appnd' read to them, and Emmy and Rattltap have been busy visiting each school at just the right moment to inspire the children. More and more children have made their bowl of things and have made a pouch – or found something they can use as a pouch – and they are learning to purl, discovering the wild web for themselves. Like Billy, a lot of the newcomers to purling get a big shock – they suddenly understand what's missing from their everyday lives, and they want it back. Computers and stuff are great, but not worth losing Nature for!

Penny and her team are ready now. During a project class, Mr Weatherstone suggests a meeting at Tom Wylder's place, and they agree that it would be good to get some help composing the letter to the PM.

"What's the letter going to say?" asks Larky.

"We'll use these questionnaires – look!" cries Penny, holding up the tally sheet. "Climate change – stop! Taking from Nature – stop! Give back to Nature! Laws for Nature! Stop money and machines destroying the planet and people's lives!"

"Strong words, Penny," says Mr Weatherstone. "How do you plan to introduce this?"

"Well, sir, erm... Oh, what do we see happening? We see terrible damage to Nature and the wild web because humans take too much. We see damage to the land and the sea and to people's lives because of wrong farming and because of conflicts and war.

"We see Nature being destroyed by machines because humans always want to take more. We see Nature being destroyed by climate change because humans burn fossil energy to make their machines work.

"There's war, and hunger, and homeless people in the world because humans are greedy and don't share.

"We children are all asking the grown-up world to do something about it all now, and if you want us children to survive, you must:

> Give us back the natural world we've lost.
> Stop trying to grow money all the time, that's a disease.
> Give back to Nature.
> Leave fossil energy in the ground.
> Stop machines destroying the planet.
> Stop war and weapons.
> Stop squabbling and grow up, like you're always telling us children to do.

"All this you must make law: Nature's Rights, up there with Human Rights, because humans haven't got any rights at all if Nature's not all right – and do it by Christmas!"

The classroom is very quiet when Penny stops talking. She is feeling flustered and embarrassed after talking more passionately than she ever has before.

"Hey! Amazing, Penny," says Stomper, in awe.

"Good work, Penny," says Mr Weatherstone. "Get that written down! When we visit Tom, we can decide how to begin and end the letter."

With a feeling of elation, the children write down Penny's words; for the first time in ages, they feel charged up and ready – to do whatever it takes.

Mr Weatherstone sends them all out for a break before reading a story, and then it's home time.

~

Later, at Tom's place, the children are outside under the lean-to roof that covers the terrace along the front of the house. On ledges and dwarf walls, Tom has placed fossils collected on his travels, and the children are examining them. Meanwhile, Tom is in the kitchen with John, putting lemonade and cake onto a tray, and glasses on another. The lemonade is home-made, with ice cubes chinking in the neck of the huge jug. The chocolate brownies are on a big plate, still warm from the oven.

"A man of many talents, I see, Tom!" says John.

"The credit doesn't go to me, John. We can thank my Mrs Sedgwick, my housekeeper, for the chocolate brownies."

"And the lemonade?"

"Oh, I made that myself."

They carry the two trays to the living room.

"Do help yourselves," Tom says, and he waits for the children to settle themselves before continuing. "Penny, you and your team have done a brilliant job with your survey. I've looked at the tally sheets, and the recent ones show how people begin to feel differently when they are given a chance to look deeper into things. Purling really does change people's perspectives. I try to do that with film making, trying to really observe the deep Nature and record it on film for people who can't get out there to see it for themselves. But it is the real looking that changes our perceptions, not watching films."

"But films can change our knowledge and our opinions," says John. "Yours certainly do."

"Thank you, John. They can, and do, but it is in the realm of ideas rather than a true feeling-sense." Tom hesitates. "Ideas that are disconnected from the natural world will not help to stop extinction from happening."

"Extinction? Extinction of what, Mr Tom?" asks David, who has been listening carefully.

"Of nearly everything, David," says Tom. "You children have been discovering how badly the wild web is torn. I've been studying this same thing my whole life. It's my view that we are living in the midst of a mass extinction event, the sixth mass extinction event in the history of our planet; most species will be extinct within your lifetimes. Many people would criticise me for saying such a thing to children, because it is depressing. I think otherwise. I think that it is only by facing up to the facts that we will find the motivation needed to do something effective, rather than just meddling around the edges of the problem.

"However gloomy this might sound, we must do all that we can to help the wild web to recover. But for this to happen, political leaders and the elite who control the economy must change their ways, and quickly."

For the attention of the PM
10 Downing Street
London
SW1A 2AA
England

Dear Honourable PM,

All of us putting our names at the end of this letter want you to know that we are the children of England and we would like you to listen to us because what we say comes from our hearts.

Because we are children we see things different to how grown-ups see things and we see that things are being done wrongly and would like to say what to do.

What we see happening is, we see terrible damage to Nature and the wild web because humans take too much. We see damage to the land and to the sea and to people's lives because of wrong farming and because of greed and war.

We see Nature being destroyed by machines because humans always want to take more.

We see Nature being destroyed by climate change because humans burn fossil energy to make their machines work.

There's war and hunger and lostness in the world because humans are greedy, and they take and take but don't give or share, not enough anyway.

We children ask the grown-up world to do something about it all, and to do it now, and if you want us children to survive, you must:

Give us back the natural world you've taken away from us

Stop trying to grow money all the time, that's called cancer

Give back to Nature

Leave fossil energy in the ground

Stop machines destroying the planet

Stop war and weapons

Stop squabbling and grow up, like you're always telling us children.

All this we want you to make law: Nature's Rights, up above Human Rights, because humans haven't got any rights at all if Nature's not all right.

This is very important and very urgent and there isn't much time, so please do it quickly, and we mean NOW!

Yours sincerely

The Children of England.

Signed:

In the silence that follows, Tom has a moment of worry that he has upset the children, but Billy steps in with enthusiasm.

"Let's 'ave a go at stoppin' that road!" he cries.

"Ah, yes," says Tom. "You're right, Billy, we need to focus on real things. Penny and her team have focused on the letters, now there's the road. What do you think we should do, Billy?"

"Whatever it takes! We'll stop it some 'ow."

"Come on!" cries Tom. "Let's research it on the internet. Right now!"

Skilful on the computer, Tom finds a government website which he navigates to find the relevant reports. He reads out loud about how the planning application for the new road has been in its final stages of consultation for the last six months. The Home Secretary has recently given it the green light, approving the amended plans and ordering that the project should go ahead at once.

"So they's plannin' to destroy our woods," says Billy, angrily. "'Ow could anybody do that?"

"Never!" shouts Stomper. "We'll stop them!"

"Billy," says Penny. "This is the time to take a stand. We'll send our letters and we'll get our new purling friends to help us stop the road being built."

"Don't we need to ask Mr Tom and Mr John for help with the letters?" says Larky.

Penny smiles. "We can do it ourselves now, I think."

"Hey! Talking of new friends," calls Tom from the computer desk. "Look what I've just come across!"

Tom has found a reference to 'Wot Appnd', as well as posts by people excited about purling and wanting to know more about it. The children crowd round the computer; they recognise some of the posts and ask Tom to follow certain links. It is soon very clear that the internet chat about purling is spreading fast and has already crossed the country, and there are some posts from people in other countries too.

Penny says that she has a few chat-friends and they are all following the story. They tell her that 'Wot Appnd' is available online, so everyone can find out about Emmy and the bowl of things and the pouches.

Stomper says that she has loads of chat-friends, and one said she's learned to purl with a pouch made from a little draw-string bag that she keeps beads in.

"Blimey." Billy's voice is strong. "It's really 'appnin'!"

"Thanks, Mr Tom, you've cheered us up loads. We'd better go now, it's getting late," says Penny.

"Penny, could I quickly copy out your letter? Would you like me to write a beginning and end for you? I could email it to John."

"Thanks, Mr Tom, we've got it sorted now, we'll do it."

"Thanks for the lush lemonade and brownies, Mr Tom!" says Larky, skipping around and laughing.

"You're all welcome, it's great to see you. Goodbye for now!"

"Bye!"

Suddenly the children are gone. Tom and John sit quietly.

"Phew!"

"Yes."

"John, would I be allowed to show a short film at your school, do you think?" asks Tom.

"Yes, I'm sure, Tom, but that would be up to Mrs Proctor."

"Of course, I'll arrange to see her."

~

Penny and her team write and re-write the letter several times, determined to get it right. They remember to be polite and to try to set everything out on the paper tidily and in the right places and put addresses and the date and things like that. Tom had suggested starting with the words 'We the undersigned', but none of the children like that, so they fish around for a while and decide on: 'All of us putting our names at the end of this letter want you to know that...'

At last they are happy with their rough drafts and start to make neat copies. There are bits where they have to change the wording because they want to send a letter to the PM, and they want to send a letter to HRH, so some of the words have to be different. Jerome remembers that they had planned a third letter – to the Secretary-General of the United Nations – and that will need different words again. Penny looks up the address on the internet; the other two addresses they can work out for themselves.

The neat copy of the letter to the PM looks like this:

So that's that one done. The next one starts off with a different address that goes:

Your Royal Highness
Buckingham Palace, London, England

The third letter goes:
> The Secretary-General of the United Nations
> 405 East 42nd Street
> New York
> NY10017
> United States of America

Penny can do the best writing, so she does two of them, but Holly's writing is almost as good, so she does the one to the Secretary-General. When they are satisfied, they carry them proudly to the school office to ask if they could have half a dozen photocopies of each one, and please could they type up three envelopes to post the letters in, and put stamps on them, and please can they have permission to pin copies of these three letters up on the school notice board to collect signatures and thumb prints.

When all this is done, Penny leads the way to the school notice board. They move other notices around to make room and pin the letters up, with a blank sheet of paper below for signatures and thumb prints. They also pin up a ballpoint pen, dangling on a long string, so that there's something to write with.

The four children stand back to admire their work.

"Hey! We must sign them ourselves before we forget!" cries Siobhan.

They do so, and their signatures are soon followed by nearly everyone's in the school, including teachers and visiting parents.

But the job isn't done yet. Earlier, in class, Mr Weatherstone had said to Penny that when the letter to the PM is ready, he could scan it and email it to teachers that he knows in other schools, asking them to get signatures as well; now they are ready, Penny asks him to do exactly as he suggested.

Now they just have to wait for the signatures to come, but meanwhile, there are other things to do. Billy wants Penny and her new helpers, and the rest of the gang, namely Larky and Stomper and David, to come with him to Pip's place.

If they were purling they could be there in an instant, but they don't like to purl too often because they like being in their bodies, and anyway, purling is for special things to do with the wild web. And so it is, they walk to Pip's, talking about how much better they feel now that they are doing something for the wild web, and Larky says that it feels like when they first met Emmy.

"Where is Emmy? I haven't seen him for ages, nor LuLu, not

since the sea purling," says Stomper.

"I's missin' seein' Emmy, 'n the old git–"

"Billy!" interrupts Penny. "You shouldn't call Mr Pip that, it must sound rude to Siobhan and Holly, and Jerome."

"Well, it would sound rude if I didn't already know how close you all are because of the mouse," says Siobhan. "Thanks for inviting us today, I really want to get to know everyone better."

They arrive at Pip's place and knock on the door. When he opens the door he laughs, seeing them crowded round with their smiling faces looking back at him. He greets them warmly.

"Ah! My long-lost friends! Here you are at last. Come in, come in, kick off those wet shoes, come and get warm. Let's see now, come through to the kitchen."

"Thanks, Mr Pip," says Billy, following Pip inside. "This is Siobhan 'n Holly 'n Jerome, they's been doin' the letters with Penny. They's finished 'em!"

"Hallo, and welcome to you all. Do call me Pip. I'd like to read those letters! Now, what would you like?"

"Is the wood stove alight?" asks Larky.

"Yes."

"Could we just have some squash and sit by the fire?"

"We've missed that, Mr Pip," says Penny.

"Go through and get settled and I'll bring some drinks."

"Thanks, Mr Pip," sings Larky.

Soon they are all warming up by the fire; Pip brings in the tray and hands out the drinks. He sits in the chair that the children have left empty for him.

"Where's Emmy, Mr Pip?"

"Emmy's been busy with Rattltap, visiting schools and all that, and he's staying with LuLu, that's why we don't see him. LuLu has been very poorly sorted, as Emmy would say, since the sea purling."

"That was last summer!" cries Larky. "Oh, poor LuLu, I wish we could see her, and help," says Larky.

"Even I can't do that," says Pip. "Emmy said he'll tell me when it's time."

Billy coughs a bit self-consciously. "Mr Pip, we's wantin' to make a plan 'bout the road, 'n we's needin' your 'elp? We was thinkin' we should 'ave two purlers on lookout, all the time, up by them machines."

"Good plan, Billy. Are there enough of you to do a rota."

"Yes, I'll sort that out," Holly volunteers.

"What next?"

"Well, Mr Pip, Penny thinks we should be gettin' lots of town people up there to the woods to see for themselves," Billy explains.

"Great idea, how about making a flier that we could put through letterboxes?" suggests Pip.

"We could design it, Mr Pip, would you help with the words?" says Siobhan.

"Well, that should be clear and simple. Let's see: 'Tillings Wood threatened by new road; some trees already cut down, come and see for yourselves. Let's stop this before it goes any further. Come to the top gate of the wood next Sunday morning. See you there!' Stuff like that. I'm very happy to do leafleting. Oh, yes, put my phone number on it, too."

"We can all do leafleting, Mr Pip."

"Good. Now, can I see your letter?" asks Pip.

"Yes, here's one you can read," Penny says, pulling a folded-up and dog-eared copy of the letter to the PM from her pocket. Pip unfolds it and reads.

"We'll wait while the signatures come in," says Penny when Pip's had time to finish. "Then we'll send them."

"I'm impressed! Strong and heartfelt, well done all of you! It will be interesting to see what response you get! Where do I sign?"

"I've got that," says Holly, rummaging in her shoulder bag and handing Pip the list of signatures. Pip signs his name.

"Thanks, Mr Pip," says Penny. "We'd better go now and keep guard in Tillings Wood."

~

Mrs Proctor approves of Tom's proposal to show his film at the school. She suggests doing two screenings, one for the younger pupils and another for the older pupils. The film is called 'Rewilding'. It begins by describing how the natural world has changed over thousands of years due to fluctuations in the climate and the effect of human activity. Different habitats all over the world have been filmed, including landscapes that look more or less natural, and landscapes that have been transformed by humans for farming, for mining natural resources, and for building towns, cities, industry and roads. The huge scale of deforestation and destruction of natural habitats is very clear, and so too is the steady increase in the human population, always making more hungry mouths to feed.

The film looks at what is known about climate change and the activities of humans that speed it up. The science says that global warming is already on the point where 'runaway climate change' begins; it's called a 'tipping point', beyond which we humans will not be able to do anything to stop it. All humans could hope to do is to slow down the process. People need food to eat and somewhere to live, but so do wild creatures and plants. The ecology of the planet as a whole must be healthy to support all life, or humans will not survive, nor anything else.

The film proposes that areas of each country, and areas of the oceans, should be allowed to wild themselves, so that Nature can recover and create oases of wilderness. This should be the sea as well as the land. Big areas of the oceans should not be fished or mined for minerals, so that fish stocks can recover and ecosystems thrive once again. There used to be so much more life in the seas – and on the land – than there is now. The sixth mass extinction event is happening around us, and it is happening because of humans.

When the film comes to an end, Tom gives a talk. He says that it is easy to forget that Nature used to be more abundant because what we see every day seems normal. In fact, the abundance of Nature has been disappearing slowly for thousands of years because of increasing human activity, and so the rate of species extinctions has been getting faster for thousands of years.

Scientists estimate that the 'background rate' of species extinction has been between one and five species per year. But that's how it used to be. Scientists now argue about how things have changed since humans started to have such a big impact on the natural world. When was that? When did it start? Perhaps it all began when hunter-gatherers hunted the mega fauna, those huge herbivores and their predators that once roamed the Earth. That process took thousands of years, but even so, it did change the ecosystems of whole continents. But the sixth mass extinction event really kicks off with the development of agriculture, about 12,000 years ago. There is debate about when exactly the Anthropocene epoch starts – that's the name proposed for the geological epoch shaped by human activity. Tom says that he doesn't like the term, as it somehow manages to suggest the old idea of the dominion of Man over Nature, as though that were something to be proud of.

Estimates of how many species disappear each year are hotly argued. Some say it is between 1,000 and 10,000 times greater now than the background rate. That could mean anything from a dozen species every day to a hundred species every day – and getting faster. But others say this is an exaggeration and there is no real evidence for it. There are ecosystems that have not been studied and countless species remain unrecognised and this makes it hard to estimate what's happening.

Tom doesn't hesitate to talk about really big issues, issues that most people don't want to talk about. He knows that the children might well get bored, but it's worth the risk. They might really hear what he's saying. He continues on the subject of extinction.

When a big mammal or bird becomes extinct, people notice, but most species are small and inconspicuous, like tiny plants or insects, snails or little frogs, fungi or lichen, bacteria, algae, krill – the little things that are too many to count. These are the multitudes that make ecosystems work, and when these species disappear, one by one, a moment arrives when entire ecosystems collapse – remember trophic cascades – causing many thousands of species to become extinct in a short period of time. This is happening right now, and is not easy to monitor, estimate or predict. Any extinction caused by human activity is an extinction too many. Extinction of entire ecosystems is catastrophic.

Tom draws his talk to an end by saying that he would like to set the older children a little homework. He asks each class to divide into five groups and each group to select a leader. He gives each leader a slip of paper with a few words written on. He explains:

"I've selected five ideas, or concepts, related to climate breakdown and to ecology in general. I would like each group to research one of them. The five concepts are:

> Ecosystem Engineer
> Shifting Baseline Syndrome
> Trophic Cascades
> Methane Plumes
> The Keeling Curve

"The film has shown you a bit about what these things might mean, but you will have to do some research. You can talk to your teachers about it, use the internet, and read books! I'd like all of you in each group to write down what you find out, but your leader will give a little talk to class just before the end of term. It's your end of term task!"

~

Tom helps Penny and Siobhan design the leaflet about the road building in Tillings Wood, asking townspeople to go and have a look for themselves and to meet there on Sunday. When it's finished, he emails it to Pip who prints out a few hundred copies. Pip drives round town delivering bundles of leaflets to his friends. He drops in on Donna to tell her what's been going on and gives her a bundle of leaflets for Larky. Then he drives to Penny's, but there's no one in, so he shoves the leaflets through the letterbox. Then over to Stomper's for a cup of tea and a chat with Linda, who is keen to catch up on what's been going on.

Later, Pip meets up with Billy and David and gives them some leaflets too.

"Please don't go leafleting alone," says Pip. "People can be funny about having things put through their letterboxes. I've said this to Donna and Linda, so Larky and Stomper will know."

"Mr Pip, I've got a map 'ere that 'Olly drew," says Billy. "It's showin' who's doin' what street, 'n yours is blue."

"That's good, well done, Billy. Looks like I'm the lucky one. The blue ones are mostly round where I live!"

"That's right, Mr Pip, we don't want you gettin' lame from walkin'!"

"Billy, are you calling me old and lame?!"

"Only teasin', guv!"

Billy and David set off to leaflet their parts of town, and Pip walks the streets marked in blue on his map. He uses up all his leaflets and returns home to print more. Later, he gets a visit from Larky and Donna who have come to get some more as well. Larky says she needs to take some for Penny and Stomper too. Holly has been helping, while Siobhan and Jerome are keeping guard in Tillings Wood – purling, of course.

The next day the phone calls begin. Local people telephone Pip, people who have something or other to say about the leaflets they've received. Some suggest that there should be a meeting in the town hall before traipsing all the way to the woods. Pip doesn't agree. Others are saying yes, let's get organised. Some people knock on Pip's door; one such visitor suggests getting up there to the woods, before Sunday, to see what might be needed by way of equipment.

"Equipment?" asks Pip.

"Yeah," says Mr Mavrik, one of the keen people. "We'll need to camp out in the treetops, chaining ourselves on. Like we did years ago to save the trees when the supermarket got built."

"So, you think we need to 'occupy' the site?"

"Oh yeah, they'll have us arrested and taken away in half an hour if we don't."

"Blimey, it sounds a bit scary."

"It's scary alright. We'll get agro and abuse. They won't be friendly, I'll tell you that for nothing."

"It's going to need a few people, isn't it?"

"No problem, I've got loads of friends spoiling for a bit of peaceful demo. We go all over the country trying to save trees and land from being ripped up."

"And you happen to live here?"

"Yeah, just around the corner."

"Couldn't be better. Shall we go and have a look at the site then?"

"You leave that to me. I understand you've got work to do with the young 'uns."

"Alright, Mr Mavrik, I'll see you on Sunday. By the way, how do you know about the 'young 'uns'?"

"Call me Jonty. Word gets around, everybody knows there's something going on."

"Right, Jonty, thank you very much."

"Glad to be of help."

~

The purlers keeping guard see the first visitors to the site in Tillings Wood. Late in the day a few men arrive with a van and park at the roadside where they can get into the wood. They carry bags and boxes through to the place where the security fence has not been finished and enter the compound where the machines are.

After a quick look around, they go back into the surrounding woods to examine the trees along the edge of the compound and decide which ones to climb. One of the men has a slingshot device for sending a thin rope, with a weight on the end, up and over a high branch. He's skilled, and in two minutes flat he has got the end of the thin rope over the branch and back down. He attaches a climbing rope and by pulling the thin rope, the climbing rope is installed over the high branch. As soon as the rope is in place, one of the other men, wearing a climbing harness, disappears up into the tree while the first man installs a climbing rope in another tree.

A bit later, just as daylight begins to fade, another vehicle arrives. This time it's a small pick-up truck laden with pallets, planks and rope. The materials are carried through to the trees where the climbers are working, and ropes are used to pull the stuff up into the treetops. By the time darkness falls, everything has been pulled up and the ground tidied, so you wouldn't know anything had happened. The vehicles disappear off down the lane, leaving a few men behind to guard the equipment overnight.

Before dawn the next day, the pick-up truck returns with another load of materials. These are carried through into the wood below the compound. The men repeat the operation of last night but this time on trees that form a line down into the woods, following the numbered marker posts. When there is enough daylight, they begin to make use of the pallets, planks and ropes to make platforms for sleeping, as high up in the treetops as they can manage. Bags containing food, water and bedding are pulled up and made secure on the platforms, with tarpaulins covering them to keep them dry. Ropes are stretched between trees to help people move from one tree to the next without coming down to the ground.

The purlers change shifts every few hours, and whoever has just come off-shift tells the others the news of what's been happening. The children are very excited and can't wait for Sunday. But there's just a little bit of school still to do.

~

On the morning of the last day of term the weather is mild, a nice change after the rainy two weeks they've just had. Mrs Weeble has organised a treasure hunt, well several really, using different coloured paper for the clues for each class. The children rush around the playground, playing field and Nature garden looking for clues; it's all a bit chaotic and crazy, and loads of fun. In the end, they find small boxes of chocolate eggs, a treat for after lunch.

Later, in Billy's class, Mr Weatherstone taps on his desk and holds up a hand for quiet. When the children have quietened down, he introduces the afternoon's challenge. "This afternoon will be the last challenge of the term. You all saw Tom Wylder's film 'Rewilding' and I'm sure you remember what he said about giving you a last task." The children groan. "It won't be as bad as all that! And it won't take you long, if I know anything about you lot. Now then, Tom divided you up into five groups and gave each group an ecology concept to research. What was the first one? And who is the

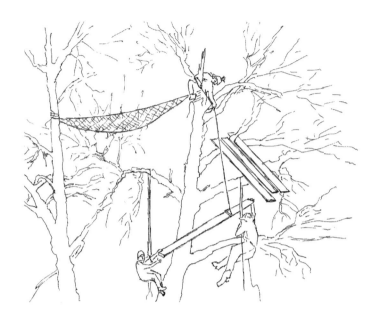

leader of that group?"

"It's me, sir," says Siobhan. "We were asked to explain what is meant by 'Ecosystem Engineer'."

"Thank you, Siobhan, and did you find out what it means?"

"Yes, sir, and lots of examples, sir, so it was difficult to choose. Ecosystem engineers are species that make habitats for other species, just by doing what they do. One example is beavers. Beavers cut down trees using their teeth. They eat the leaves and twigs and use the branches to build dams across the streams and rivers where they live. The dams make pools that flood the banks and make the ground wet all around, and this makes lots of different habitats that wouldn't be there without the beavers. And all this slows down the water flowing in the stream, so it doesn't rush down and flood villages lower down.

"Other ecosystem engineers are elephants and wild boar, but they don't have to be big. A very long time ago when life on Earth was just getting started, there were the first tiny algae-like things that made oxygen and that changed the whole planet and it took two hundred million years before the ground stopped soaking up all the oxygen."

Mr Weatherstone is impressed. "So, an ecosystem engineer is

a species that changes the environment, creating more habitats for other species?"

"Yes, sir."

"Good, thank you, Siobhan, well done to your group. It makes me wonder... Humankind is a species that changes the environment, but we are reducing the diversity of habitats, and causing extinction of other species. We are ecosystem demolition engineers! Now, who's next?"

"Me, sir," says Jerome. "We got given a tough one I reckon. What is 'Shifting Baseline Syndrome'? Well, we didn't have a clue what any of those words meant, so we had to ask around and look on the internet and everything.

"It's like my Dad saying that when he was a kid there was loads of birds and insects and flowers, lots more than now. But when I ask my granddad he says no! When *he* was a kid, there was even more birds and flowers and trees and everything. So, what it's about is scientists not looking back far enough when they decide how many fish there should be, like cod for our fish 'n chips. They're saying that cod numbers are back up to 1980s numbers so it's alright to fish them again, but some bloke did research and found 1980s numbers of fish is only a tenth, no, less than that, of what they used to be.

"We've forgotten how much wildlife there used to be, so we just say 'when I was a kid there was loads of...', as if that was alright, but it weren't."

"Very good, Jerome," says John. "Well done to you and your team. Right, who's next?"

"Erm, me, sir," says Billy, feeling nervous and shy. "Like Jerome, we 'ad a really 'orrible one cos we 'adn't a clue. We was asked: 'what's Trophic Cascade' mean?

"Well, we 'ad to do a bit o' work 'n research 'n all that malarkey. It's about food chains, where the little things at the bottom is gettin' eaten by bigger things, 'n the biggest things is at the top; trophic means the levels in between, like rungs on a ladder.

"Cascade is like a waterfall 'n trophic cascade is like when a creature on one level dies out 'n this is bad news for everythin' else. We found an example of sea otters eatin' sea urchins in the kelp forests in the sea. Kelp is seaweed that grows big 'n tall 'n is eaten by sea urchins. 'Umans kill off the otters 'n the urchins gets too many 'n they eats all the kelp 'n everything dies off."

"Very good, Billy, well done to you and your team. It shows how things are all linked together. Right, who's next?"

"I am, sir," says Penny, "and we were asked to explain 'Methane Plumes'. We didn't know so we had to look it up and it's a bit complicated.

"A methane plume is when methane gas bubbles up from the bottom of the Arctic ocean. Methane gas is made when plants and animals die and sink to the bottom of the sea and go mouldy and rot. Because the Arctic has been frozen for thousands of years, the methane gets frozen solid inside the ice and it's called methane hydrate, because of the ice. But the ice is melting, and the sea is getting warmer and the frozen methane hydrate is melting, and the methane gas is bubbling up and going into the air. What's really bad is that methane is a lot worse greenhouse gas than carbon dioxide. It's a hundred times worse, well, about eighty-four times, in fact.

"Methane plumes are natural, but as the sea warms up they are getting bigger and bigger and are happening more often, making climate change go quicker. We also found out that methane and carbon dioxide gases are being released as permafrost melts."

"Thank you, Penny, well done to you and your group. Is there one more group?"

"Yes, sir, the Keeling Curve," says David, a little nervously. "Like the others, our group didn't know anything about the Keeling Curve, so we had to look it up. Mr Wylder gave us some clues where to look. Anyway, Olly suggested we ask in the office for some photocopies, so here's a drawing we made of the Keeling Curve." David walks around handing out a copy to each person in the class, including Mr Weatherstone.

"What it is," David explains, "is – and I'm reading out from something we found – 'a graph of the accumulation of carbon dioxide in the Earth's atmosphere based on continuous measurements taken at the Mauna Loa observatory on the island of Hawaii from 1958 to the present day.'

"That's the end of the quote. It was Doctor Charles Keeling who started doing it and kept it going. It's still going now. Other scientists got interested because the increases in carbon dioxide in the air matched the increase in fossil fuel burning, and this was the first time a scientist had said it – that humans are causing climate change.

"I forgot to say, CO_2 is one of the greenhouse gases that are building up in the atmosphere and absorbing heat from the sun and warming the planet. You won't know this, but I read it along the way that half of all human CO_2 emissions have happened since 1990 – get your heads round that! We can't blame history for climate change – it's all of us alive NOW that are doing it, and we could fix it, we have to fix it."

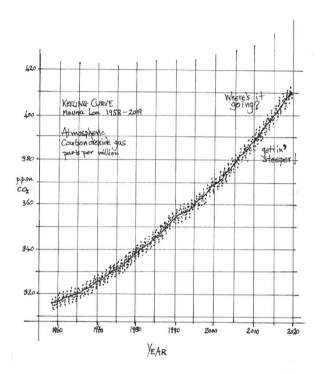

A shocked silence follows David's speech. His friends look at him with admiration, for they know how hard it has been for him since he met the mouse. The others in class are surprised by David's performance, and shocked by what he says. Mr Weatherstone is very impressed.

"Thank you, David, that was a remarkable presentation, well done to you, and well done to your group. I must say, I am really proud of all of you, and I am proud of everything that you've done this term. I think things are going to be busy for you over the holidays. I hope you have a good time! Class dismissed!"

"Thank you, too, sir, for all your help with our projects!" cries Penny, as the children stampede out of the classroom and down the corridor, and out into the April air.

~

On Sunday morning, Pip and Billy walk up through Tillings Wood to the compound where the road-building machines are lined up. As they draw near they hear raised voices, and they hear a siren as a police car speeds up the lane towards the gate. There are police officers inside the compound already, and men in hi-vis jackets and hard hats – the road builders. Outside the compound, on the woodland side, a group of local people wait to see what's going to happen. The police have formed a cordon across the gap in the fence, and an officer with a loudhailer is telling everyone to go home.

The townspeople don't show any sign of moving and some shout out in protest that they have only come to see what's going on, so why all this bother? The response is yells from the workmen that they're trespassing and will get arrested.

Billy and Pip keep their distance, having a discreet look around, trying not to attract attention. They can see that platforms have already been built in the trees, and rope bridges too. All the leaves have fallen, so the tree dwellers are easy to see. Billy sees purlers high up in the trees around the compound, keeping out of sight. Anyone not looking for purlers wouldn't notice them.

"Larks!" he yells, but his voice is lost in the racket from the crowd, but Larky feels his call, and after a while she purls down.

"What's 'appnin', Larks?" Billy asks.

"Some people have been here for days," says Larky, "up in the trees, chained to branches high up. There's some chained to the machines too. That crowd from the town have only just come."

"The Occupation of Tillings Wood!" says Pip. "We must call the local radio and TV and get them here as soon as we can. I should've thought of that sooner. Larky, could you go and ask the tree dwellers if they need anything?"

"Right away, Mr Pip!"

Larky purls back to her friends up in the trees. The purlers have been getting to know the tree dwellers, causing quite a stir, but they've soon made friends, and the purlers are perfect for taking messages from one place to another without being seen.

As the day wears on, the townspeople drift away, uncertain how to deal with the situation, which is turning out to be more aggressive than they had expected. Not at all happy at what they have seen, they grumble and mutter about being better prepared next time.

126

Pip and Billy keep hidden in the nearest undergrowth. They watch as the workmen begin to go to their vehicles and drive away – but not before they've helped the police to cut the chains from the protestors locked to machines. These protestors are arrested and bundled into the police vehicles waiting nearby. Their only offence has been trespass, as they've caused no damage or disturbance. Pip hopes that they will be released before long.

The remaining workmen shout at the tree dwellers, swearing at them and saying they'll get them down tomorrow – if any of them are stupid enough to stay up there. One of the men revs up a chainsaw, threatening to cut into a tree at the edge of the compound to show they mean business, but a police officer stops him.

Larky returns.

"They're alright, just bring all the help you can tomorrow!"

"Right! Come on, let's get home," says Pip. "Take care, Larky."

"See you later!" yells Larky, disappearing back to the treetops.

"What can we be doin', Mr Pip?" says Billy, as they make their way back down through the woods.

"Well, Billy, I'll try to contact the media people – I know it's Sunday but it's worth a try – and prepare for tomorrow and get there early with as much food and water as possible. There might be some townspeople wanting to meet up and hatch a plan."

"Should I be purlin' tomorrow?"

"Might be best, Billy. I think we are going to need the purlers, and you would be good at communicating. Put out the call, Billy, we'll need as many purlers as possible."

"Alright, I'll call 'em. See you there tomorrow, Pip."

"Yes, Billy," says Pip, noticing the seriousness in Billy's voice, and the fact that, for the first time, he didn't call him 'Mr Pip'. "Take care of yourself, my friend."

Billy gazes at Pip for a moment, then turns to run along the road to his Nan's house; Pip continues his walk home. He wonders about Emmy and LuLu, deciding to visit them later even though Emmy has not said that it's time yet.

Once at home, he looks up the phone numbers and makes calls to the local radio, TV and newspaper. He has to leave messages, which he does in some detail so that if they are interested they can go straight there to the woods. Having done all that, he puts his coat and boots back on, and walks to LuLu's place. He taps on the door.

"Allo?" comes Emmy's voice through the letterbox.

"Emmy! It's Pip, may I come in?"

"Iyzll b askin LuLu."

Pip waits; eventually there's the sound of a key being turned in the lock and the door slowly opens.

"Hallo, Pip, come in," says LuLu quietly, closing and locking the door when Pip has stepped through.

Pip takes off his boots and coat and follows LuLu to the sitting room. He feels awkward; perhaps he shouldn't have come.

"I'm sorry to come uninvited. Emmy did say I should wait until it was time, but I really couldn't wait any more..."

"It's alright, Pip, you're here now."

"I've been worried, LuLu. Emmy has told me that you've been poorly sorted. Are you feeling any better?"

"It's true, I've not been well," says LuLu. "Not ill, but heartbroken. Emmy calls it being re-knitted."

"Like what happened to me – after I saw Emmy and Scraggy in their homeworld?"

"Yes, like that. Purling under the sea has broken my heart; as Emmy says, I am being re-knitted. But I'm finding it harder and harder to be in the world of humans. Emmy took me to the Glade and we talked with Rindill, and that helped. I stayed in the Glade and later, after night had fallen, I slept; I dreamed, finding myself purling and looking at my own sleeping body. When I'm purling there is a sense of beingness – a sense of being one with all other creatures. It is an oceanic awareness. I am at home there, being in the unwords.

"As I watched, my body faded and after a while it disappeared. I understand that the children long to be back in their bodies after purling a long time. That seems perfectly right, as they are young and strong and vital, but I am not; it is such hard work for me to be in the world, I would rather purl.

"Since then, my body fades in and out of the world, and I have come to accept that this is so."

Pip takes a moment to let what LuLu says sink in. Some of what she says is familiar to him because of his own struggles, and he, too, finds the human world difficult; he is tired of the noise and speed of it all, and the relentless disappearance of Nature is a constant wounding. But his body has never ghosted. Well, not yet.

"LuLu iz bein re-knut, Pippee, n sheezll b invizibl wun."

"LuLu, are you leaving us?" says Pip.

"Not leaving, not until it is time."

"I feel like crying."

"Pippee, singin iz betta."

"I will be both, for a time," says LuLu. "Perhaps we are both for much longer than we are ever aware. Perhaps we have always been both. The children now have the chance to be aware that they are both, and to continue to have the awareness that purling has given them."

"Sorry, both what?" asks Pip, perplexed.

"Bein inna boddee n bein invizibl. Umanz iz lernin xcept theyz avin to b re-knut."

"Anyway, Pip, that's enough about me. Tell me what's been happening."

Pip is worried because he doesn't understand and wants to ask more about it, but he decides to leave it until another time. Instead, he describes what he knows of the children's work writing the letters and getting signatures; he talks about seeing many more children purling, seeing the protestors making camp in the woods and up in the trees, and seeing the angry road builders. When he describes the plan for tomorrow's demonstration, LuLu speaks.

"I won't be there tomorrow, Pip, I am not strong enough yet. Please tell the children that I think of them with love. They are all in my heart."

"I will, LuLu."

"And you – please be careful."

"Pippee, yooz avin to b careful. Prapz yood betta b stayin ome."

"I must go, Emmy, I must help the children. It's dangerous anyway now and will get more so, I'm sure. The authorities don't like direct action like this and will want to stop the media getting involved. We'll see what happens."

"Yip, wot appnz. Weezl b seein wot appnz."

They sit in silence for a while. Emmy is in LuLu's bowl of things, on a small table in the middle of the room.

"Look after each other, won't you?" says Pip.

"Weez lyke that, Pippee," says Emmy, pressing his paws together tightly.

"I know... I miss you both..."

"Everything is changing, Pip, please be careful. And come to see me again when you can."

"Thanks, LuLu, I will. Thanks, Emmy. You are both here, in my heart."

Pip leaves LuLu's place feeling churned up; he cries as he walks, glad of the dark and the cool air. He realises that the apprehension he has been feeling is not just about the demo in the woods tomorrow; as LuLu has said, everything is changing. He has been feeling something creeping up on him in recent days, like a tide coming in at night.

~

During the dark hours people continue to gather, arriving on foot at Tillings Wood, or purling children appearing out of thin air. The full-sized people make camp in the woods, and as the camp grows, new people make their way further into the woods, following the line of the surveyor's yellow-topped posts that show where the road will go. People in the camp don't go into the compound, except for a few who chain and padlock themselves to the digging machines and bulldozers. Purlers that are newly arrived are guided to the Glade by other purlers so that they can learn the wild talk and get used to purling.

At daybreak the road builders arrive in pick-up trucks. Leaving the people padlocked to machines for the police to deal with, they start up generators and turn on the flood lamps. Organising their chainsaws, ladders and bolt croppers, they walk out of the contractors' compound and into the woods, through the gap where the section of fence has not yet been put up. The police officers are pushed aside, their shouts ignored, and the crowd of townspeople looking on are roughly forced aside. People are knocked over and trampled, people trip up, become angry, start shouting and yelling – it is very frightening.

The purlers swarm down in their thousands; they have been watching from above, hidden in the misty air. Seeing the townspeople in danger, the purlers press in on the crowd of angry road builders. There are so many purlers, the men are confused and can't see where they are going. They trip up on rocks and fallen branches; they yell and swear and thrash about, trying to swat the swarming things as though they are insects. The purlers manage to stop the angry men, and hold them back, so that the townspeople can pick themselves up and get to safety. Two men in the compound start up a bulldozer and excavator – that don't have anyone chained to them – and drive through the gap in the fence. As they come down the slope, the purlers swarm around them, making it impossible for the drivers to see where they are going. They need to stop, but they don't stop in time, and the machines crash into each other.

A television crew arrives just in time to see the cloud of purlers descend from the sky; they manage to get some footage of the diggers, but only from a distance.

"Hurry up, guys!" yells Specky Spender, the one who does the talking. She's ready to jump into any fray to get good footage. "Come on, Will!"

Wobble-Cam Will is the cameraman.

"What on earth is that?" yells Specky, pointing at the swarm of purlers surrounding the road builders.

"Look at it on camera!" calls Will. Looking at the small camera screen, Specky sees that the swarm of purlers is glowing.

"How weird is that! What *are* those little things? It's like a swarm of locusts, but they're too big to be insects."

"Where's someone to talk to?" says Will.

"Over there, in the woods, I can see people there."

Will is already moving that way, filming as he goes, with Specky following and talking into her mobile phone at the same time.

"Are you guys getting all this?"

"Yeah, yeah, we're cool," says someone in the TV van.

Will is filming people in the camp and in the treetops. Jonty Mavrik walks over to say hallo.

"What's happening here? asks Specky, holding out the

microphone to pick up Jonty's reply. Jonty is smiling.

"Hallo, Specky Spender, we meet again. What's happening? You can see with your own eyes, and the camera's eye too, I hope."

"What *is* that cloud? I can hear singing, what's going on?"

"You're witnessing a miracle, Specky," says Jonty, laughing. "It's a revolution, I can tell you that much now. This'll run and run!"

"But what on Earth is it?"

"Come, I'll show you."

Jonty leads the TV crew to the camp and on down the hill a bit.

"Billy?" he calls out.

"Over 'ere, Jonty."

Sitting round a campfire are several protestors, including Pip and Tom Wylder. Purling in the air are Billy, Larky and Penny. They have been making plans.

"What's 'appnin', Jonty?" asks Billy.

"Here's the TV people. This is Specky Spender, and Will with the camera."

"Er, hallo. Hallo, Billy. Erm, what are you?" stutters Specky, hesitant for the first time in her life.

"I's Billy 'n I's 'uman 'n I's purlin'," says Billy, proudly.

"Er, right, but what does all that mean? Why are you so small?"

"That's cos of Emmy, 'e's the mouse."

"Mouse? What mouse?"

"Hallo, Specky," says Pip. "You've got some homework to do if you want to understand the answers to your questions. I'm Pip."

"Ah, right! You're the crackpot that left the garbled message on my phone?"

"Very succinctly put. Yes."

"Time I interrupted, I think," says Tom. "I know a bit about filming. Have you got live transmission now? We need to give you the backstory – here, sit down and we'll tell you. You may want to get another camera out there to keep up with what's happening."

"Alright, good, let's hear it!" says Specky, sitting down on a log. "Yes, we're transmitting live now, and the team will get another camera out there, don't worry about that."

Wobble-Cam Will continues filming and sound recording while Specky is given a brief history of how purling came to happen at all. The team in the TV van are listening and get to work looking up 'Wot Appnd' on the internet.

"Where's the mouse you mentioned?" asks Specky.

"Emmy's not here," says Pip. "He says that humans have to sort themselves out; he's done his best to help us, and now we have to get on with it."

"He's helping us all the time," says Penny, "and the wild creatures are too."

"And the invisible ones!" cries Larky.

"Oh dear, this is getting a bit fanciful, isn't it? Who are you two?"

Will comes in close to get shots of Billy, Larky and Penny.

"I'm Penny."

"I'm Larky!"

There are yells from up the hill. "Police! Police!"

More police arrive and set about arresting the protestors chained and padlocked to the digging machines. One of the road builders uses huge bolt croppers to cut the chains, and the protestors are dragged off to the police vehicles. The second camera team manage to film this, and soon Will and Specky are there too, so the editors have images from two cameras to choose from. The police then try to catch the purlers, but it isn't possible – the purlers dodge and swoop about like mist being blown about in a breeze. The police are surrounded by yet more purlers, so many that the police can't see where they are going, and stumble about in confusion.

Purlers arrive in their thousands; they are coming from everywhere. They are coming from towns and cities far away, from industrial areas, from hospitals, care homes, and schools; they come from factories, prisons and detention centres – and they come in their thousands. There are people of all ages: children, grown-ups, and old people; there are disabled people of every sort, for whom purling is a miracle of freedom; there are people who have never seen the countryside in their lives, never been in Wild Nature, because where they live is just roads and buildings and concrete.

People come who have only known hardship: refugees from war-torn places who are frightened and isolated; people who have never played barefoot in the mud or climbed trees in the middle of a wildwood; people who have never opened a conker casing to find the treasure inside. Not a single one of these people has talked with wild creatures before, and so when they hear about purling, they want it, they want to learn how to do it. People in prison can learn how to purl, and with their sleeping bodies still locked up, they are here, now, free to purl in Tillings Wood, and they have already been to the Glade where they learned the wild talk and have even felt the unwords – their lives are transformed!

There are so many purlers now, the magic of the Glade grows and spreads far and wide. The great wave can be felt by all: the people in the camp and in the treetops, the townspeople who are looking on in amazement at it all, even the police and the road builders are affected and moved, without knowing what it is. The officer in charge of the police, DI Luckham, sees the cloud of purlers lifting a little, clearing the way for the road builders to see their way back to the compound, their anger drained away, for the moment.

He orders the police officers to retreat as well, following the road builders. The purlers do not enter the compound but surround it on all sides except the gateway to the road. The afternoon comes to an end and the road builders get into their vehicles and drive away. DI Luckham posts four officers to keep an eye on things overnight, then returns to the police station to report to his boss. The TV crews pack up and leave, saying that they will be back in the morning.

Purlers are disappearing, each with a little pop, but new arrivals appear too, and the sound is like rain falling on dry autumn leaves. The townspeople are reluctant to go home because they have felt something special today, but it's getting dark, so they eventually wander off down the road, or through the woods if they are familiar with the paths. The people in the camp, and the tree dwellers, prepare for a long night.

~

The police station has been busy ever since the Superintendent became aware of the flier circulating in the town – the leaflet about the Sunday meeting in Tillings Wood. Superintendent Bowden had a feeling that it might become a difficult situation and she wanted her team to be well prepared. Once the demonstration in Tillings Wood had got underway, things at the station got a lot more chaotic very quickly.

When two small boys are brought in for 'breaking and entering', Superintendent Bowden decides to interview them herself, with a WPC in attendance, as the other senior officers are all out. Bottl and Luke have been caught, or 'apprehended' as the police say, trying to break in to Tom Wylder's house. Tom had gone to Tillings Wood and left the alarm on, as usual, because of all his filming equipment; the alarm automatically alerted the police. The two small boys were caught red-handed trying to force the back door open, using a car jack and a lump of wood jammed against an adjacent wall.

Bottl and Luke are not very talkative. Superintendent Bowden talks to them about the seriousness of the charges against them for criminal damage and criminal intent.

"Why did you try to break in to that particular house?" she asks.

"Dunno," says Bottl.

"Do you know the owner?"

"Nope."

"What did you hope to find?"

"Dunno."

There's a knock at the door and an officer pokes his head in.

"'Scuse me, Ma'am, they're back from Tillings Wood."

"Ah, yes, thank you."

Superintendent Bowden stands up and is about to leave the interview room to hear how things have gone at Tillings Wood when Bottl suddenly speaks.

"We knows a bit 'bout that."

"About what, Brian?"

"The purlers."

"The what?"

"The purlers, Miss, we knows who they is 'n where they's livin'."

"Who do you mean, Brian?"

"Ones what started it."

"I see. Who are they?"

"If we's tellin' 'bout what we was doin' at that 'ouse 'n 'bout the purlers, you could let us go 'ome."

"Brian and Luke, understand this: I do not negotiate with criminals. However, if you are able to help the police with their enquiries, I might see fit to recommend leniency."

"What's that mean? Ma'am, we's juniors, ain't we?" says Luke.

"Ah! You have a voice after all, Luke, good. Now listen to me, both of you. I'm not going to make deals with you. You have been apprehended breaking and entering, which is a very serious matter. If you have useful information, it is in your own best interest to speak now or have withholding evidence added to the charges against you."

"Well, Miss–"

"Ma'am, please."

"Well, Marm, we's been watchin' 'em all since a year or so.

There's an old bloke, who's friends with Mr Wylder who makes films 'n it's 'is 'ouse we was tryin' to get in."

"Yes, I know his name. Who's the 'old bloke', and what's he got to do with 'purlers', whatever that is."

"They's callin' 'im 'Pip', or 'Mista Pip', 'n it's 'im what's got the mouse."

"Mouse? What mouse?"

Superintendent Bowden is glad that she decided to interview the children herself. Before interviewing the two boys she had been in her office watching a television news update on her computer. She saw the footage of the swarms of miniature creatures that stopped the road builders and police in their tracks. She had no idea what the phenomenon could be, but now she might be about to find out.

Bottl describes what he knows about Emmy and Pip and LuLu, and how the story, 'Wot Appnd', is the mouse's story and gets told at schools and is on the internet. He tells the Superintendent the names of the children that were the first to be brainwashed by the mouse, and they were the first 'purlers'. He explains that the 'purlers' are children, and they'll be asleep somewhere, dreaming into their little pouches.

"But, Marm, there's loads of 'em now, 'undreds, fousands. It's gone viral."

"Alright, Brian, let me worry about that. Are there other adults involved?"

"Yeah, well, there's Mr Wylder, 'n there's Mr Weatherstone our teacher, 'n Larky's mum, Donna..."

"And, Brian, do you know these people's addresses by any chance? I can find out easily enough, but if you know–"

"Yeah, the old bloke, Pip, lives..."

Bottl and Luke between them remember all the addresses, and Superintendent Bowden writes everything down. When they are finished, she sits quietly watching the boys.

"What's you doin' wiv us, Marm?"

"Brian, you must promise me that you won't try to break in to Mr Wylder's house again, or anybody else's house for that matter. If you think you have evidence of something important, come to me personally. I'll ask the desk sergeant to look out for you. In certain circumstances, the police may get a search warrant to search specific premises, but we need evidence to support the request."

"Is we goin' 'ome, Marm?"

"Soon. First, tell me more about Mr Pip."

~

Later that day, after the WPC has taken the two boys home, Superintendent Bowden watches the news updates on her office computer; she is astonished by what she sees. The purlers appear to glow with a pale light, and there are so many they swarm like giant luminous bees. It is easy to see why the police have been stopped in their tracks.

She looks up 'Wot Appnd' on the internet and begins to read, soon realising that she'll have to do that later. She buzzes through to Detective Inspector Luckham, asking him to come to her office.

"Ma'am?" he says when he arrives.

"Sit down. Tell me what you've seen today."

DI Luckham describes the day in Tillings Wood. Superintendent Bowden listens carefully, and when DI Luckham has finished, she is quiet for a while before she speaks.

"I would like you to set up a watch on certain people, Detective Inspector. Take some men off Tillings Wood–"

"But, Ma'am, we're overrun already!"

"I know, that's what I mean. Back off. Stop pushing. Pacify. Meanwhile, I want round the clock surveillance of these people."

She slides a piece of paper across the desk. DI Luckham scans it.

"You may not be aware, as yet," she continues, "that these miniature beings are actually humans, children in fact, that are asleep somewhere, probably at home in their beds, and they are dreaming themselves as flower fairies or elves or whatever they are.

"I want to know when these people meet up, when they sleep, where they go to sleep, everything about them, but don't be noticed.

"I also want you to give your special attention to finding out about the mouse."

"Mouse, Ma'am?"

"Yes, the mouse. I've written the info you'll need on that sheet of paper. Good luck."

"What about the contractors at Tillings Wood?"

"Let's see what happens with minimal police intervention, and we'll review it tomorrow."

"Yes, Ma'am, goodnight then."

"Goodnight."

~

The next morning, TV crews arrive before daybreak and get set up. Specky Spender and Wobble-Cam Will walk down to the camp in the woods to hear the news from Jonty Mavrik. The next arrivals are the police, allowing the officers who have been on duty all night to go off-shift at last. There are fewer police than yesterday, and DI Luckham has told his officers to keep the peace and intervene as little as possible.

The road builders arrive in force, making a great noise with their 4x4 vehicles, and yelling and shouting. They are angry again. The site foreman has heard from the boss of the company that there will be no pay until the road building begins. That's not exactly what the workmen want to hear, and they behave like a bunch of berserk bears. There are more of them than there are police, and when they surge towards the police cordon, they simply push the officers aside and charge down the slope, carrying their chainsaws, ladders, metal bars and bolt croppers, heading for the protestors' camp.

People from the camp leap up and run towards them, but before they clash together, the purlers come down from the sky in a cloud so dense that the road builders are engulfed, unable to see where to go. They stumble and trip on stones and roots, knocking each other over. One of the men is carrying a flamethrower and he manages to get it going, brandishing the thing and spurting flames up into the cloud of purlers, trying to burn them up. But the purlers slip sideways faster than he can move his machine and anyway the flame would not burn them, just as purlers are not made wet by rain, so they swarm around his head to stop him.

From outside the cloud of purlers, the protestors looking on see the tongues of flame leaping up into the air while the purlers slip easily out of the way.

The road builders roar as the flamethrower's mad antics fire up their rage and frustration.

"This could get really ugly!" says Jonty, leaping up from beside the campfire. "Specky, come with me, you've got to interview the road builders, let them know they are on live TV, let them know this is being taken seriously, try to defuse it. You like a bit of adrenalin, don't you?"

"OK, let's go!" shouts Specky, and she, Will and Jonty run into the cloud of purlers who allow them through, like a tunnel opening

and closing in again once they have gone through.

Superintendent Bowden watches the television news on her office computer. The reports are live from the scene and she has just witnessed how angry the road builders are and how helpless they are inside that cloud of tiny purlers. She buzzes through to her secretary and asks her to get the boss of the construction company on the phone ASAP. She sits back watching the news report, and waits. The phone rings.

"Buckfast here, what the hell are you doing about this fiasco, we've got a road to build."

"Mr Buckfast, your men are behaving like mercenaries. Are you paying them to be violent or are you threatening them with no pay at all?"

"That's not your concern, lady–"

"You will call them off, Mr Buckfast, or I will have them all arrested."

"What?"

"I want them back in your works compound in the next five minutes. Any outside the police cordon after that will be arrested and charged with disturbing the peace and aggravated assault. It's live on the news, I am watching it as we speak."

"You're siding with the protestors! Are you off your trolley?"

"I am looking for a strategy that will work, Mr Buckfast, and your men are breaking the law, live on TV. Do it now!" She slams the phone down.

DI Luckham comes into Superintendent Bowden's office. He smiles, having heard the last bit of this conversation.

"What strategy might that be, Ma'am?"

"Nothing that Mr Buckfast would understand."

"Likely not, Ma'am."

"Send a few more officers to the site and arrest any road builders that try to get through the cordon. Let's have a stand-off. Defuse the situation, Detective Inspector."

She waits while DI Luckham phones the order through to his next in command.

"Now," she continues, "have you any information resulting from your surveillance?"

"It's early days, Ma'am, but we've located the people known as Pip, LuLu and Billy. Billy's a schoolboy, the other two are older. Oh, and the mouse, he's with LuLu, we think."

"Alright. Well done, that was quick work. I want them all arrested tonight and put in separate cells. Charge them with incitement to riot and lock them up. Oh, on second thoughts, bring the mouse to my office."

"Right." DI Luckham raises an eyebrow, trying hard not to smile. "Anything else, Ma'am?"

"We need to think of a way to control these so-called 'purlers', which means we must find and control as many of their sleeping bodies as possible. There must be thousands of worried parents out there; they may have gone to doctors or hospitals for advice. Work with them. Find out, find out everything."

"We'll need to work with other forces, Ma'am."

"Of course, yes."

"Right, I'll get to it."

~

Late in the night, the police visit Pip's house and bang on the door. Pip is instantly awake as he isn't purling and he's a light sleeper. Without further ado, he is arrested and bundled into the police transporter vehicle.

Next is Billy's place. The door is opened by Nan, who takes

exception to this intrusion and becomes furious when she realises that the police are going to carry off Billy's sleeping body. She jumps up and down and screams and hollers, but they take no notice and drive away. Grandpa sleeps through it all because he is purling over in Tillings Wood, enjoying the campfire and company.

The next, and last, stop is LuLu's house, where there is no answer when they bang on the door. They are about to burst it open when LuLu finally opens it. She is confused, and doesn't understand what is going on, but somewhere inside herself she had been expecting something like this. She calms herself and does what they want. They demand to know where the mouse is, and she says, simply, "He's in my pocket", and she shows them, whereupon she and Emmy are escorted to the police vehicle and driven to the station.

The prisoners are not allowed sight of each other; each is charged as directed by the Super, and put into a cell for the night – all except for Emmy, who is taken to the Super's office and handed over.

"Has the mouse been charged?" asks Superintendent Bowden.

"Just like a real person, Ma'am!"

"You never know, he might just be."

Superintendent Bowden puts Emmy on her desk in a bowl of paperclips. She looks at him gravely for some minutes. Emmy slowly turns his head until he is looking directly at her. Superintendent Bowden feels a tingle of fear and excitement run up her spine and the back of her neck.

"Have you anything to say?" she asks, feeling suddenly awkward about talking to a toy mouse. It's quite absurd to imagine that it might talk back.

"Iyz sayin nothin till yooz readin 'Wot Appnd'."

The Super gasps, staring in astonishment at the mouse. "I don't understand. How is it possible that–"

"Mi naym iz Emmy, n Iyz a mowse wiv an eart n real feelinz, xcept Iyz toy mowse in uman world."

"So, it's really true."

"Really real, n yooz pleez to b readin 'Wot Appnd' so yooz kno-in."

"May I call you Emmy?"

"Yip."

"Emmy, all these tiny children...?"

"Purlaz."

"Yes, 'purlers', as they seem to be called. It is my job to control mass demonstrations and to keep the peace–"

"Purlaz iz nevva urtin nothin," Emmy interrupts.

"But they are stopping the building of the road! It is my job to remove the protestors from Tillings Wood so that the work can proceed."

"Yooz ad betta b findin anuvva job, Soopa Intent Bowden."

Superintendent Bowden's face flushes; she feels humiliated and embarrassed. Here she is, sitting at her desk and talking to a toy mouse that has just told her she will not be able to do her job.

"Iyz feelin in mi eart yooz trubbld. Pleez b readin 'Wot Appnd' so yooz kno-in wotz appnin, coz umanz as to b changin kwik."

Superintendent Bowden is exhausted; she needs to bring this interview to an end.

"I trust that you will not try to escape?"

"Iyzll b ere wen yooz returnin."

"Thank you, Emmy, I believe you will. I'll say goodnight then." She picks up her laptop to read 'Wot Appnd' at home.

~

In the night, Pip, LuLu and Emmy eventually manage to go to sleep. LuLu purls straight away; she looks at her sleeping body, watching as it ghosts away to nothing. She smiles, thinking how mystified the police will be when they check on her next. She disappears from her cell with a little pop, reappearing in the Super's office where Emmy is purling above the desk.

"Hallo, Emmy, are you alright?"

"Allo, LuLu, yip, Iyz orite. Iyz lukin at mi sleepin boddee."

"Mine has ghosted already."

"Emmy's boddee iz nevva ghostabl."

"But you are free to purl!"

"Yip, letz vizzit Pippee."

They find Pip asleep, but not purling. Emmy purls close to his face, calling him with his heart. After a little while, Pip wakes and rubs his eyes.

"LuLu! Emmy! How wonderful to see you! I've been having horrible dreams, I'm so happy to see you're both alright."

"Pip, my body has ghosted already," says LuLu, "so you needn't worry about me, but Emmy's body is in Superintendent Bowden's office. Billy is in the cell next door to you and he's purling in Tillings Wood, so he's fast asleep."

"Yooz ad betta b stayin ere, Pippee."

"Hmm. Why is it always me? Only joking. Yes of course, I'll keep an eye on Billy, and you, Emmy – well, your bodies – as best I can. Let me know what's going on out there, won't you?"

"We will, Pip," says LuLu, "and we'll tell Billy what's been happening, so he can purl back to see you."

"Will Billy's body ghost away?"

"No, Pip, it's only me so far."

"Alright, please be careful."

"Weezl b orite, Pippee. C u innabit, bi."

"Bye, Pip," says LuLu.

Pop, pop, and they are gone. Pip feels suddenly very alone.

~

The road builders are in a rage, stumbling about in the woods unable to see where they are going because of the thousands of purlers. The man with the flamethrower waves the torch around madly, making spooky shadows and silhouettes. Jonty, Specky and Will appear through the mass of purlers as if by magic, and the road builders converge on them with a roar.

Jonty holds his arms in the air, and shouts at the top of his voice: "We bring word–"

The road builders crowd in, making a tight circle around the camera crew and Jonty.

Specky speaks up. "This is live television, you're on TV right now. This whole situation is being taken very seriously, and you should know that from the outside it looks like you are the bad guys. Why are you so angry? Why are you being so aggressive?"

Wobble-Cam Will pans the camera round, waiting for someone to answer. Eventually a big bear of a man pushes through to the front.

"I'd better answer that, bein' site foreman. We all 'as to earn a livin'. If we don't work, we don't get paid."

"Everyone can understand that," says Specky Spender. "The delay in the work isn't your fault, and it isn't your job to sort it out. You have your voice on television now, how would you like this situation to be resolved?"

"I don't want my men threatened with no pay because we can't work."

"Well said!" says Jonty. "Let's go up to the compound and discuss this calmly."

The road builders shift about uneasily, but their foreman agrees. The purlers move aside to make a clear way back up the hill to the compound. The foreman watches the purlers anxiously.

"What on Earth are these things?" he says, to no one in particular.

"We don't know yet," says Specky, "but they could be your own children."

"If they be mine, they'll be feelin' the back of my 'and."

"Don't be too hasty to judge them."

"My kids were bigger than these things the day they were born! These are like midges."

"Look, they're moving away," says Will.

As they walk through the gap where the police cordon is, the purlers hang back, staying outside the compound. The road builders are free from the cloud of purlers at last.

"Thank goodness for that! They were drivin' us mad," says the foreman.

"What will you do now?" asks Specky.

"I'll send the men 'ome."

"We'll keep up the reports on television. Make sure you keep up too!"

"I never thought I'd want to thank you TV people, but thanks."

"You're welcome... But you should thank these little fairies."

~

The road builders have gone, except for the night watchman, and the police cordon is down to two officers. The TV crew have gone too, and everything is quiet. As dawn brightens the eastern sky, Emmy appears in the midst of the purlers. When thousands of purlers come together, they rise up into the air like a luminous mist; this is called a Rising.

The sky is clear but for thin threads of cloud that begin to light up with the approaching dawn. A pink glow catches the wisps of cloud and the multitude of purlers turn to face the rising sun.

Emmy loves being part of the Rising; it feels like home to him and he feels a surge of joy. At last! This is the way home!

On the ground, the camp people are waking, and those who have a view of the sky watch the Rising as it ripples with light.

Emmy purls down to the camp to see if Tom and John are still there. Like birds dropping down from the sky to their favourite roosts, Emmy's friends follow him down, forming a miniature Rising in the firelight. Emmy says that the rippling light is the unwords happening. He tells the story of the arrests as best he can, and tries to explain about LuLu's body ghosting, and that she is safe at home again, but don't tell anyone.

"Iyz wurrid for yoo, Billee," says Emmy.

"I's alright Emmy, I's right 'ere!" says Billy, purling just beside Emmy.

"Iyz wurrid bout wot theyz doin to b wakin yoo."

"Is Mr Pip purlin'?"

"Pippeez waykfl."

"I should go back, wake up I mean, 'n be with Pip," says Billy.

"Yoo b tryin, Billee."

"Tryin'? What's you sayin', Em?"

"Yooz onli abl wen invizibl wunz iz appi."

Billy tries. He brings his attention to the eye of his heart and asks to be back in his body so that he can help Pip, but straight away he can feel that his pouch will not do it.

"You's right, Em, I can't do it. Why?"

"Invizibl wunz az reeznz."

"Let's do a gaol break!" cries Larky.

"Now, now," says Tom, "that's not the way. We should go and talk with the police and tell them what we know. There's no way that there has been incitement to riot."

"I'm too angry to do that!" says Stomper Jack, crossly.

"Steady on, Jack, you's knowin' anger's no good," says Billy.

"There must be another way," says John. "Look, here come the TV crew."

Specky and Will are walking down the hill towards them. They have been allowed to cross the compound and the police cordon.

"Good morning, everyone!" says Specky chirpily. "Any news?"

"Any news!" yells Stomper. "They's arrested Pip and Billy and Emmy and LuLu!"

"Where? When? What happened?"

"Iyzl b xplaynin–" says Emmy.

"Oh, heck! The mouse!" cries Specky.

Tom introduces them properly, to give Specky time to calm down and interview Emmy properly. Wobble-Cam Will films the interview with Emmy and the little group of purlers floating by the campfire in the woods. When Emmy's finished explaining, Specky has some questions.

"What are you going to do?"

"I know!"

"And you are...?"

"Stomper Jack!"

"What do you suggest then, Stomper Jack?" says Specky.

"They arrested the wrong ones! They should arrest the bosses 'n the politicians that destroy everything to make money."

"Steady on, Jack!" says Billy. "You's angrier than me!"

"We'll strike!" says Stomper, ignoring Billy. "That's what we'll do. That's it, we'll go on strike – till they let them go."

"Strike? But you don't work, you're too young," says Specky, puzzled.

"Children's strike, we'll call it. We'll not do what grown-ups tell us and we won't go to school!"

"Hey, what about me?" says John Weatherstone. "I won't have a job!"

Stomper purls close to the camera, eyeballing the lens.

"We'll strike! Release 'em, or else!"

Stomper backs off from the camera, becoming aware of the silence around her.

"Right," says Specky, slowly. "Thank you for that. I don't know if the news editors will use today's footage, but I'll try to put something together that they want. We are not on live broadcast any more because this is old news."

"Old news!" cries Penny.

"Well, it's quieter, put it that way. We'll not be staying, but do call me if anything changes, won't you? Here's my card."

"Old news, indeed," says Tom Wylder, as they watch the TV crew repack and leave. "They couldn't be more wrong."

~

Over the next few days, the protestors reduce the size of the camp because things have calmed down a lot. The Rising of purlers is a constant reassurance and is always there in the sky ready to defend the woods against any attack. Individual purlers disappear when they need to return to their bodies and to their families. Other purlers arrive to replace them, and, in fact, more arrive than leave, so the Rising grows every day.

The campers want to reduce the impact they are having on the woods. They have needed fires to keep warm and have taken firewood from the woodlands. Too much scavenging of firewood is not good, because rotting wood is essential for the ecosystem to thrive. Decaying timber is food and habitat for fungi and invertebrates, good for the soil and food for larger creatures.

Some of the tree dwellers go home, too, to rest and wash and eat, but they work out a rota to make sure there's always a good team there in the woods.

The holidays come to an end, and on the first day of the summer term the children turn up to school as a Rising of purlers, remaining in the air above the school. No children turn up for lessons except for Bottl and Luke, and when they see what's happening, they simply turn around and go away again, thinking *'Yes! more holiday!'*

All this attracts the local press and the TV cameras appear again; there is news of sympathy strikes at schools across the country.

Some parents have been interested in what's been going on and have found out enough not to be worried about their children's sleeping bodies that won't wake up. But many more parents are very worried and frightened. They try to wake their children up, and when they can't, they panic, and carry them to the doctor or to A&E, or to a private clinic, but nobody is able to wake them.

In some private clinics and treatment centres, experiments are being done. Technicians in white coats try electric shocks, sudden loud noises, pinpricks, heat and cold, water jets, and drugs. Even so, the children do not wake up.

Sometimes a child wakes up because they stop purling, wanting to be in their bodies. Maybe they need to eat, or go to the loo or something like that, or just have a run around on the ground. It's nice to be back in their bodies – or it used to be. Now, when they wake up, the technicians or parents do all that they can to keep them awake!

At the police station, experiments are done on Billy and Emmy, but they don't wake up either. Superintendent Bowden doesn't get told about these experiments at first, but later she hears rumours and it worries her.

The media people get to hear rumours too about the clinics, and the word 'torture' appears in print in the local paper. The TV crews jump into action and try to get access to the clinics and the police station, but without success. But they make good television out of the fact that there must be a cover-up.

Specky and Will return to Tillings Wood to find out more by talking to the purlers. The Rising of purlers is still there, and David and Penny purl down to meet the TV crew. Specky says that she has done some homework.

"I've read 'Wot Appnd' online, don't understand most of it but I get the gist. So, tell me about the letters."

"There's been no reply," says David. "We put our hearts into those letters, and Number Ten can't be bothered to reply."

"Could you explain about the letters? Could I have copies?"

"Tom's got a copy in his pocket, I think!" says Penny. "He's down there by the campfire."

"Let's walk down," says Specky.

"If you've read Emmy's story," says David, "you'll already know – Emmy gave us purling. Well, we had to work hard at it, and now we see Nature in a different way to normal. We feel that we are part of everything, and not separate like grown-ups tell us. The wild web is awake in a way that humans are not. Maybe they were once, but humans use Nature and take from it without giving anything back. Nature gives, humans take, and there will be nothing left.

"We don't want to live in a world without Wild Nature right on our doorsteps. We don't want to live in a world where people are cheated and bombed and treated like slaves. It's time all that history gets left behind. We're rebelling. You can see it happening everywhere. It's not only us children. Find out, Specky, find out how many purlers there are now, and how many more every day, find out where they come from and what their lives have been like!"

"I will, David. That was quite a speech. Ah! Here we are."

"Hallo, Specky! Digging in the mud again?" says Jonty, with a laugh.

"Mr Tom," says Penny, "have you got the letter on you?"

"Well, young lady, I believe I have!" Tom pulls the letter from the back pocket of his trousers.

"Please, give it to Specky, Mr Tom," says David.

"Ah-ha! Going public with it, eh?"

"Yes, we've had no reply, and with Pip and Billy and Emmy arrested, we've got to do something."

"I agree, David," says Tom. "All the same, I admire your courage, all of you. What will you do with it, Specky?"

"Read it!" she says, holding the letter for Will to get on camera.

She reads the letter out loud, carefully and clearly. When she is finished, she looks at Penny. "This is great! We can work with this. Do we have your permission to broadcast this? We aren't live now, but we'll prepare a news item the editors can't resist."

"Yes!" say Penny and David at the same moment.

"Good. Who did you send this letter to?"

"Erm, the PM, HRH and the Secretary-General of the United Nations," says Penny, solemnly.

"Hmm. Good. We can make some mileage out of that. Oh, and I recommend that you write your manifesto," says Specky.

"Manni, what?" asks David.

"Manifesto. It means to make your views and ideas known to the public. It means 'to make obvious'."

"But we've done that with the letter, haven't we?" says Penny.

"Well, you wrote the letter to three specific people, not to the public, not to everyone."

"Penny," says John Weatherstone, "I'd be very happy to help with that if you'd like."

"I would, too!" says Tom.

"Thanks, Mr John, thanks, Mr Tom, good plan," says David.

"Right, everyone, we'll be off now," says Specky.

"Wait!" cries Penny. "Please do something to get them released, please. They can't be kept locked up without a trial, can they?"

"They are waiting for the court hearing," says Specky.

"Specky, please, do something!" says Penny.

"I'll think of something!" says Specky, and she and Will walk up through the wood towards the compound. Will pauses and looks back, filming the group down by the campfire – Tom, John and Jonty sitting on logs, and Penny and David purling between them.

Chapter Five

Crisis

Specky Spender and Wobble-Cam Will prepare a news item for TV, using a copy of the letters sent to the PM, HRH and the Secretary-General of the United Nations. Specky tells newspaper friends about it, and the next day the television news and the newspapers challenge the authorities to reply to the children's letters.

The first phone call she gets is from the Public Relations Officer at Buckingham Palace, who explains that no such letter has been received.

Next, she hears from a clerk at the London office of the UN, in Whitehall, who says the same thing; no such letter has been received in New York either, apparently.

She does some more 'digging' and discovers that letters sent to 'Very Important People' are examined by security officers before they get anywhere near their destinations. So, the letters must have been intercepted and stopped, but who told the security people to stop these particular letters, and why? Specky contacts 10 Downing Street and is put through to the Public Relations clerk. He is polite, but gives nothing away; Specky suggests that it's beginning to look like a cover-up. She's fobbed off with an assurance that the children will receive a reply to their letter in due course. When she asks what happened to the other letters, the PR clerk says, "no comment".

~

Billy and his friends are spending most of their time at the camp in Tillings Wood. They like it there; they can be in their bodies and enjoy sitting by the campfire or purl up to join the Rising. Right now, they are all – except Billy – in their proper bodies. Billy is purling all the time because his body is locked up in the police station, and he doesn't want to wake up there.

The townspeople have set up tents and benders, and a sort of home-made tipi, where they can sleep and shelter from the rain, and they have helped the children put up their own shelters. The children like it when they are sitting round the campfire with some of the protestors, talking and singing and listening to stories. It's comforting to know that the Rising of purlers is always there above them, keeping guard.

"I'm hungry," says Larky.

"There's spuds baking in the embers, Larky, won't be long," says David.

"Burnin' more like!" cries Billy, purling just out of reach as David takes a swipe at him with the poker stick he's holding.

Earlier in the day, Siobhan sneaked through the woods back to town to get supplies from home. She got butter, salt and pepper for the baked potatoes, and cheese, lemonade and some other things her mum could spare.

"Spuds are ready!" calls David, flicking the blackened potatoes out of the fire with the stick.

"Thanks!" says Jerome, picking up a blackened lump from the ground. "Ouch! Watch out, they're really hot."

They sit round the campfire, prodding holes in their potatoes with sticks and melting butter into them; their hands get black and greasy and salt sticks to their fingers. At last, they are ready to eat.

"Awe! That's yummy!" says Stomper.

"Good one, David," says Penny. "You can be camp cook."

"Not on your life, Penny."

"Hallo! May I join you?" a voice calls from the woods.

"That's Mum!" cries Larky. "Mum! Over here!"

"Hallo, Donna," says David. "We haven't seen you in a while, have you been alright?"

"I'm alright now, David, thanks, but it was hard after our sea purling. I know it seems a long time ago now, but it's been difficult; I just had to get on with ordinary things for a bit and try not to think about it. I'm sorry not to have made an effort to see you all. I got a bit down, to be honest, but Emmy visited me a lot and helped me."

"I's glad you're 'ere now, Donna," says Billy.

"Thanks, Billy. I've wanted to see you all, but couldn't come out, didn't want to be reminded... you know?" Donna's voice breaks a little.

"Yes, Donna," says Penny, gently. "We know."

"Would you like a spud, Donna? There's plenty."

"Yes, please, David, that would be great. I've come today because I met your mum, Penny. She gave me this letter to give to you." Donna pulls an official-looking letter from her coat pocket and holds it out for Penny.

"What – hey! It looks posh, I wonder if it's..." says Penny excitedly. "Wait, my hands are black and greasy, I'll have to clean up a bit."

"Is it from the PM?" says Jerome.

"Let's have a look. Is there a clean knife?"

David wipes the blade of his penknife on the T-shirt they are using as a towel – it's already looking like a rag. Penny rubs her hands as clean as she can, takes the knife and carefully slits the envelope open. She sits there with the envelope in one hand and the knife in the other.

"Come on! Read it!" cries Siobhan.

"Alright." Penny gives the knife back to David and unfolds the letter.

"Yes, it's from Number Ten! Erm... It's signed p.p. somebody, I can't read the squiggle."

"So, it's not from the PM," says Stomper grumpily.

"It means it's signed by the personal secretary to the PM," says Donna. "The PM can't do everything personally."

"Should've done this personally! Get on with it, Penn!" cries Billy, purling close, trying to read it for himself.

"Alright. Here we go:

"Dear Children of England,

"The PM has asked me write to you expressing thanks for your impressive letter.

"It is clear that you feel strongly about the issues that you mention, and the large number of signatures indicates how important these issues are to a great many children.

"Please be assured that the government is doing all in its power to negotiate with the leaders of other countries to achieve: an end to war, an end to poverty and social inequality, and a limit to the effects of climate change. Targets have been set, and all these issues must be addressed in order to slow the degradation of the environment.

"The PM hopes that this assurance will restore your trust in the process of democracy and the rule of law.

"For the benefit of the communities you live in, it would be helpful if you were to discontinue your demonstrations and to begin negotiations according to the proper procedures.

"Yours sincerely,

"p.p. squiggle."

Silence.

"What?" says Larky.

"What the 'eck's that all about?" cries Billy.

"Well," says Donna. "The letter says that they're doing

everything they can, and so you must stop being such a nuisance."

"Ha! We haven't even started yet!" cries Stomper.

"We've been fobbed off. They're not hearing us," says David, crossly.

"They're politicians, David," Donna says, "of course they don't hear you, not in the way that you mean."

"Why 'of course', Donna?" says Penny quietly. "We have to find a way to their hearts, that's the listening we're asking for, isn't it? That's the listening we must have."

"How do we do that, Penny?" says Siobhan. "We've written our letter and had loads of signatures and we've been shoved aside – it's back to business as usual."

"Bubble normal," says Penny.

"Right, then!" cries Stomper fiercely. "Like I said before, we'll strike!"

"Aren't we on strike already?" says Jerome.

"We'll strike more!"

"Calm down, Stomper Jack," says Billy, purling close to her. "We'll find a way."

"We have to go to them, take it to them," says Penny, thoughtfully.

"Take what to them, Penny?" says David.

"Wildness, heartspeak, the unwords... We must take what we love to them – and show them."

"How do we take wildness to politicians, Penny?"

"The purlers, David, the purlers!"

"Penny, what..."

"We do our thingy, what's it called?"

"Manifesto?" suggests David.

"That's it, or whatever we call it, and take it to where all the politicians are, and we'll ask the purlers to come too."

"Of course!" cries Siobhan. "We've seen what happens here when there's a Rising – even the road builders ended up with smiles on their faces!"

"Let's ask Tom and John to help with the manifesto," says David.

"I should go back now," says Donna. "I'll phone them up when I get home, if you like, and let them know."

"Thanks, Mum. Mum, do you want me to come home now?" says Larky.

"Only if you want to, dear, I know you're safe."

"Thanks, Mum, I'll stay a bit more." Larky gives Donna a hug. "Love to Dad!"

"Bye, everyone, and thanks!"

"Bye, Donna!"

~

The Magistrate frowns as he watches the accused being brought into the courtroom. A bearded man is led in and shown where to stand; a boy of about eleven years of age is brought in, lying on an ambulance trolley, apparently asleep or unconscious; a clerk approaches the bench with a small wooden box in his hand, a cigar box with the lid removed, and inside lies a toy mouse.

"Why on earth do you bring me a toy mouse in a box?" demands the Magistrate.

"Your Worship, this mouse is responsible for inciting the children to rebellion, or so I am informed by the police."

"Don't be absurd, man, what's got into you? And what's that corpse of a child doing here?"

"Your Worship, this is the sleeping body of the boy named Billy. He is one of the principal ringleaders."

"Well, wake him up, dammit, so he can account for himself," says the exasperated Magistrate.

"Your Worship, it is impossible to wake him. Doctors and scientists have been trying every possible means."

"Have they indeed? Has the boy been charged?"

"Yes, charged with incitement to riot, Your Worship."

"Please would you not say 'Your Worship' every single time you speak! What about the mouse?"

"Y... The same charge."

"Extraordinary. Absurd. Now then, who is the gentleman who appears to be awake?"

"Pip is his name, Your Worship, the main conspirator in helping the mouse to carry out his plan."

"The mouse has a plan then, eh?"

"It would seem so, Your Worsh–"

"Alright, alright. Let him speak."

"With all due respect, sir," says Pip, "it seems clear to me that you have not been made fully aware of the facts in this case. This will make it difficult for me to give an account of myself, or indeed of Billy or Emmy, who lie here asleep.

"However, as I have also been charged with incitement to riot, I wish to lodge our collective plea of not guilty, citing in our defence the simple fact that we, and all the other children involved, have merely exercised our right to peaceful demonstration."

"Hmm. Very well. Is there anyone present representing the police?"

"Yes, Your Worship. I am Superintendent Bowden."

"Please enlighten me, Superintendent."

"In view of the health concerns that the doctor has expressed for the accused, and in acknowledgement of the fact that they have shown no malice or unpleasantness at any time, may I recommend that they be released on police bail."

"How long have they been in your custody?"

"About a week, Your Worship. The mouse has been awake most of that time and has spoken at length and been cooperative. He has also appeared purling."

"Purling? What is the meaning of this word?

"Purling is–"

Pop! Emmy appears, purling, in front of the Magistrate.

"Allo, Yor Wurship, mi naym iz Emmy n Iyz a mowse wiv an eart n real feelinz, eevn if Iyz only toy mowse in uman world."

Emmy goes closer. "Yooz askin wot iz purlin n purlin iz flowtin inna powch like Iyz doin, n uman cubz iz purlin n uman cubz iz cummin ere for yoo to b seein wot purlin iz."

Thousands of little pops all happening at the same time make a big pop, and suddenly the courtroom is filled with purling children.

The Magistrate stares in astonishment, frightened by this abrupt invasion, but the expression on his face slowly changes to a smile. The Rising of purlers brings such joy to his heart, he can't stop smiling.

"Remarkable. I haven't felt like this since – since I was a child!"

"Yor Wurship, yooz abl to b purlin too wen yooz reddee. Bi!"

Emmy and the purling children disappear from the courtroom as suddenly as they arrived. The Magistrate sits quietly for some time, the smile lingering on his face.

"Your Worship?" says the clerk.

"Ah, yes," says the Magistrate. "Superintendent, I now know that you spoke truly of these... these things; they show no malice or unpleasantness. I order that the suspects be released on police bail pending further enquiries. The boy must be escorted home; as for the mouse, I entrust this box into your hands, Superintendent."

The court rises, and the Magistrate departs. Superintendent Bowden asks DI Luckham, who also attended court, to arrange for Billy's sleeping body to be taken home to Nan's place. She then goes up to the bench for the box with Emmy's sleeping body in it. She looks wistfully at the mouse and turns to Pip.

"I'm reluctant to part with him, but you'd better take him," she says, offering the box to him.

"Thank you, Superintendent. You won't lose him. If you ever need him, just call."

"How do I do that?"

"You will know. Thank you for what you did for us."

"There's pressure on me to end the demonstration and get the road builders back to work. What happened in court was – I don't know – unprofessional? I may be in trouble."

"The road will not be built, I'm sure you realise that by now. But you can't be blamed for that."

"The system has to have its scapegoats. I don't know what's happening, everything is changing, I feel quite dizzy."

"Yes, it can be very uncomfortable. Become a purler, then you will know what you need to do."

"Can grown-ups do that too?"

"Oh yes, there are thousands of grown-ups in the Rising. It used to be more difficult to begin purling, but now it's easier because the way is clear to see. But it does need to be your heart's wish."

"Thank you."

~

Pip puts sleeping Emmy into his coat pocket. He wonders what to do with the cigar box, deciding to put it in the other jacket pocket to take home. It could useful when he builds another bug hotel. He goes to LuLu's to tell her about the court hearing.

"You weren't even mentioned, LuLu, even though you were arrested and charged as well. I think Superintendent Bowden arranged that."

"Where's Emmy?" says LuLu.

"Oh, sorry, he's here in my pocket." Pip puts Emmy into LuLu's hands and straight away the sleeping mouse stretches and wakes up.

"Allo, LuLu! Weez free! Weez free!"

"Oh, Emmy, you smell of tobacco!"

"He was put in an old cigar box," says Pip. "Well done, Emmy, thanks for getting us out of there..." Pip tells LuLu of events in the courtroom.

"What happened to you and the other purlers, Em?" says LuLu.

"Weez all purlin to Risin."

"At Tillings Wood?" says Pip.

"Yip."

"I'd like to purl there too, Emmy, with your help. Would you do that with me?" says LuLu.

"Yip. Wen yooz reddee."

"Thanks, Em. Pip, why don't you have a sleep, then you could purl there too if you feel like it? There's a blanket on the back of the sofa."

"Good plan, I'll do that. Yes, I am tired; I'll have a sleep first and see you later."

LuLu lies down in her room and is purling straight away, and even as she and Emmy pop off to Tillings Wood, her body fades until it can only just be seen.

~

While the court hearing was happening, there was some excitement at Tillings Wood: a group of heavily armed security men arrived in the compound and barged their way through the police cordon. The moment they broke through the cordon and moved towards the woods, the purlers closed in, packing themselves so tightly together that no light could get through at all. The security guards were unable to see and stumbled about in the dark before giving up trying to move. The purlers then opened a narrow way for light to get in, leading the guards back to the compound.

The police detained the men while they investigated who they were and where they had come from. It turned out that Mr Buckfast had hired a security firm to get rid of the protestors at Tillings Wood. Mr Buckfast was arrested and taken to the police station for questioning.

~

Tillings Wood is quiet today. Tom Wylder and John Weatherstone are sitting by the campfire with David and Penny. Purling around them are LuLu, Billy, Emmy, Larky, Stomper and Siobhan.

"Pip might come when he's rested," says LuLu, "but I'll tell you what he told me about the court hearing..."

"Hooray! Mr Pip's free!" cries Larky when the story is told.

"'N I's got me body back!" says Billy.

"N Emmyz boddeez owt ov prizn!" says Emmy.

"LuLu, Emmy, it's good to see you, it's been ages. We've missed you very much," says Penny.

Emmy and LuLu purl down close to Penny and David.

"Weez orlwayz togevva in our eartz," says Emmy.

"We've missed you all too," says LuLu. "It's good to be back with you, and I really want to know what's been going on here while I've been away!"

"Well, where to start? There's so much going on!" says Tom.

"What's happening right now? Let's start there."

"We've been talking about what a 'manifesto' might be, and where to start," says John.

"The letter is a good start."

"Yes, it is, LuLu, I agree! But is there anything we could compare it with to try to make it even better?"

"Let's think of famous manifestos or charters," says Tom.

"Do you mean old stuff?" says David.

"Old, new, anything," says Tom.

"Erm, what about the Declaration of Human Rights?"

"Good, Penny," says John, "that's probably the best historical model, but can you think of any others for comparison?"

"You make this sound like a history class at school!" says Tom.

160

"You's right, Mr Tom, but we's in wild school so we's not mindin'!" cries Billy, purling around with the other purlers.

"Urm, what about the Ten Commandments?" says Siobhan.

"Good, Siobhan. What can we remember about these things?"

"There's nothing about Nature in them," says Penny.

"True. Any other models of what a manifesto might be like?"

"What's that Old English thing called?" says Tom. "King John wasn't it, and the Barons?"

"Magna Carta," says John.

"Yes! That's it."

"Again," John explains, "that's not about Nature, but about property and taxes and protecting wealth. In other words, protecting people from other people trying to rob them."

"Is Magna Carta the beginning of democracy in England?"

"Arguably, Tom. But perhaps the ancient Greeks should be credited with starting the debate about democracy, and incidentally, predicting its end!"

"What are you two on about?" complains David. "What's all this got to do with us now?"

"Well, David, I just think it might be helpful if you could see some examples. Maybe the best example is, as Penny said first of all, the Universal Declaration of Human Rights. It's quite modern, 1948 in fact, just after the horrors of the Second World War. Here, I've got a short version of it..."

David reluctantly takes the bit of paper from John; Penny reads it with him to encourage him.

"You've done some thinking, John, eh?" says Tom.

"Yes, well, I am a teacher."

"Let's see if there are ideas here we can use for our manifesto," says Penny.

"I bet there's loads of people in the world trying to help Nature and poor people," says Larky. "But all I ever hear in the news when Dad's got the telly on is about terrible things happening."

"There's good things in this," says David, "like 'No slavery' and 'No torture'."

"And the first one is good. 'Articles' are they called?" says Penny. "It says: 'We are all born free and equal. We are all born free. We all have our own thoughts and ideas. We should all be treated the same way.'"

"They're talking about people, aren't they?" Siobhan says.

"Yes, all the different sorts of people in the world," says Tom.

"It's saying that all humans should be treated the same way, in other words, have the same rights."

"So, if we say, 'all creatures'," says Penny, "or 'all living things' are born free and equal and have the same right to exist..."

"That's it, Penny!" says Siobhan. "Humans aren't separate from Nature."

"I think your manifesto needs to name ways for Nature to be protected," says Tom, "and that has to include people, because they are part of Nature."

"That'll never be doin' it Mr Tom!" cries Billy. "They's breakin' laws all the time! We needs people to feel it in their 'earts."

"That's right, Billy," says John. "How can we bring that about?"

"When we read the letter from the PM," says Penny, "we felt that we'll never get them to hear us – the politicians and money people, I mean. We need a change of heart, as Billy says, then they'll hear us. Our idea is that we take our manifesto, or Charter, or whatever we are going to call it, to them – with all the purlers."

"I agree, Penny, good plan," says Tom. "You children have all you need already. Where's that letter you sent to the PM? That's your manifesto, isn't it? You have it already, as LuLu said."

"I've got a copy," says John, rummaging through the papers in his bag.

"I'm fed up with all this history stuff," says David. "It's always getting in the way."

"It makes people what they are, David," says Tom.

"That's the whole problem, isn't it? What if history came to an end?"

"What's you thinkin', David?"

"Don't know, Billy, just wondering. I've got a feeling."

Billy watches David, curious to know more, but David remains silent and thoughtful.

"Ah, here's that letter," says John. "Let's have a look at it again, maybe we could just change a few bits here and there."

"And what then?" says Penny.

"Well, then I shall go with you to Westminster," says John, "and you will hand in the manifesto publicly to parliament. I'm sure Specky Spender would like to help out."

"Alright!" cries Larky.

"But they's never listnin', is they?" says Billy.

"So-o-o," says Penny, slowly, "some of us go in our bodies so we can read it–"

"Yes!" cries Billy, "But who?"

"It's alright, Billy, I think that's a job for me and David. David?" says Penny.

"Yeah, count me in."

"As I was saying," says Penny. "Some of us go in our bodies and everybody else – purling!"

"Awesome!" says Siobhan.

"Right," says David. "Let's have another look at that letter."

"Hallo, everyone!" says Jonty, just arriving back at the camp. "I heard some of that. Would you like to know what I think?"

"Hallo, Jonty, come on then, tell us," says Tom.

"Well, I think your letter is fine as it is, I would just change one thing."

"What's that?" says Billy, purling round and round Jonty's head.

"You are Children of the World, not only England!" Jonty pauses to let that sink in. "You could call it 'The Children's Charter for Nature's Rights'."

"That's a bit of a mouthful, isn't it?" says Tom.

"I s'pose it is."

"Children of the World!" says Penny. "Yes! There's so many purlers now, and they are coming from everywhere."

"Good!" says John. "You've got some work to do on your letter, but let's plan a trip to London, shall we?"

"It's all a bit scary," says Penny.

"I'll come with you, Penny, if you'll let me," John reassures her.

"I'd like to come too, if that's alright?" says Tom.

"Thank you, Mr John; thank you, Mr Tom; please do come, I don't think we could do it without you."

"We *couldn't* do it without you," agrees David.

"When shall we go?" says John.

"Any time... I s'pose," says Penny, anxiously. "What will happen when we get there?"

"It'll be alright, Penny," says John. "We'll go to Westminster and do the camera thing with Specky, outside the Houses of Parliament, and then we'll go to wherever the 'handing-in' is done. Then we'll get something nice to eat and come home."

"What about the purlers?" cries Larky, whizzing about happily.

"The purlers'll do what purlers do," says Billy.

"What does that mean, Billy?" cries Stomper.

"You's seen what 'appens in Tillin's Wood, purlers just does what 'as to be done."

"You'll be with them, Billy, won't you?" says David.

"Yep."

"Good. Erm, Penny, are you willing to do the reading? That's a bit too scary."

"Yes, David, it is scary. Just have to hope I can do it."

"You were awesome in the Glade, Penny!" says Larky.

"Hmm. I shall try to remember the Glade, and all that energy. I'll need you with me, David, and you, Tom, and you, John."

"We will be!"

"Can we come to your place, Mr Tom, to work on the Charter thing?" says David.

"Of course. Coming, John?"

"I'd better get home. I'll come over later."

"Larky, would you make sure that Emmy and LuLu and the purlers know where we are?"

"Course, David, we'll go now. Come on, Billy! Come on, Stomper! Come on, Siobhan! Hey! Where's Emmy and LuLu? I thought they were here!"

"They purled up to the Rising a while ago. Emmy's done all he can for us; it feels strange not having him with us so much," says Penny.

"LuLu's needin' 'is 'elp," says Billy.

"Come on! Let's find them!"

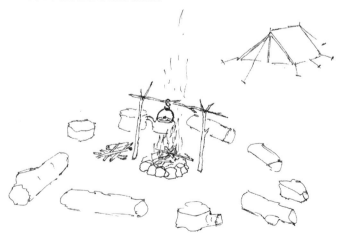

Larky leads the way, purling towards the Rising.

The others make their goodbyes.

"Bye, Jonty, call us if anything happens, won't you, or if you need anything?"

"Thanks, Tom, I'll do that. Good luck to you all!"

~

Penny and David go back with Tom to begin work on the computer. They sit on the sofa and watch the screen as Tom makes the changes to the letter that they ask for. Penny wants quite a lot of changes; she wants to make it much stronger than the letter to the PM.

"We could go on forever doing this," says David.

"This is the moment to refine your message, make it as clear as you can," says Tom.

John arrives, flopping down in an armchair; he reads what he sees on the wall screen.

"That's fine. It's bold, and I think that's necessary, well done," he says. "Let's go next Wednesday, it'll be PMQs, and that's usually well attended."

"What's pee em queues?"

"PMQs, David, is Prime Minister's Questions. By the way, I like the title: 'Children's Charter for the Rights of Nature'."

"That was Jonty's idea," says Penny. "We just changed the words round."

"It works alright, I think."

"Now then, Penny, and you, David," says John Weatherstone, in his 'school' voice. "We will need to have your parents' permission for you to go to London, and to travel with Tom and me. They could come too, of course, if they want to, couldn't they?"

"Er... I s'pose," says Penny, not feeling very keen.

"I'll write letters for each of you to take home. Please would you ask them to give you a written reply?"

"Yes."

"When we get permission, I'll order tickets online," says Tom.

"Thanks, Mr Tom. Oh, and sir... I mean, Mr John," says Penny, "what will you say in your letters to our parents about why we are going?"

"I'll tell them the truth: it is the completion of your school project and you want to hand in a petition to parliament."

~

Penny is worried about what she has agreed to do; her tummy is fluttery. She thinks of how good it is to be with other purlers, or to be in the Glade; she decides to purl when she sleeps next. That night, she finds herself purling above Tillings Wood with the Rising. Floating in the midst of thousands of purlers, her fears and doubts fade away. It is always a wonderful surprise to feel the unwords again after being in the normal human world. She remembers how Emmy has been around to remind her and her friends, to look with the eye of her heart. But being in the normal world makes it very hard to do that, and Emmy hasn't been around nearly as much.

Penny gazes down on the landscape below, recognising the town she lives in and the surrounding countryside. It seems so small from here, delicate even. She has a feeling memory of purling with dolphins, and she shudders as the great wave ripples through her; the natural world is small and finite, and it is dying. Her resolve grows strong, she knows what to do.

She opens her heart to the unwords. She tells the purlers of the plan to go to London and the request for the purlers to come too. The ripples of light that pulse through the Rising grow brighter and faster as this news is welcomed, and her friends gather round, reassuring her with unwords, 'yes, we'll all be there with you, close to you'. Penny feels reassured and strengthened, and when she has been long enough in the Rising, she and her friends descend to the camp below.

Finding no one, they purl close to the camp fire which is now just fading red embers. Billy asks Penny, "Why's you 'avin' to be outside parliament for readin' the wotsitcalled, Penn?"

"John says that's the way it's done."

"Ain't they filmin' parliament?"

"Oh, yes," says Siobhan. "That's always on television."

"Let's do it in there, then."

"Billy, we can't just go inside the House of Commons, just like that!" says Siobhan. "No one can do that."

"We can! Purlers can!" says Billy, defiantly.

"Oh-oh! Billy's got a plan hatching!" says Penny.

"Erm, maybe somethin'. Penn, can I 'ave a copy of... what's it called?"

"The Charter?"

"Yeah, that."

"Of course, Billy. Tom will have a copy with him I expect."

Over the next few days everything is made ready. Specky

Spender is told what the plan is. She panics a bit, because she's already scheduled to be somewhere else that day, but after a hectic few hours of phoning, she gets things rearranged. She wants to be in London, doesn't want to miss that!

Tom chooses an early train so that they can get to London in time to walk to Westminster from the railway terminal. They sort out what they need for the day, packing maps, food, water, and of course the Charter to be handed in; they take two other copies, one to read and one to give to Specky Spender.

Early on Wednesday morning, Tom drives around, picking everyone up. It's still dark as the four of them walk from the car park to the station. They don't talk much. Penny is sleepy and a bit cold; she can't help thinking about what's going to happen and it makes her heart skip a beat every now and then. In the train she watches the light growing as the day begins, and she can see more detail of the world outside, flashing past the window.

Tom is thinking of when he was young, when trains used to make the rhythmical clacketty-clack sound as the metal wheels went over the joins in the rails. Now the rails are welded, and there is only a steely ringing sound, except when the train goes over points.

As the train approaches the outskirts of Greater London, the landscape outside the window changes rapidly. Buildings crowd up to the railway; there are more bridges and factories; there's more mess and rusty old machines. David has never been in a train before and watches, fascinated, as the scenes move past the window. Penny has only once been to London before, with her parents, to see a West End show. It's exciting, and a bit scary too.

When the train arrives in London, Tom suggests that they have breakfast in a cafe before walking to Westminster. They study the street map of London to figure out the way they will walk. Penny has such butterflies, she can't eat a thing.

They walk past Marble Arch and into Hyde Park, going down by Park Lane where posh people live. Further on they walk past Buckingham Palace and eventually Westminster Abbey. Penny is tired and has had enough of walking, but it looks like there's nowhere to sit down. The streets are crammed with cars, and it's very noisy and smelly – quite a shock after the campfire in the woods.

"Where do we go?" asks Penny, nervously.

"We carry on down this street to Parliament Square," says Tom.

Tourists are milling about in Parliament Square, taking pictures of the famous buildings that can be seen all around. There are fantastic views of Big Ben and the Houses of Parliament, and Westminster Abbey too. Specky Spender and her team have arrived already, and she calls out.

"Over here!"

"Hallo, Specky; hallo, Will," says Tom.

"Hi! Can you go just there, please," says Specky, pointing, "so we can film you with the Houses of Parliament behind."

"Won't we be going closer?" says David.

"You will, to hand in the petition, but right now we need space and light, and I'm a bit worried that the purlers in the sky will block all the light out."

Above Parliament Square, the Rising of purlers has been gathering all night and is already vast. Now that Penny and David have arrived, the Rising moves lower and daylight does get blocked. The film crew rush about organising more lights for the filming, but they need not have bothered; the cloud of purlers begins to glow and pulse with its own light, plenty of light for filming.

The purlers arrange themselves so that there is a clear line of sight to the Houses of Parliament, but all other directions are blocked. The Rising glows – ripples of light seem to move over the surface, mesmerisingly, and light pulses through the vast cloud. Drivers of cars, buses and lorries that have been stopped sit quietly, entranced by the effect of the purlers.

When Specky's television crew are ready, she signals Penny to begin. David stands next to Penny; Tom and John stand either side, protecting them. Penny closes her eyes; she feels the energy of the hundreds of thousands of purlers flowing down into her, giving her courage, enabling her. When at last she speaks, her voice is changed; no longer is it just her voice – it has become all of their voices.

"We are the voice of the Children of the World and we come to submit to parliament the Children's Charter for the Rights of Nature.

"This is not a petition. This is a declaration that speaks for all these purling children, here and everywhere in the world."

Penny pauses, her eyes closed as she gathers herself; in her heart she asks the Rising of purlers to give her strength and inspiration. She holds the piece of paper with the words typed on it, but she doesn't need to look at it when she speaks.

"The Children's Charter for the Rights of Nature.

"Because we are children we see things differently to how grown-ups see things, and we see things being done wrong and we need to say to grown-ups how we see Nature dying.

"What we see happening is: we see terrible hurt to Nature and the wild web because humans take too much; we see terrible hurt to the land and the sea, and to people's lives, because of things being done wrong and because of greed and war.

"We see Nature being destroyed by machines because humans always want to have more, and so they make more machines.

"We see Nature dying because of climate breakdown, and we see that humans can't stop burning fossil energy to make their machines work.

"There's war and hunger and fear and lostness in the world because humans are greedy, and they take and take but don't give or share – and the more they have, the more they want.

"We Children of the World ask you grown-ups of the world to open your hearts and feel again that you belong in the heart of Nature. We ask you to do the following things, and respect them, and make them law for all the world:

"All living things are born free and equal and have equal right to exist and be healthy.

"Give back land and sea to Wild Nature so the wild web may heal.

"Give children back the Wild Nature you've taken from our lives, so that we may heal.

"Give us back our open time, unclocked and untimetabled daydreaming time, so that we children may imagine into being the future we see in our hearts.

"Stop growing money all the time. Turning Nature into money is killing our future and is a crime against life.

"Using fossil energy is a crime against life, it must stop now.

"Stop machines destroying the planet because this is a crime against life.

"Stop making weapons and stop making wars because these things are crimes against life.

"Stop squabbling, and grow up, like you're always telling us.

"All of this we want you to make law, and to call it the 'Universal Declaration of the Rights of Nature', up above Human Rights, because humans haven't got any rights at all if Nature's not all right.

"This is very important, so please will all the countries in the world have a special meeting and agree to do these things, and please do this straight away. We Children of the World are watching, and we will be waiting, and we will do whatever needs to be done for you to understand how urgent this is.

"Signed

"The Children of the World."

Swooning, she reaches out to David for support. Wobble-Cam Will keeps the camera focused on her as a thousand purlers come down and surround her. Penny's head slowly clears and when the strength returns to her limbs, she stands again.

"Now we will hand in this Charter to the Government of our country. May they hear us!"

The film crew, the gathered tourists who have been watching, and all the purlers cheer as Penny and her friends turn to walk through the tunnel of purlers towards the Houses of Parliament. The camera crew follow to the entrance gate, which is as far as they are allowed to go, and film the handing over from there.

Almost at once the Rising of purlers lifts, releasing the traffic to flow again and clearing the pavements for tourists to walk about. The Rising divides, moving and pulsing with waves of light. Some of the Rising moves towards that part of the building containing the House of Commons, suddenly dropping down and disappearing from sight.

At the same moment, inside the House of Commons, the PM has been asked the question, 'what will be done about the children?'

The PM is about to speak when something very strange happens. A thud happens, a really deep thud, that makes tummies wobble in a not very nice way. Every single person in the House rubs their tummy, looking down as they do so, and when they look up again, the House of Commons is crammed with purlers, from the highest roof timbers down to the level of the suspended microphones.

Even though it is contained within a building, this is a Rising, and it glows and pulses, rippling with beautiful pale light, emitting a tantalising sound like, well, like nothing on Earth.

The politicians are astonished, speechless, shocked into immobility. Their fear subsides as the benign influence of the Rising calms them. Emerging from the Rising, Billy and Siobhan move downwards a little, followed by Larky, Stomper and Jerome. Larky can't help whizzing about, she is so excited, but Billy and Siobhan are in more serious mood. Siobhan moves to a microphone.

"Honourable Sirs and Madams," she says fearlessly into the weird silence of the House of Commons, "we've come to tell you

about what happened outside this House just a minute ago, because you won't know yet and you should know straight away.

"The Children of the World have handed in the Children's Charter for the Rights of Nature. So that you don't have to go out and find it, we have come to read it to you, here and now, just in case it should get lost."

The politicians are mesmerised, unable to speak. The PM is unable to speak; even the Speaker is unable to speak.

"Before the Charter is read out to you, Billy would like to say a few words. Billy..."

Billy moves closer to the microphone. He looks upwards to the Rising and the rippling light gives him courage. He looks at each of his friends, and then faces the PM.

"'Onerable Ones, I's called Billy 'n I's got some things to say 'n it ain't just me talkin', it's all the Children of the World.

"Grown-ups is 'avin' rules tellin' us young ones what we can be doin' 'n what we can't ever be doin', 'n we's gettin' a tellin' off when we's lyin' or cheatin' or bullyin', or bein' selfish.

"What ain't right is, we's seein' grown-ups is not avin' to do like they's tellin' us to be doin'. Be listnin' 'n we'll tell you what's true.

"You politicians is tellin' us we 'as to work 'ard 'n get exams, 'n get money, 'n 'ave everythin' we's wantin' 'n be rich 'n everythin'. Now we's seein' grown-ups is not 'avin' rules at all, grown-ups is gettin' what they's wantin' by lyin' 'n cheatin' 'n trickery, 'n they's greedy, never 'avin' enough of anythin' 'n always bein' frightened of losin' what they's 'avin' already. Everythin' they's doin' what makes 'em richer is urtin' other people, 'n 'urtin' creatures 'n plants, urtin' the Earth, urtin' the water in the sea 'n urtin' the fishes 'n all the millions of things what makes the livin' skin of the Earth.

"'N what we see 'appenin' is, some's gettin' richer 'n lots of folks is gettin' poorer, 'n all this 'more is good' stuff is killin' Nature 'n breakin' the Earth, 'n poor peoples is starvin' 'n 'avin' no 'omes 'cos of war 'n drought 'n floods, 'n there's so many millions 'n billions they's killin' the wild web 'coz they's 'avin' to eat wild things, 'n they's killin' wild web 'n not knowin' it.

"'Umans is too many, 'n they's wantin' more 'n more stuff, 'n they's not stoppin' 'avin' more, 'n not stoppin' growin' is a disease wot's killin' children's future.

"We's not goin' no more to school, wastin' our lives bein' brainwashed with your lies 'n trickery just so we's growin' up like you with disease 'n greediness 'n not 'avin' a lovin' 'eart for all creatures, 'n all the people, 'n all the Earth.

"We Children of the World is wantin' you grown-ups to see you's killin' wild web 'cos you's finkin' yoo's different 'n seprat, you's finkin' you's ownin' everyfin', 'n can use everyfin' up. But you's wrong, 'n you's 'avin' to be givin' wildness back before it's too late, 'n we children is tellin' you now we's not 'appy with your rules no more, weez not 'appy with wot you's doin'. We children is luvin' our mums 'n our dads but we's not luvin' wot 'umanz is doin' 'n lettin' to 'appen.

"'N we's not 'appy that millions of us children is 'avin' nothin' but concrete, 'n roads, 'n orrible houses for livin' in – or no houses at all – 'n no Nature, 'n no wild web.

"'N we's not 'appy when grown-ups is sayin' they's right 'n we's wrong. Every country's sayin' they's comin' first, 'n others comes last. Every country's sayin' god belongs to them, 'n not no other, 'n wars and sufferin' is 'appnin' 'cos grown-ups is 'avin ideas in their 'eads what are killin' life on Earth 'n making people suffer too. It ain't right. It ain't right at all. We's not 'avin' it no more.

"'N you's believin' machines 'n techno stuff is solvin' all problems, but you's not seein' 'ow machines 'n techno is separatin' you from Nature, 'n separatin' you from your 'eart, makin' you numb so's you ain't feelin' like you's killin' 'n murderin'.

"We's no more doin' wot we's told. We's no more goin' to school. We's strikin'!

"You's sayin' you's doin' wot you's doin' for your children's future, 'n every mum 'n dad is workin' for a better future for all we children, so they's thinkin' everythin's all alright. But it ain't alright.

"You's 'avin' to be changin', quick, 'n doin' what's written in our Charter, so we children won't 'ave to be forever purlin', 'n so's all livin' things 'as a future.

"You's thinkin' already there'll be more children bein' born so you don't 'ave to care 'bout us, but you'sll be wrong, cos all babies wot's birfin' now is seein' with their 'earts, 'n'll be seein' wot's wot 'n'll not be 'appy, 'n'll be followin' the purlers 'n the great wave.

"We's askin' you grown-ups to open yor 'earts 'n stop killin' Wild Nature, 'n be doin' it now! 'Ere's what 'as to 'appen..."

Siobhan moves closer to the microphone. Slowly and solemnly, she recites the Children's Charter for the Rights of Nature. Once or twice she hesitates because she forgets a bit, but by way of the unwords from the Rising she remembers and continues. When all is said, she moves to Billy's side.

The recitation of the Children's Charter is met with absolute silence. Nothing stirs. Not a breath can be heard. Suddenly, with a great gasp, the politicians suck air into their lungs as though they'd been holding their breath for all this time, and with that in-breath, they snap out of their trance.

"I'm sure that I speak for all those assembled," says the PM, able to speak again, "when I say that you have presented a remarkable spectacle. A somewhat unorthodox means of approaching parliament, but we admire your courage and your passion.

"I am worried that by your extraordinary behaviour you are causing great suffering to your parents, who will be distraught, and all this time you are missing school and the learning that will enable you to thrive in the competitive modern world. It would be better for everyone if you were to all return home, and to school.

"You have contributed greatly to the debate on the need for legally binding international agreements on human rights and the environment. The negotiations required to take the debate forward are complex and very sensitive, as different nations have different needs and views. However, such negotiations are under way, and we accept your contribution of the Children's Charter for the Rights of

Nature gladly and will incorporate its substance into the process.

"I understand your feelings of frustration with the adult world, and I am sure my colleagues will agree that we can acknowledge you by stopping the road development that has affected you so much, and also give you assurance that great efforts are being made to strengthen the international laws protecting the natural world.

"I trust that this will reassure you all sufficiently that you feel able to return home."

The PM's speech raises cheers, in the traditional way of politicians showing support for their leader, but the applause is not enthusiastic. The PM's speech seems to fall on stony ground.

"'Onerable PM," says Billy. "You just ain't gettin' it. Time's 'xactly what you 'ain't got no more of. We's not goin' back to school to be trainin' for future, cos there ain't no future if you ain't doin' what we's sayin' you's 'avin' to be doin'. You's 'avin' to be lookin' in yor 'earts 'n changin' – changin' everythin' now – like so!"

POP!

Billy, Siobhan, Stomper, Jerome, Larky – and half a million purlers – suddenly disappear from the chamber.

~

Outside in Parliament Square, Penny is exhausted and hardly able to stand. David and John support her, and Tom leads the way as they make their way through the crowds to begin their journey home. Specky arranges for one of the television vans to take them to the railway station; the driver is called Steve and he says how impressed he is with what's happened, and he congratulates Penny.

She recovers a bit in the warm van, and Steve offers to drive around a bit and show them the sights, but Penny says she needs to get home. Tom says he should have made a booking at a hotel, so they could all stay the night.

"No, Mr Tom, I would rather go back anyway, if it's possible."

"Yep, plenty of time to get the train you mentioned," says Steve.

Penny sleeps on the train. David daydreams, thinking about the drama of the day. Tom and John talk in low voices. The countryside passes by in darkness as though they are travelling in a tunnel. All they know of the outside world is the singing of the wheels on the steel tracks. David thinks of all those lives being lived in the bushes and fields beside the railway, and in the houses in the villages. He feels he needs to say hallo to them all, but the landscape goes by too quickly, much too quickly.

When the train arrives, Tom fetches the Land Rover from the car park; John helps Penny into the back of the car and covers her with a blanket. Making a beeline for Penny's house, Tom carries her in and makes sure that her mum is at home to care for her. He explains what has happened, that it was all a great success, and will be on the news. Penny is just very tired.

Next, he drops David off, then John, and so back to his own place. He makes himself a cup of tea, and flops down on the sofa to watch the late news on the television. The events in Parliament Square are well reported by Specky; she and Will and the team did a good job.

What comes next takes Tom by surprise. He had no idea about the events inside the House of Commons, but here it is, on television for all to see. Tom laughs out loud listening to Billy's rant, as the commentator calls it, and he snorts when he hears the PM's response to Billy, and to the Children's Charter.

But what makes Tom gasp in surprise is what the reporter says next. News is coming in of exactly the same things happening in other government buildings in other countries across the world. Not only that, but Billy's rant and the Children's Charter were recited at exactly the same time by purlers speaking their own languages. The news goes on into the night and Tom makes himself some soup and toast and settles down to watch.

Within a few hours, nearly one hundred countries are calling for an emergency summit meeting of leaders. Most of these countries are saying that they believe the Children's Charter for the Rights of Nature, alongside the Universal Declaration of Human Rights, would be the perfect place to start negotiations to fix the problems the world faces.

Tom smiles sleepily. "A good day's work! Well done, you kids," he says out loud, and promptly falls asleep.

~

After sleep, and a few days of rest, Penny visits LuLu and Emmy to ask if they would take her to the Glade.

"Hallo, Penny, how lovely to see you," says LuLu. "I've heard how well you did in London. Well done!"

"Thanks, LuLu, it was a big day. I need to go to the Glade, but I can't do it alone, would you take me, please? And Emmy too, if he's here. I'd love to see him as well."

"Yes, Emmy's here, Penny. He helped me to get to the Glade when I was very weak after the sea purling. We'll take you there, don't worry."

"Allo, Pennee Unwurdz, Iyz verri appi seein yoo."

"Hallo, Emmy. It's good to see you, too."

"Letz b goin Pennee, weezl b purlin n elpin yoo."

"Thanks, Em."

Emmy is already purling, and LuLu lies down on the sofa and is asleep, and purling, within two seconds.

"LuLu! How do you do that?" cries Penny.

"It's quite natural for me now, Penny, I'm more comfortable purling than in my body."

Penny walks while LuLu and Emmy purl with her, a little in front and to either side. Having their company feels good and the walking is easier. Once they get out of town her spirits lift, and by the time they reach the Glade she is feeling much better.

She sits close to the talk-stone. Emmy and LuLu purl close by. Penny calls Rindill with her heartspeak, and when he appears from the undergrowth he flies to his favourite perch; he looks at her inquisitively, whispering his song. Penny closes her eyes. She sees her own body asleep, sitting in the Glade close to the talk-stone, with Rindill whispering to her and Emmy and LuLu purling close by. She sees her own body ghosting.

"Penny, you're purling," says LuLu gently. "Your body is ghosting, don't be frightened."

"I feel relief," says Penny, sighing.

"I did too, when it happened to me."

"Yooz simila," says Emmy. "LuLu n Pennee Unwurdz iz simila, yooz both avin purlniss."

"Penny Unwords," says Rindill, "you have done a great thing, and Billy, too, and all of you. There will be much for you to do before it is time, and you must be strong. The Glade will strengthen you, and all the creatures will strengthen you."

"Rindill, thank you. You say, 'before it is time'. What do you mean?"

"We creatures do not know what the great wave brings, but we know that what is happening will mark the end of the age of human separation. That is the time that is meant."

"What will happen?" says Penny.

"There will be a great migration, but we creatures cannot yet see what that means, and we can't yet see beyond it."

"Thank you, Rindill, and thank you, Glade, and all the creatures and plants, and the Earth itself."

"This is your home, too, Penny Unwords," says Rindill, leaping into the air, trilling his trill and tumbling down to disappear into the undergrowth.

Penny purls quietly around the Glade sharing the unwords with Wild Nature, and she feels heartened. When she is ready, purling Penny disappears and sleeping Penny wakes up.

"Hallo, Penny," says LuLu. "Are you alright? Will you be able to walk home?"

"Yes, LuLu. Thanks to you and Emmy and Rindill, I'm feeling better."

"Letz b gettin ome, Pennee. Laa la laaa la laaa laaa!'

"Ah, Emmy! I haven't heard you singing for such a long time!"

~

The radio and television news programmes are full of Billy's rant and the Children's Charter for the Rights of Nature. No one can explain how it is possible for the Charter to have been recited all over the world, in so many different languages, all at the same time. But everyone likes to talk about it, endlessly suggesting how it might have been done, thinking it's a hoax like crop circles.

There are reports of purling happening more and more all over the world. Huge Risings are appearing above the cities and towns where there are government buildings, even where there are no towns, only a village hall, and Risings form above the headquarters of large companies and corporations, the companies that cause so much suffering to people and to Nature in their operations. The Risings continue to get bigger as new purlers join them.

There are reports, too, of the purlers' sleeping bodies ghosting, and stories of babies purling in tiny socks and mittens, and how they laugh and recite the Children's Charter in 195 different countries, and many more different languages, around the world.

The sky begins to glow with the light of the many Risings, the colours shimmering.

~

LuLu and Emmy purl along with Penny as she walks back from the Glade. When they are nearly home, purling LuLu disappears – she wants to be at home to welcome them to her door.

"Emmy!" she exclaims. "There's a parcel in the bowl of things!"

"Parsl for Emmy? Oorayee!"

Emmy purls to the bowl and looks at the parcel.

"LuLu, itz from Flimzee n Iyz xcited n mi tummeez wobblee."

"Let's take it to the table and open it," LuLu suggests.

The parcel is tatty, but the words can still be seen; Emmy reads them out.

"'Mowzl Emmy, Portl Post, uvva side ov fog, uvva side ov Ilnd ov Myst'."

"Emmy! It's from your homeworld!" cries Penny. "How amazing is that?"

"Pleez b opnin parsl, LuLu," says Emmy, trembling with excitement. "B urryin!"

"Alright, Emmy, keep your fur on!" says LuLu, laughing.

She carefully unties the heartstring that binds the birch bark wrapping. The outside layers of birch bark are brittle, and break apart, but the inside layers are still flexible and can be unrolled. A creamy-white birch bark strip is wrapped around a twig, and when LuLu unwinds the bark she finds writing all the way along; under this birch bark strip are lots of woollen threads wound round the twig.

"What's the message saying, Em?"

"Weez orl missin yoo, Emmy, pleez cum ome kwik wen wurldz iz singin saym kulla soon. B reddee. Luv Purl n Flimzee n Dreema n evreewun ooz luvin yoo."

"Emmy?" Penny's gentle voice breaks the silence.

"Emmy's eart iz burstin n teerz iz appnin."

"Do you know what it means, Emmy?" asks LuLu.

"Emmy's waytin."

"What's this, Em? May I unwind these threads?" says Penny.

"Pleez b doin."

Penny picks out the ends of the threads, holding them together with one hand, and with the other hand she turns the twig, unwinding the threads. At the other end, the threads have been knotted into a pattern.

"It's woven!" says LuLu. "Or maybe knotted."

"Yooz rite, LuLu, itz nottid, not wovn, n itz Dreema wotz dun it n evreewun az nottid sum.

Emmy is very still and quiet.

"Theyz mayd speshl fredz wishin Emmy to b cumin ome, n itz appnin wen wurldz iz singin saym kulla."

Quiet again, he floats in his pouch, gazing at these wonderful

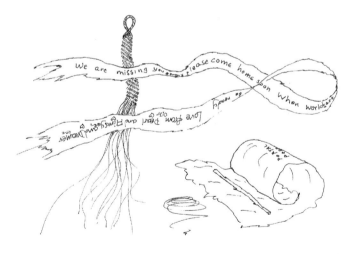

things that have been made by Flimsy and Pearl and Dreamer and everyone at Burrow Cave. He touches the woven threads.

"Wen wurldz iz singin saym kulla – Iyz merembrin, Iyz

merembrin!" Emmy purls around the room excitedly. "Iyz merembrin Snugweed! Now weez purlin to Risin – pleez b feedin yor boddeez n sleepin."

Emmy breathes some chocolate fumes from the little bowl on the table, while LuLu and Penny eat. They wrap themselves in blankets, curl up on the sofa, fall asleep, and are purling within moments; their bodies ghost away until they can only just be seen.

Pop! Pop! Pop!

Emmy, LuLu and Penny join the Rising above Tillings Wood, merging with the cloud of purlers and feeling the pulse of the unwords. Emmy unwords his memory of Snugweed to the Rising, and how Snugweed showed him the many worlds happening; Emmy wants all the purlers to see for themselves.

The Rising responds by ascending higher into the sky, and into space beyond the atmosphere of the world. Looking back, the Earth shines, colourful and beautiful: blues and greens, whites, browns, reds – a multitude of colours. These colours begin to blur and become jumbled. The purlers can see that behind the jumble of colours there is another jumble of colours, and behind that another, and another. These are the many worlds, each with its own particular colours, and the many worlds appear like a rainbow and the purlers see and feel and hear these colours; the colours are singing. The purlers are hearing a rainbow of sound where the many worlds meet and part in a mesmerising dance.

Emmy remembers how he felt when Snugweed showed him the many worlds happening. He remembers how each world has its own isness – not only the sound and the colours, but also the countless other qualities that are needed for a world to exist at all, and he remembers how these qualities of isness made him feel pulled closer or pushed away. He remembers how he felt when Snugweed showed him the world that he knew to be his own home world, and how his heart leapt in his breast, and he remembers his disappointment when he was shown the human world, which didn't feel quite right, but that's where he had to go.

Emmy's heartspeak spreads with the unwords to all the purlers, and they feel this as though it is their own lost memory re-awakened, for now they see it for themselves.

~

Standing on the mountainside on the Island of Mist, One-Eye'd

Tooby is gazing at the sky in wonder. He runs to Bamboo Cave, calling everyone to come and look, and he runs to the rat cave, calling Bart and Carl. They are all outside now, watching marvellous colours glowing in the sky, rippling and pulsing, and as they watch, the colours slowly fade. The mice and two rats on the Island of Mist are left with a mysterious sound ringing in their ears, a sound so fine and so high that it is almost out of reach.

"It'll be soon," says Tooby. "Be ready!"

~

Standing under the silver birch trees, on the hill above Burrow Cave, Flimsy is watching the sky. She sees colours ripple and dance, and there is a sound that she feels rather than hears, and she is reminded of her vision of the many worlds happening.

Flimsy smiles, reassured; she is certain now – Mowzl Emmy is coming home, and it will be soon.

~

The Rising descends slowly through the littered layers of space, where all the broken satellites orbit the Earth, and down into the thin and fragile envelope of life that hugs the world. Taking up its station again above Tillings Wood, the Rising settles, and the purlers consider the meaning of the wonders they have seen. By means of the unwords, the Risings and purlers all over the Earth now know the feeling-sound of the many worlds happening.

Chapter Six

The Great Rising

"LuLu? Wakey time!"

"Oh! Emmy, hallo," says LuLu, sleepily. "I've been dreaming we were in the sky with the Rising."

"Yooz rite, LuLu, weez been sky purlin n seein mennee worldz appnin. LuLu, Pennee'z poorli sortid, sheez needin yoo."

LuLu shakes off her sleepiness and checks on Penny, stroking her forehead and feeling her temperature.

"She's very hot, Em. Penny? Can you hear me?"

"LuLu," whispers Penny. "I'm so cold."

"I'll make you a hot water bottle. I'll just make you a bit comfier."

LuLu rearranges the cushions and stretches Penny out on the sofa, spreading extra blankets over her and tucking them close; she strokes her forehead, talking softly, explaining that a fever makes your body get hotter, and that makes you feel cold and shivery. When your temperature stops going up, then you feel hot and sweaty.

"Emmy, keep an eye on Penny, please, while I make a hotty and some medicine for her."

"Orite, LuLu," says Emmy, beginning to la-la a little tune.

LuLu prepares a special tea with dried herbs and honey, and while the kettle is heating up for the hotty, she boils up other herbs and roots in a saucepan, straining the liquid through a sieve into a bowl. Returning to Penny she slips the hotty under the blankets; Penny holds it to her tummy. LuLu dips a soft cloth into the liquid in the bowl, squeezes it out and gently holds the warm, damp cloth to Penny's forehead. With a twist of cotton wool dipped in the special tea, she moistens Penny's lips.

"Emmy, she may be like this for a day or two, we need to tell her parents."

"Orite, LuLu. Iz we tellin Billee n uvva cubz?"

"Not yet, Em. Let's let her come back to herself first. Tell Penny's mum to come whenever she wants, she knows where to come."

"Orite, LuLu. Bi!" Pop, and he's gone.

"LuLu?" whispers Penny.

"I'm here, Penny. Try to sip this." LuLu spoons a little tea to her lips, and Penny manages to sip enough to moisten her mouth and throat. LuLu bathes her forehead with the cloth, the herbs filling the air with their aroma.

"This is how a chrysalis feels," whispers Penny.

"You should rest."

"A caterpillar showed me how it makes a chrysalis, and how it turns to liquid inside." Penny pauses, recovering her strength. "I was purling; I could feel her isness changing as she melted into liquid... Her caterpillarness disappeared, and her butterflyness began to appear in the liquid..." LuLu strokes her forehead. "That's how I feel now, LuLu, I am liquid."

Pop! Emmy returns and purls close by. Penny makes one more effort to whisper.

"I'm dying – and being born." She sinks down into feverish sleep once more.

"Penneez bein re-knittd, LuLu," says Emmy, quietly.

"Why, Emmy? She's been re-knitted before, after the ocean purling – we took her to the Glade and she seemed so much better."

"Yooz rite, LuLu, n sheez stronga in er eart. Now sheez feelin great wave stronga, n feelin wotz avin to appn, n itz urtin'."

"Emmy? I don't like the sound of what you're saying."

"Yooz kno-in orlreddee, LuLu, n yooz been urtin deeplee. Penneez undastandin wot Rindillz sayin n wot great mygrayshn iz meanin."

"You've known for a while, haven't you, Em? Why haven't you wanted to talk about it?"

"Uman cubz aznt bin reddee."

"I see. But you told the Rising, didn't you? When we purled up into space?"

"Yip. Theyz orlreddee feelin unwordz, n theyz reddee."

"Please, tell me, Emmy – I felt the unwords too – but I want you to tell me."

"Wen Iyz in Risin Iyz feelin verri appi, n Iyz feelin Iyzll b goin ome inna bit. Iyzll portl ome wen worldz iz singin saym kulla."

"Will we be coming with you, Emmy? Can we purl with you?"

"Umanz iz purlin wiv Emmy n Iyz verri appi, but umanz iz avin no boddeez wen theyz portld. Evvee stuff theyz leevin ere. Penneez kno-in, n sheez urtin."

"Emmy, I want to come with you, and Pip does too; we won't mind not having bodies, but the children – their lives are only just beginning – they aren't thinking that their rebellion will lead to dying!"

"Tiznt dyin, LuLu, leevin evvee stuff ere iznt dyin."

"Oh, Emmy, this is getting difficult, perhaps we shouldn't talk like this with Penny unwell. She'll want to talk about it too, with us."

"Yooz rite, LuLu, Penneez needin kwiet."

"Let's talk when she can join in. I'll stay with her if you want to go, Emmy."

"Fankz. Iyzll b findin Billee n uvvaz."

"Alright, Em, see you soon. Oh, Em, before you go, is Penny's mum coming?"

"Sheez cummin innabit."

"In a bit today?"

"Yip."

"Good, thanks."

"Bi, LuLu!"

"Bye, Em."

Pop.

~

Penny hears the familiar sound of their voices from far away, voices that she knows and loves, but muffled; she doesn't hear the words. She feels wrapped in darkness, warm and friendly, and she is at peace.

The unwords call her softly, slowly becoming clearer as the meaning grows in her awareness; the meaning is carried by a voice inside, unlike any she has heard before. The voice she hears, or feels, if it can truly be called a voice, is a bit misty and at times a bit peppery, like someone with a sore throat whispering.

"I do have a name," says the misty, peppery voice, "otherwise I wouldn't be a voice at all, but you gave me a new name which I like very much."

"What is the new name I gave you?" Penny asks, very curious because she can't remember any such thing. She does not speak out loud; this conversation is inside – it is the unwords.

"The narrator! Do you remember now?"

"I remember! I remember asking Mr Pip, 'who is the narrator?' in 'Wot Appnd'."

"Exactly."

"How do you make it happen? The writing I mean. How does Mr Pip manage to write when he's asleep?"

"It's just a bit of mischief of mine. Somebody has to write it, and Pip is fun to tease."

"Yes, Emmy likes to tease Pip, too. Does Emmy know you?"

"Yes, everybody knows me, but not personally."

"Are you... God?"

"Bless me, no. I don't know what that would be at all. No, I'm like the invisible ones but not quite there yet, I'm an inbetweener. I've still got a name, in fact two names, which may not quite be the right direction to be going, but I have no body, or 'evvee stuff', as Emmy is fond of calling it. I still have work to do, relating dimensions.

"My job is to bring the wisdom of the invisible ones to the physical world, and it's my job to help the mouse – well, to help all of you."

"So, you are narrating 'Wot Appnd'!" says Penny. "I knew there must be somebody–"

"Not somebody, some – hoo."

"Some who?"

"No, hoo, that's my name. It's a different sort of hoo to who. You try it for me – say them! You must say my name with an in-breath."

"hoo is different to who, who to hoo, hoo to who too!" Penny laughs, trying to get the breathing right.

"Ahh! It is a very special pleasure to hear my name said by you. You are the first one ever to be able to say my name. Can you feel how different the words are from each other on your lips? I wish I had lips, then I could taste the words too."

"Yes, hoo. I can taste the difference, but I would never have guessed. But, hoo, we have so many questions – do you know things? Do you know the answers?"

"hoo may, hoo may not. You may ask."

"Why is Emmy's world exactly eight thousand one hundred and twenty-eight years in the future?"

"Ah! It is a special number. The sum of all its divisors, not including itself, equals itself."

"What? What on earth do you mean?"

"It's a perfect number. I like that sort of thing, and I had to choose one number or another, so I chose that one. You see, there's a great deal of time in my dimension, and not much else, except numbers, so I've become fond of them. Try twenty-eight! That's an easy one: one, two, four, seven, fourteen..."

"Hmm. I'm not sure that I understand what a perfect number is, hoo, maybe I could ask you again sometime?"

"Yes, of course, but do you have another question for now?"

"Was it an accident when Emmy came to the human world?"

"hoo doesn't do accidents."

"Do you mean that you made it happen?" cries Penny.

"No, not exactly; the invisible ones feel every ripple of the great wave, and it is they who set things in motion; it's my job to cross the t's and dot the i's, which is the fun bit of course."

"You mean, you make it all up?"

"No, no! Emmy does that for himself, as it happens. He named Snugweed and talked with him – that wasn't scripted. He invented purling, without which none of this would be happening – that wasn't scripted either."

"What about Uncle One-Eye and the Island of Mist?"

"The portal happened because of the invisible ones. The Island of Mist appears differently to everyone who finds themselves there. The Ocean world is a world of potential; it is where the many worlds meet. I think humans call it a paradox."

"What *is* 'scripted', hoo?" says Penny, fearfully. "What *is* 'scripted' to happen?"

"Ahh. Now we are getting somewhere."

"Well?"

"Patience, dear. We have an abundance of time, and little else."

"You might have, hoo, but I think I'm dying."

"Why do you think that, Penny Unwords?"

"Because I am not worthy to be alive."

"Why ever do you say such a thing?" cries hoo.

"Because I have seen the way that humans are going, seen what we do, and I am ashamed, and do not want to grow up like that."

"Then don't grow up like that."

"What? How?"

"No, it's hoo."

"No, I mean HOW."

"That's an anagram of 'who'."

"Oh, hoo, you're driving me crazy!"

"You and the other purlers will suspend history; you will exist between the old and the new ways of being."

"And that isn't dying?"

"No, Penny, it is dying and being born, just as you said to LuLu a moment ago when you woke up and spoke of the chrysalis."

"I'm not going to have a body any more, am I, hoo?"

"You will not. You will be leading the great migration. Many others will choose not to migrate, but to stay and do what they can to help the humans that do not migrate. All this has to happen, Penny. It isn't personal, as humans would say, you just happen to be the one for the job."

"So why do any of us have to migrate? We don't want to be invisible ones!"

"You will be inbetweeners, like me, for a time. It will need a certain number of purlers to be able to make the sound that bridges the many worlds. It is this that will transform human destiny, and, incidentally, allow Mowzl Emmy to get home."

"What is a 'certain number', hoo?"

"About five or six. Five, er, billion, that is, give or take."

"Five billion? That won't leave many behind, will it?"

"Two or three billion, plenty for a few wars!"

"Oh, hoo! That's a terrible thing to say. So, we fail. Then what's the point?"

"You will not fail. It is this history of conflict and fear that inspires the transformation, in you and all the others. You are being re-knitted, Penny Unwords."

"What *does* that mean? Emmy is always saying that, as though it makes it alright to be in terrible torment!"

"Penny Unwords, I have no body and so I have to imagine feeling joy – and now I am feeling joy! It is my great honour and pleasure to be with you in this moment of eternity.

"To be re-knitted, as the mouse calls it, is when the courageous young love of the heart is woven with the wisdom of the invisible ones. It happens to be true that this hurts – physically, emotionally and, if I dare to use the word, spiritually. You are stepping into your full humanity."

"I won't have a body to step with," whispers Penny.

"Bodies don't last long in any case – you needn't worry about that."

They don't say anything – or unword anything – for a long time. Time enough for hoo to discover another five perfect numbers.

"You are ready, Penny Unwords. hoo will leave you now."

"Wait! hoo!"

"Wait? I am the essence of waiting."

"Oh, hoo, I'd stamp my foot if my body worked."

"Only a bit of fun."

"Tell me about Emmy's home world."

"What would you like to know?"

"Are there humans there?"

"There are and there aren't."

"Grrrr!"

"Oh, Penny Unwords, I haven't had so much fun in – well, it doesn't bear thinking about."

"What do you mean 'there are and there aren't'?"

"The future is shaped by what you do now. As I have already said to you, the great migration, if it occurs, will transform human destiny. The billions of purlers who go with the Rising to follow the great wave will be drawn to other worlds where they are needed; they will become invisible ones."

"Do you mean that there are invisible ones in Emmy's home world?"

"Of course."

"Is it only humans that can become invisible ones?"

"No, no. Awareness doesn't belong to humans. On the contrary, humans are a little wanting in that department, mistakenly thinking that awareness is the same as intelligence. That's why humans have to be re-knitted."

"What other beings become invisible ones?"

"Everything, everyone – creatures, plants, stones."

"Oh, hoo, I don't understand; it's too much, too big. It's unreal."

"It is very simple, Penny Unwords, as you already know in your heart, but you have yet to give yourself to the great wave. This is your time of awakening, and you do this for the world. This is true for all the purlers, but you are the first, and you will lead."

"Are there humans in Emmy's home world?"

"Ah!"

"Well?"

"The answer is not yet born."

"You mean it depends on what happens?"

"Y-e-e-s, something like that."

Penny sighs. "Will Pip be writing about our conversation in 'Wot Appnd'?"

"Yes, do you mind?"

"No, I'm glad. Thank you, hoo."

"hoo thanks you, too!"

~

There's endless talk on the TV and in the newspapers about the Children's Charter for the Rights of Nature, and, of course, about Billy's rant and the PM's inadequate reply. Some of the journalists are calling for the politicians to respond, accusing them of avoiding the issue. The question 'what's to be done about the children?' is still not answered. One of the journalists refers to the children who presented the Charter as 'Penny's Pirates', and this catches on. Some journalists write about Penny's Pirates bringing a refreshing new force into politics; others write fierce criticism, claiming that the pirates are trouble-makers and terrorists and should be disciplined and forced to return to school. Nobody seems to understand the idea of ecological emergency.

Billy and his friends are worried about Penny; they know that she's unwell and is being cared for by LuLu, but Emmy says it isn't time to visit yet, so they haven't been to see her. The children get bored and fed up with the news, which never seems to get anywhere; they feel that they haven't been listened to, they haven't been heard.

The news gradually moves on to other things, as this becomes 'old news', and the weeks go by. The children often walk to the woods, needing to touch the wet earth and smell the mushroomy smell of the soil and leaf-mould. They want to run and shout and get muddy and wet. They can't do these things when they are purling.

The road-making machines have been taken away from the compound in Tillings Wood and, after removing the security fencing, the contractors finally leave. The site is abandoned and untidy – a huge scar in the woodland. The machines had pushed over the trees and scraped the soil, bulldozing everything down the hill in a tangle of earth and rock and broken trees.

The camp-dwellers want to do something to help the woodland recover. Planning a big tree planting campaign, they appeal to the townsfolk for donations of tree saplings, tree stakes and tree-ties – and help with the work! Volunteers start digging through the compacted rubble to make planting pits for the new trees. They carry soil in buckets up from the tangled heap to the planting pits, making sure that the new tree saplings will have their roots in good soil. It's not a good time of year to plant tree saplings because it is summer, but they can prepare everything for planting in early autumn.

About one thousand planting pits are prepared, each with a stake and tree guard lying next to it. The children busy themselves finding all the surveying stakes and pulling them up, taking them to the compound where they are used as tree stakes.

The Rising, hovering above the woodland, is constantly visited by new purlers who come to be with the unwords to re-charge. Those new to purling learn from the creatures in the Glade before they join the Rising, which continues to grow larger every day.

This is happening everywhere, not just in Tillings Wood. Risings are forming everywhere, all over the world. Purlers learn from each other because they come from all walks of life, and all places, and each purler has their own story to tell.

The purlers are coming to the Risings from towns and cities, from hospitals, care homes, schools, factories, prisons and detention centres; they come in their thousands. There are people of all ages: children, grown-ups, and old people; there are disabled people of every sort for whom purling is a miracle of freedom; there are people who have never seen the countryside in their lives, never been in Wild Nature because where they live is just roads, and buildings, and concrete; there are people who have only known hardship, refugees from war-torn places who are homeless and isolated; people who have never played barefoot in the mud or climbed trees in the middle of a wildwood; people who have never opened a conker casing to find the treasure inside. Certainly, none of them have talked with wild creatures before, and so, when these people hear about purling, they want to learn how to do it. People in prison learn how to purl, and with their sleeping bodies remaining locked up, they are now free to purl in whatever Rising they have joined, and their lives are transformed.

You may have a sneaking feeling that you remember reading this before. Well, you are quite right. It is repeated because it matters so much.

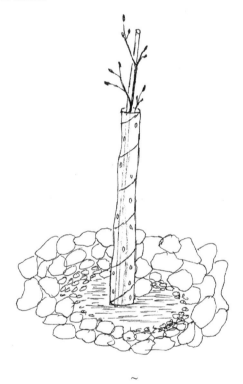

~

There are lots of countries in the world that are inspired by the Children's Charter. They want to take the opportunity to start new talks, and the first thing to do is fix a date for the first summit meeting of all the countries of the world. Even the big rich countries want to be part of it, mostly because it would look bad if they didn't, so an agreement is reached for the first meeting of all the countries of the world. The second thing to do is to agree where the meeting should be, and this takes another round of negotiations. These things take a long time. At last it is agreed that the first summit should be in Hawaii, partly to honour Dr Keeling, but also to acknowledge that islands everywhere are at particular risk of inundation by rising sea levels.

When the big day arrives, leaders of most countries deliver strong speeches, saying that we must all do something immediately; we must be courageous and ambitious in stopping climate change in order to save the future for our children and grandchildren and all of Nature. They call it The Climate Action Agreement. When they have made their speeches and attended the photo shoots, they return home, leaving their delegates to do the work of negotiation.

Days and days of talks, going on late into the nights, eventually result in some sort of agreement. With great pomp and ceremony, the summit is declared a success and all the delegates go back to their respective countries.

In the weeks that follow, the thousands of pages of The Climate Action Agreement are scrutinised and endlessly discussed on the radio and TV. It is soon noticed that nothing at all in the agreement is binding in law. The delegates from the richer countries refused to agree to any plans that might harm their economies.

Even though their leaders had said such strong things on the first day of the summit meeting, the rich countries do what they always do, showing that it's 'business as usual' for them; subsidies and tax breaks continue to be given to the mining and drilling companies, weapons continue to be made, and more weapons are sold. The Children's Charter might as well never have happened.

But not all countries are like that. More than half the countries of the world agree to a second meeting of nations, and nearly one hundred countries attend: countries that are not so rich, countries that are exploited by the big corporations, countries that are most affected by floods, or drought, or sea-level rises – or other effects of climate change and ecological collapse; countries suffering upheaval and warfare because of the struggle for control of oil, gas and minerals; countries at war because of religious disagreements fanned into flames by the politicians.

These countries form a coalition and present the United Nations with a strong case for Nature's Rights and Human Rights, with climate justice being a strong theme. It is made very clear that this new legislation must be binding in International Criminal Law.

The rich countries, who are also Members of the United Nations, vote against doing any such thing. They are not willing to let go of the power and control that they have and so they don't support the idea of new laws. The arguing goes on and on, not getting anywhere at all. Months go by. The children feel betrayed.

~

Penny's fever passes; she slowly returns to herself, drifting through twilight worlds on her way, hearing echoes of hoo's curious voice. It takes many weeks before she can be taken home.

For the next few months, Emmy purls to see her every day; she talks about hoo, the narrator, and of her new understanding, and Emmy realises how much she has changed. Penny's meeting with hoo changes everything.

Emmy has been keeping in the background for quite a while, so that the human cubs can make their own decisions and find their own way. He has been worried because of the difficult challenges the children have had to face, but now he knows that Penny has gone beyond everything that he knows about. It's true that he wants to get home, but he loves his friends, and he cares about what will happen to them, and to humans and the wild web. He looks at Penny, and sighs.

"Pennee, yooz seein deeplee, mor deeplee than Emmy. Yooz trulee brayv."

He purls close to her eyes and they gaze at each other.

"Emmy, it's a great mystery to me, and I've sometimes been very frightened of what might happen. But now I feel clear, and I'm ready. I am not frightened any more."

"Iz yoo reddee to b seein orl yor frendz?"

"Yes, Emmy, yes! What I'd like to do is to go wool gathering with them, to Cloud Common! I need to do that, and with all our friends!"

Emmy arranges everything, calling with his heart to summon people; he purls to Donna's to ask if it would be all right to meet at her house. She is overjoyed; it has been so long since the whole gang has been together, and she misses that.

When the day comes, the children turn up not knowing what to expect. Emmy hasn't mentioned anything about a wool gathering expedition, just that it would be good to meet. When everyone is there, Emmy appears in their midst, purling. He is the only one purling.

"Uman cubz, Iyz verri appi to b seein yoo orl agayn–"

"All except Penny!" cries Larky. "I wish we could see Penny."

"Here I am!" says Penny, standing in the doorway.

"Penny! You're better!" says David. "We've been so worried, and we've missed you."

"Thanks, David. Yes, I've had a bit of a tough journey being re-knitted; I need to be with you all. I feel like doing the wool gathering walk with you all, would you do that with me?"

"Wool? We don't really need any more wool, Penny," says Donna.

"That's not why I need to do it, Donna. Do you remember how we felt when we did it the first time? No need to answer that – just remember."

"Yes," Billy says uncertainly. "We's all gettin' soakin' wet 'n Pip's tellin' the story of Beechnut dyin' 'n Flimsy gettin' ill – it was depressin'."

"Yes, you're quite right, Billy, but that's when we cracked open, that's when we first really felt the great wave."

"Well, I wasn't there, and I'd like to know. Let's do it!" says Siobhan.

"I want to come!" cries Larky, and all at once everyone cries out, "Yes! let's do it!"

"Thanks, all of you," says Penny. "I need to be with you, and I have a feeling that Cloud Common is a good place to be."

Donna and LuLu sort out water, food and bags. Pip has his backpack with him, so they stuff that with snack food and bottles of water. Everyone else can carry a shopping bag to put wool in. It's a gorgeous day and the sun is climbing in the sky as they set off, chattering away, making their way to the footpaths that lead to Tillings Wood and Cloud Common. It feels like a holiday to be doing this; it feels good.

They have a wonderful time exploring Cloud Common and collecting wool. It's not the wool that's important – it's being together. They picnic, lounging about in the sun, and play games until they are so tired they can't run any more, and when the sun goes down they wend their way home through the woods in the twilight.

~

In the dead of night, when most people are asleep, aircraft fly over making such a racket that even Billy's Grandpa wakes, shouting in alarm. Planes are taking off from military bases, heavily loaded with weapons, fuel and supplies, their engines straining as the planes gain height. There are smaller planes too, fighters and bombers, and there are heavy bombers and heavy transport planes; all these machines roar across the sky, slowly curving round to their correct bearing.

These planes will fly all night, re-fuelling in mid-air. All this technology will deliver death and destruction to people in faraway lands. Television will show images of smart weapons delivering with pinpoint accuracy the so-called 'surgical strikes' – the explosions visible on the screen as remote clouds of fog, obscuring the fact of death and injury. That is supposed to make it all right. But it's not all right, and everyone who has been woken by this noise of war lies awake for a long time wondering why this is happening. Who wants it? We don't want it. There are many who feel so upset that they purl to the Rising and stay there. What else can they do?

These nights of warplanes setting off and returning become a regular occurrence, increasing in frequency as the weeks and months go by.

~

A few weeks after the walk on Cloud Common, Emmy purls to the camp to see who's around; Larky is purling and, seeing him, she calls out.

"Emmy! Come and join us!"

He purls down, Larky whizzing round him excitedly. Tom Wylder and John Weatherstone are sitting with David and Penny on the logs beside the fire pit. No fire is lit as the day is hot and sunny. This is the first time they've been back to the camp in many weeks.

LuLu and Siobhan walk down from the compound where they've been looking at the preparations for the tree planting.

"Hallo, Emmy!" cries Siobhan. "Where have you been? We haven't seen you since Cloud Common."

"Iyz bin owt n abowt. Wotz appnin ere?"

"Hallo, Emmy," says John. "It's good to see you. We've been talking, trying to understand what's going on – or what's not."

"Allo, Mista John, yoozl ave to b xplaynin to Emmy pleez."

Tom and John tell Emmy what they have heard on the TV and radio news. The richer countries are not agreeing with the countries that want to make international laws to protect the Earth and all of Nature, including humans.

People are divided by the Children's Charter; some people say 'yes, we agree, let's do it', and other people say 'what a lot of nonsense! We'll never do that, good riddance to the lot of you.' It's these people – the ones that say 'what a lot of nonsense' – that are pushing their weight around.

"You remember, our own government voted to bomb a faraway country," says Tom. "We all heard the warplanes that first night, and since. If you look for the beginnings of that conflict, you'll find that it goes back into history. Countries with more military power control weaker nations by force, usually in order to control natural resources. It's always been the same."

John describes some of what he's seen on the television news, about how people are being forced to flee their own lands because of conflicts and climate change. These refugees, or migrants, as they are now called, try to reach safety and a new life in other countries. The number of migrants grows greater every day. Many countries are saying no, we don't want you living here, so the migrants have nowhere to go and live in huge camps where they have nothing at all except, if they are lucky, food aid sent from far away. Some countries are building walls, or razor wire fences, along their borders to stop people coming in, and putting soldiers on guard.

That's why so many millions of people are purling, and the numbers grow every day. Women are no longer becoming pregnant; there have even been reports of early pregnancies being re-absorbed. People are frightened by what is happening, and there are many who want to find solutions to the problems and to help each other, but leaders don't seem to be able to make agreements with neighbouring countries. The arguments get worse.

It is becoming clear that it is the poorer people in the world that will suffer most from climate breakdown and ecological collapse. The richer countries – the very ones who have created the problem – are defending themselves, rather than cooperating to find solutions.

The conversations in Tillings Wood have been about these huge events and the tragic stories of human and wildlife suffering.

"I can't bear it," says Penny. "What we did with the Children's Charter has only made things worse."

"'Ang on a minute, Penny!" cries Billy. "What's you gettin' at?"

"Already, people are being more horrible than they were before!" cries Penny, her voice breaking. "We've made it worse! No one is hearing us!"

"I think they are hearing you, Penny," says Tom. "It's because people are hearing you that they find the courage to challenge how things are. As a result, disagreements and arguments are happening more."

"But why not cooperate and find solutions?" says David.

John speaks up. "There are lots of people who believe technology will solve the problems. They will go on thinking that way and go on using technology to succeed at any cost. That is the story of history, that is what humans do."

"I think technology has created ever more complicated ways of enslaving people," says Tom.

"That may be true, Tom," says John, "but there are positive things about technology too–"

"What about the migrants?" interrupts LuLu. "Couldn't we help them? Any of us could become climate migrants!"

"We could try to get them purling!" says Larky.

"Why aren't they purling already?" Penny asks.

"Because they don't want to give up being in their bodies," says LuLu. "Not everyone is ready or willing to do that. There are people inspired to help others, and there are many ways of helping. What do you say, Tom?"

"Humans can't just stop the old ways, even with all the children in the world purling and saying they must stop! It's not easy for humans to change, because people *are* their habits, and traditions – they are *defined* by their history. Emmy, what do you say, how can the old ways change?"

"Iyz finkin orl uman cubz iz avin to b leevin."

Emmy's words are met with an uncomfortable silence.

"Emmy," says LuLu, whispering. "Where would they go?"

"Weez nevva kno-in wot great wave iz bringin. Umanz iz purlin, wotchin, n waytin'."

"But what are we waiting *for*?" cries Siobhan. "If no babies are born, there's no future anyway! For humans, I mean."

"We are waiting for the end," says Penny, her voice low. "We are waiting for the moment of change – when the old history dies and the new way of being is born."

All eyes on Penny. Everyone feels the chill of fear – a rippling of the great wave across their skin and down their spines.

"What happens to the purlers?" whispers Larky.

"Theyz goin wiv great mygrayshn," says Emmy.

"Where?" says Larky.

"Mennee wurldz iz appnin n yoozll follo yor eartz."

"And our bodies?" says LuLu.

"Yoozll b leavin evvy stuff ere."

Larky cries out, sobbing; the others look at the ground, feeling awkward.

John clears his throat. "Emmy, how long have you known this?"

"Iyz merembrin littl bi littl. Wen weez in Risin n seein mennee wurldz appnin, Iyz merembrin."

"Yes," says Penny, sighing. "We saw, too – me and LuLu."

LuLu nods, a faraway look in her eyes.

Emmy continues. "Wen Iyz arrivin in uman wurld, creechaz iz showin Emmy wild web torn n brokn. Iyz kno-in umanz iz avin to b waykin up."

"Technology has always helped humans to survive," says Tom, "and to be more comfortable. But when you look deeply into that, technology evolves because people want to change the environment – to be more comfortable, make life easier and wealthier, and have power over Nature. Power, also, to defeat their enemies, power to control resources and to control the people themselves."

"There's nothing that will change that history," says John, "nothing that we can do will change those values and traditions."

"So, the age of machines will fight itself to death, is that it, Emmy?" says Tom.

"Xaklee rite, Mista Tom. Purlaz iz elpin coz great wave iz needin elp kwik."

A new voice speaks from the edge of the woods. "Will the birds still be singing when we are gone?"

"Pip!" cries Larky.

"Hallo, Pip," says Tom. "Welcome back."

"I've been listening. I know it's true. I've known it like a weight on my heart since I saw Emmy and Scraggy in their home world. Emmy told me that his world is our world in the future – eight thousand one hundred and twenty-eight years – and there are no humans there. The wild web in his world is not torn and the great wave is strong. If there is a great migration, that's where I want to be. I feel ready, now, positive even."

"You won't have a body, Pip," says LuLu, quietly.

"I know. I have come to terms with that because I am old and tired, but the children are young and–"

"Pippee, yooz nevva kno-in wot great wave iz bringin."

"I know, Emmy, yes, I know, but that doesn't change the fact that we have to do it – don't we?"

"Do what exactly, Pip?" asks Tom.

"We have to go to the edge – and a bit further."

"Riddles, Pip, you're talking in riddles! What exactly do you mean?"

"The fact that all the children are purling – and that no babies are being born – you might have thought would be enough to wake every human up to the state of Nature. But no, the human world polarises, and fear increases. We must all go, as Emmy is suggesting, and give ourselves to the wave. It is this that will create the space into which a new way of being may arise."

There's a quiet while the meaning of this sinks in, a quiet full of apprehension. Then Penny speaks, her voice slow and serious.

"This is the great migration that Emmy speaks of. When the number of purlers is so great that their singing bridges the many worlds, we shall go. I would like to share the unwords with you all, because I have learned of things that cannot be said in any other way. To do this, it would be best for us to be in the middle of the Rising, so that all purlers are joined. Are you ready for this? Are we together? Will you come with me to the Glade, and purl to the Rising from there?"

For some moments her friends are speechless with surprise. Penny has shocked them: the waiting is over; now it is time for action.

"We will come, Penny Unwords!" says Pip.

"We will come," say the others, all at once.

~

They walk in silence from the Camp to the Glade – Billy and Larky purling along with them – each deep in their own thoughts. They are surprised to find Rindill already alerted and waiting for them. Many wild creatures are assembled, and the humans settle themselves carefully so as not to harm or frighten them.

"We welcome you to the Glade," says Rindill. "The great migration is beginning, and we creatures are here to give you our blessing. We too shall go with the great wave when our time comes, and so we are all of one will."

The creatures able to make sounds and cry out in whatever way they can; the creatures that can't make sounds cry out with their heartspeak, and with this surge of energy the humans leave their bodies and purl to the Rising. By means of the unwords, Penny shares with the Rising that the waiting is over – now is the moment.

Purlers are arriving in countless thousands to this and every Rising throughout the world, each Rising rippling and pulsing, lighting the sky.

The Rising above Tillings Wood divides into two, one cloud larger than the other; the smaller cloud, shining brightly for a moment, abruptly vanishes, reappearing in that place of the politicians; once again the Rising appears inside the House of Commons, and once again the will of the purlers strikes dumb the throats of the politicians.

In every government building across the globe the same scene unfolds, and as Penny purls downwards, preparing to speak to the assembly, so too does her counterpart in each and every other place. As she begins to speak, so too do they, speaking the same meaning but in their own tongue, wherever they may be.

Penny speaks slowly, gently, with the voice of one who has lived for a thousand years.

"It is our story, as humans, to believe in ideas of a better world, and to struggle to get there. Such beliefs have driven humans to strive in competition, conflict and fear. We are now so many we are destroying the Earth, which is our home, which is us, which is everything.

"These beliefs come from our history and it is time to take from our history those things which benefit all life and the living planet, and to leave all else behind. It is time we stepped wholly into our humanity.

"We Children of the World have begged the grown-ups and politicians to make this leap. We have said that we cannot live without love for all beings in our hearts, yet we see the stronger nations of the world responding by becoming even more selfish and cruel.

"We humans have become very clever – so clever that we can dream of going into space to look for another Earth. We dream such things, while people starve and die under bombs and bullets, and while the world is ripped apart in the search for minerals to make the machines that separate us from our humanity.

"We no longer need to make bombs and bullets and machines of destruction – now that we are so clever that we can see there is no enemy but ourselves.

"Now that humans are so clever, we can see, if we choose to, that we don't have to conquer Nature to prove that we exist. We don't have to destroy Nature's abundance and create starvation and war, deserts and fishless oceans just to have power over others.

"We are clever now, so clever that we can see, if we choose to, that we don't have to be frightened any more, and we don't have to be bullies any more.

"We can see that all humans and all beings have the same right to their place in Nature's abundance.

"We can see that we no longer need to struggle to create paradise on Earth, because it is here already.

"We can let go of the fearful history that we have lived for so long, we can let that story go, now, if we choose to. It is time, it is the right time, and the only time remaining.

"We Children of the World know that it is the right time; we know that this Earth is home, our most precious and only home.

"We children see how the wild web is dying and how the great wave retreats from the Earth, and this is breaking our hearts.

"We children have seen what it is that we must do: we must leave this Earth we love so that the history of fear and separation may come to an end.

"It is very hard for us to bear the pain of this because we love our bodies and we love Wild Nature, and our lives are just beginning. We love Wild Nature with all our senses and with all our hearts – but the history of fear has made a world of machines and false hopes, and we are dying in our hearts. We cannot remain in bodies denied a wild heart.

"We shall all go from you. All the children, the newly born and even the unborn, shall go from you. Many grown-ups will follow the great wave – refugees and those who suffer and have no hope left in their hearts, the dispossessed, the abused, the neglected, the exploited, the enslaved, the vulnerable, the unwell in body or mind.

"We shall all go away from you, bringing an end to the history of fear, for that history will have no future. We will exist between two histories and we shall bear witness to your deeds.

"We shall witness your awakening to the hurt of every creature, every living thing and every place that has been sacrificed in the name of progress, and you will know that you are the same as those creatures and places and things, and that this is exactly what you are, and there is nothing more you could be or ever will be.

"Your awakening will mark the end of history, and into this

emptiness something other will be born. In the moment of that birthing, it may be that some of us return."

Penny pauses, her breath slow and deep. She feels the will of the Rising, and she speaks again.

"We rise now, the greatest Rising that has ever been. This is the Great Rising, and you will marvel and be horrified; you will feel abandoned; you will feel a great tearing in your being – the wound which marks the beginning of transformation. You will glimpse for a moment the many worlds happening and you will hear the voices of angels.

"We depart now, in our billions. In this moment, we rise up."

The Rising ascends, disappearing from the House of Commons and mingling with the vast Rising outside. The sky is alight with purlers as far as the eye can see; indeed, an unbroken Rising brightens the sky over the entire Earth. The remaining humans are interrupted in whatever they are doing, compelled to look upwards and to witness this extraordinary event. For some, it is cause to be frightened, for others it is a shock because they had believed it would never happen, and yet for some, it is a moment of intense happiness.

The sky, seen from the surface of the Earth, ripples and pulses with soft colours. Wild creatures are watching too, from their burrows or thorn hedges, or gazing up through the waters of the sea into the shining sky – excited and hopeful to see this happening at last.

The host of purlers begins the singing, making a sound so difficult to hear that the humans, listening below, strain their ears, wondering what the mysterious sound might be; but for the purlers the singing inspires, and the sound grows, becoming ever finer and ever higher. The Earth, seen from the sky, dissolves into colours that shimmer with the singing and, as the sound becomes finer, the colours open, revealing the many worlds.

The purlers feel their hearts responding to the isness of each of the many worlds; to some they feel attraction, to others repulsion, but little by little, each purler is drawn to the world of their heart's choice and towards this they drift, with all those drawn to the same. They become fallings of purlers, falling towards their chosen world in rippling cascades of light.

~

On the Island of Mist, Tooby and his companions watch the sky. Drifts of colour fall in hazy skeins, like birds dropping down to their roosts at dusk. The watchers feel warmth in their hearts and they hear the singing, the sound tugging at them, inviting them.

Tooby opens the light tube and invites the light to emerge, which it does at once, pouring out and forming into an Orb. He asks the Orb if it will portal them all to Burrow Cave. As before, he says that he will hold the light tube open so that the light may return to the tube if it wishes to. The Orb slowly flattens itself, then widens into a thin disc, large enough in diameter for Carl, the largest of their company, to fit through. In the centre of the disc a black spot appears, growing gradually larger until the blackness fills the disc and the light is reduced to a ring around the edge. Tooby thanks the light, saying that he is waiting for a sign before they step through, something to mark the moment of stepping out of the Ocean World where the many worlds meet, and into the awful blackness of the portal.

The watchers are dazzled for a moment by a sudden flash, and they hear a voice shouting out, a voice familiar and welcome to some.

"Yikes! Where am I now?" cries Emmy, crashing to the ground and bumping into Scraggy.

"Emmy!" cries Scraggy. "You's alive! 'Ooray!!" and he hugs

him so tightly that Emmy has to protest.

"Scragg! I can't breathe! Not so tight!"

"Come on, quick, through the portal!" shouts Tooby. "Now!"

"Uncle One-Eye! It's good to see you, and all of you–"

"Enough o' that, get movin'! Hey, what's wrong with your legs? What's that thing?"

"My pouch!" says Emmy, scrambling to get out of it. "I don't need to be in it now I've got my body back, and–"

"Hurry up!" yells Tooby, or Uncle One-Eye as Emmy likes to think of him. "Through the portal!"

Scraggy goes first, then Whip-Tail Jack, Sieve-Brain Sally, Ruby, Marigold, Black-Boot Bess, Gaol-Break Jim, Sad-Eye'd Suzee, Cutlass Kate and Stump-Leg Stew.

"Go on, Bart! Quick now!"

Black-Eyed Bart goes next, followed by Coal-Face Carl. Tooby grabs Emmy's arm, dragging him into the portal. Emmy clutches his pouch, which he will never part with.

The next moment the whole gang spills out onto the ground outside Burrow Cave, squealing and yelling as they try to untangle themselves. Tooby holds the light tube open, inviting the light to return if it wishes to. The circle of light shrinks towards the centre of the disc, and at the last moment it disappears, like a rabbit down a burrow.

"It'll be returnin' to Crystal Cave," says Tooby, quietly to himself. But Emmy hears.

"Is that the last of the light, Uncle?"

"We'll 'ave to be seein' what's in me den! Mowzl Emmy, get you all to Burrow Cave, I'll be findin' a new 'ome for Bart 'n Carl, they's too big for our cave."

~

Flimsy and Dreamer had spent the night up on the hill above Burrow Cave watching the sky. They felt sure that something was about to happen, and they waited, watching the stars move slowly across the sky above them. With dawn came a brightening in the east and this light grew and grew until the entire sky pulsed and rippled with colours. They heard the exquisite singing of the host and watched the purlers rain down from the sky in drifting showers, like slow-moving sparks.

A flash of light and ground-shaking rumble bring Flimsy and

Dreamer back to the present; they hear excited voices below, at the foot of the cliff, and running to peer over the edge, they see Tooby and the company from the Island of Mist, tumbling about in a heap, crying out in excitement and happiness to be home again.

"They're back!" says Flimsy. "Emmy's home at last!"

"Come on! I want to give my brother a hug!" cries Dreamer, running off down the hill with Flimsy chasing behind.

~

Burrow Cave has never seen such a celebration. In no time at all the party is in full swing, thanks to Threeda, who knew very well to expect visitors and she had prepared lots of good things, and thanks too to Stumpy, who remembered to bring the last of the pickled raisins from Bamboo Cave. Cutlass Kate has her whistle, and soon she is piping a jig, and everyone is dancing about like mad things.

One-Eye wanders off to have a look in his den, where he finds

the Orb of light – the small one that used to be in the lantern – floating above the table, just as it was when he portalled back to the *Wreckless*. He speaks softly to the light, thanking it for all the help and guidance it has given; he invites the light to stay, if it so pleases, and he would be honoured if it did, but probably it will prefer to go now that the adventures are over.

Or are they? The light pulses gently and elongates itself, before

threading back into the lantern that hangs from the ceiling above.

"Ahhh!" sighs One-Eye, closing the little window in the side of the lantern. "Welcome home!"

The End

Epilogue

You might have guessed that the narrator would have the last word – hoo else? Actually, hoo's work is done, or nearly so; hoo will graduate – to become an invisible one. There will, of course, be a job going for someone who would like to be the next narrator. There has to be a narrator on duty always for all dimensions.

You'll have some questions, naturally, but it's not possible to explain everything, and anyway, what happens depends upon you; what happens depends upon your imagining.

So, what happens to all those purlers? Billions of purlers who gave up their bodies, gave up their physical existence, where have they gone? What have they achieved? Does it matter?

We can trace some of them, especially those closest to our hearts. There are some purlers who have unfinished business in the human world, and so it was their heart's wish, during the great migration, to return to the human world. Most of them returned as invisible ones, falling like dew into the wild web, returning to help heal what is broken and to help open the eyes of humans. Some returned to their bodies because it was their heart's wish to help their fellow humans, to help those who had remained to make the leap, to break the mould of history.

Of our friends, Billy is one of these. It was his heart's wish to return to find his father and to care for Nan and Frank, who would not join the great migration leaving Billy's father behind.

David, too, follows his heart's wish back to the human world; he loves the beauty of the world too much to leave it and he wants to help the wild web to recover. There are many like David, including Tom Wylder, the wildlife photographer, and John Weatherstone, the teacher. People bursting with ideas to help humans break the mould of history.

As for the rest of our friends, it was their heart's wish to go to Emmy's homeworld, which, as you may remember, is the human world eight thousand one hundred and twenty-eight years in the future. Witnessed by Flimsy and Dreamer, they could be seen raining down from the brilliant sky in showers of sparks, cascading down into the wildwoods, the oceans, the hills and mountains, the valleys and rivers. These purlers have become invisible ones with no names or faces, beings that flow with the great wave, united in the unwords.

Perhaps Ping Ling could make crocheted bodies and pouches

for those who were Emmy's friends so that they could show themselves; perhaps the invisible ones could wrap themselves with seaweed, just as Snugweed wrapped Emmy.

Perhaps they can be anything we imagine they can be. Perhaps they have no need to have any shape at all but only to be free to fly in your imagination. And so it is we imagine them: LuLu and Pip, Larky and Stomper, Siobhan and all the others; and Penny, dear Penny, the only one to speak my name...

The end is now very near and hoo will have to melt away. Perhaps one of our dear friends would like to take over the job of narrator?

There is a final little something hoo should tell you, before dissolving away completely, something that you may not have imagined yourself – yet. When Flimsy and Dreamer are watching the sky from the hill above Burrow Cave, they feel the ground shake. In fact, there is an earthquake at that moment, and inside Burrow Cave rocks fall from the walls revealing the opening to the tunnel into the mountain. Digga Bill and Burrow Bill happen to see this happening and, quick to investigate the extent of the damage, they go into the tunnel; they don't yet know that Tooby and his companions have returned. They find nothing serious, and Burrow Cave is not about to collapse. Just as they decide to return to the cave, Digga stumbles on some loose stones – one of which bangs into something hidden in the darkness, making a loud clang.

They investigate by touch and smell: it's a metal tube, crushed at one end and broken open at the other. Strange objects lie scattered about, some of which are too heavy to move, but some are light enough to consider carrying back to Burrow Cave. They decide to carry just one of the objects back to Burrow Cave, planning to go back to collect more later. They are thinking that they'll have to clear up the fallen rocks in the cave, but when they get back, they find the welcome home party already in full swing. Digga puts the thing from the tube down in the corner against the wall, and he and Burrow Bill join in welcoming Tooby and Emmy and their companions.

A little later, when Emmy is tired from partying and in need of a bit of a lie-down, he wanders over to the pile of dry moss in the corner of Burrow Cave and flops down. His paw touches the object that Digga had put down; he picks it up and examines it. It's a book, a very old book, a human book, but small, miniaturised to fit into the time capsule, for that is exactly what the metal tube is. *'They must've found another time capsule,'* Emmy thinks to himself, *'another book for Dad to study! He'll like that.'*

The cover of the book is blackened and damaged, and whatever might once have been written there has become unreadable. Emmy carefully lifts the cover; the title page inside is readable! He gasps. He says out loud the words he sees printed there: "'The Adventures of Horatio Mowzl, The Great Rising'."

hoo is disappearing now, leaving you with a little poem that came into Emmy's heart one day, who knows where from. He said it out loud one day when he was purling in the Glade.

Returnin iz ow great wave moovz

Softniss iz ow great wave wurkz

All fingz iz birfd ov bein

Bein iz birfd ov nuffin

The End
(Ha-ha! Yooz nevva kno-in!)

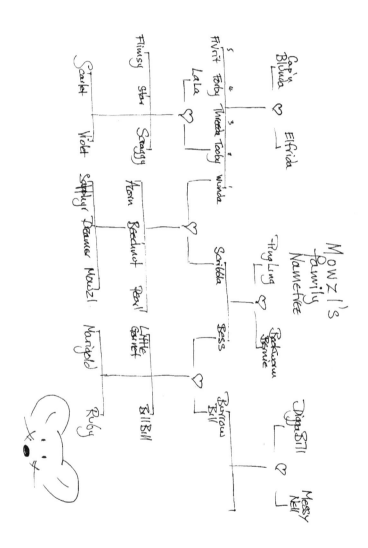

Mowzl's family Namechee

Cap'n Bluda ♡ Elfrida

5. Flivrit 6. Toby Theeda Tooby 4. Wunda 3. Lala 2. Wunda 1.

Flimsy Star Staggy

Scarlet Wolit

Lala ♡

♡

Rosin Beechnut Pearl

Sulphur Beamer Mowzl

Scribbla Bess

Ruggling Beckrow Bennie ♡

Little Bennet

Manifold Ruby

Bill Bill

Borrow Bill ♡

Digga Bill Messy Nell

A Space for Your Mowzl Notes:

Author's Notes

Being outdoors in Wild Nature has been essential to me since childhood. As a student in the 1970s studying biological sciences and ecology, it was clear to me even then that Wild Nature is in big trouble. Habitat loss and species decline has escalated since that time to become the industrial scale destruction of the natural world that we now see happening all over the world.

Human beings, and particularly children, have less and less access to Wild Nature. There are ever more sophisticated means by which children are enclosed and separated from Wild Nature, including the increase of technological substitutes. As successive generations benefit less from contact with Wild Nature, they know less about it and hence care less for it. The continued degradation of the natural world goes mostly unchallenged, even unnoticed.

This novel, to be published in three volumes, is devoted to bringing these issues into the children's domain, inviting children to ask the questions and to see for themselves – see what is missing that their hearts yearn for – and to support them in creating a platform for rebellion.

Paul Thornycroft
Stroud, Gloucestershire
October 2017

~

I wrote the above in October 2017 when preparing the Mowzl manuscripts for publication. Since then there have been many dramatic changes in public awareness of, and attitudes to, the climate and ecological emergency.

Young people are now becoming aware of the chaos escalating all around us, and it is they who will suffer the consequences of ecological breakdown. People with the power to change things are trapped by outdated values and beliefs; they are paralysed into inaction. But children are not limited by the idea that humans are more important than any other life forms. It is the young who are making the leap that is needed, and in so doing awakening the rest of us.

The Mowzl trilogy is a contribution to the growing call for us all to open our hearts and listen once again to Nature herself, listen for the wisdom of life itself – rather than merely the mind of mankind.

Paul Thornycroft
Stroud
December 2018

~

Source references:

The following links are to specific Wikipedia pages which give clear summaries of ecological subjects – such as *Shifting Baseline Syndrome*. Each of these pages include a list of books and scientific papers that allow more detailed research.

https://en.wikipedia.org/wiki/Extinction

https://en.wikipedia.org/wiki/Ecosystem_engineer

https://en.wikipedia.org/wiki/Shifting_baseline

https://en.wikipedia.org/wiki/Trophic_cascade

https://en.wikipedia.org/wiki/Arctic_methane_emissions

https://en.wikipedia.org/w/index.php?search=methane%20plume&title=Special%3ASearch&fulltext=1&ns0=1

https://en.wikipedia.org/wiki/Keeling_Curve

There are many books I would like to recommend but there is one especially.
'Feral' by George Monbiot

Printed in Poland
by Amazon Fulfillment
Poland Sp. z o.o., Wrocław

53494022R00129